# DANIEL
## AND
# NEPHI

A Tale of Eternal Friendship in a
Land Ripening for Destruction

by

# Chris Heimerdinger

Covenant
Communications, Inc.

*For Dale Christiansen*

*Who called me one day from Connecticut to say, "What if Daniel and Nephi had known each other as children?"*

*"A great idea," I replied. "But I'm far too busy to ever write it."*

*And then I thought about it . . .*

Also for Franz Werfel, Hugh Nibley, John Tvedtnes, John Gee, Brent Hall, and a host of other scholars and authors, living and dead, in and out of the Church, whose writings have inspired numerous scenes and descriptions in the book as well as a profound appreciation for the world of 609 B.C.

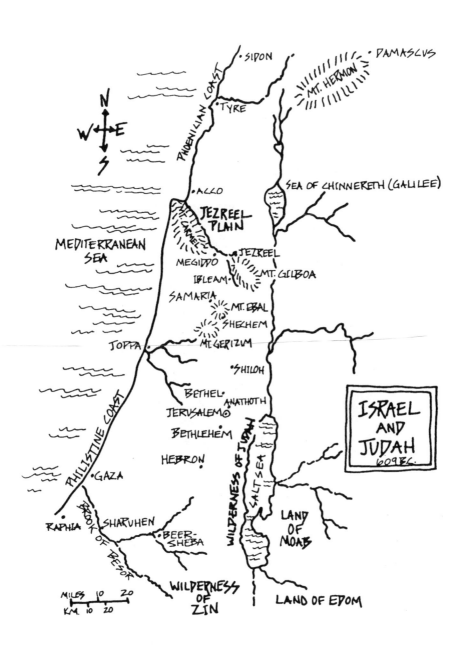

# PRINCIPAL CHARACTERS

(Persons in bold are mentioned by name in the Bible or Book of Mormon.)

## Lehi's Household

**Lehi**—estate owner and trader
**Sariah**—wife of Lehi
**Laman**—first son of Lehi
**Lemuel**—second son of Lehi
Hannah—first daughter of Lehi
**Sam**—third son of Lehi
**Nephi**—fourth son of Lehi
Leah—second daughter of Lehi
Zeruah—third daughter of Lehi
Orpah—fourth daughter of Lehi

Shamariah—servant of Lehi
Dagan—bailiff of Lehi's estate

## Ishmael's Household

**Ishmael**—Lehi's cousin
Mocheleth—wife of Ishmael
Gad—first son of Ishmael
Jumanah—first daughter of Ishmael
Amnor—second son of Ishmael
Abisha—second daughter of Ishmael
Shemima—third daughter of Ishmael
Shereen—fourth daughter of Ishmael
Nadira—fifth daughter of Ishmael

# The House of David

**Josiah**—king of Judah
**Hamutel**—queen of Judah
**Eliakim**—first son of King Josiah
(changed his name to Jehoiakim)
**Jehoahaz**—second son of King Josiah
**Mattaniah**—third son of King Josiah
(changed his name to Zedekiah)

**Maaseiah**—governor of Jerusalem
**Daniel**—son of Maaseiah

**Ahikam**—son of Shaphan and secretary to King Josiah
**Assasiah**—commander of the royal bodyguard
**Elnathan**—commander of the king's cavalry
**Shaphan**—Daniel's instructor, former scribe to the king

**Hananiah**—friend of Daniel
(Babylonian name—Shadrach)
**Mishael**—friend of Daniel
(Babylonian name—Meshach)
**Azariah**—friend of Daniel
(Babylonian name—Abednego)

# Other Characters

**Laban**—garrison commander at Jerusalem
**Necho**—Pharaoh of Egypt
*Solon—caravaneer from Athens
*Thales—caravaneer from Miletus
Zaavan—a Moabite, an assassin

*Though not in the Bible or Book of Mormon, these persons can be found in the annals of Greek history.

# AUTHOR'S NOTE

Alas, this story will never be more than fiction. Though I've striven to be accurate, I was doubtless influenced by scholarship that the next generation will consider obsolete or by my own twentieth-century, western perceptions. Only by encouraging a greater appreciation of the Bible and the Book of Mormon, and by inspiring the reader to seek out the true adventures contained in holy writ, can its telling be justified.

Chris Heimerdinger

# Prologue
## THE STILLNESS OF THE BABYLONIAN NIGHT

THE DARKNESS BEFORE DANIEL'S EYES WAS LIKE THE VOID THAT existed before God touched off His first spark of light. Daniel might have imagined his hand grasping out at the blackness and retracting with a residue of primordial muck. Yet in darkness such as this, Daniel the seer often saw clearest of all.

Barriers of mortar and stone repelled any refreshing breath of the Persian night. Nothing diluted the stench of death and decay, an odor so vile it crusted on the lungs. Yet to Daniel's nose, the air smelled as fresh as a gust of sea-salted wind on the western plain of Jezreel, in the land of his boyhood.

The stone that covered Daniel's subterranean chamber had been sealed by the king's own signet, a king who tonight lay tossing upon his bed, terrified at the prospect of reprisal by Daniel's God. The tomb had also been sealed by the signets of several sub-presidents and princes of Babylon, conspirators who'd found Daniel praying to his God despite a firm decree forbidding such practices.

Had the stone been set aside, as on other nights, starlight might have defined the roving shadows of the beasts. As it was, the chamber echoed only a beastly breathing or an occasional snarl as one of the animals roused to defend a fragment of human bone. These kingly cats had been raised to prefer human flesh. But for some reason, they found Daniel's scent unappealing.

The ancient Euphrates flowed a stone's throw to the west. The wall on which Daniel propped his back bled cold moisture from the river. Still, Daniel was warm. One lion lay at his right and another at his left. This was where the angel of the Lord had told the beasts to sleep.

The seer's eyes remained fixed on the spot where the heavenly messenger had stood. A whisper of the angel's features remained in Daniel's vision, like the ghost-image that stays on the eyes after pondering the shape of the sun.

A parade began in Daniel's mind. Mental processions such as this were not unfamiliar to Daniel. Visions had come to him before, but usually between wakefulness and sleep on nights when his thoughts reeled with the affairs of the Children of the Captivity, or with the affairs of the various kings and nations who made Babylon their capital, or with the burden of his own curiosities. Rarely had Daniel seen such visions while fully alert. The seer's heartbeat quickened.

As the vision unfolded, Daniel thought back on a festival parade he'd seen once as a boy while visiting the Egyptian capital at Noph. Similar visions had reminded him of the annual spring parade in Babylon which ended at the steps of E-temen-anki, the seven-story ziggurat that the Jewish exiles believed to be the infamous "Tower of Babel."

But the visionary processions of Daniel the seer included no mirror-bald priests, incense-choked altars, swooning maidens, or ecstatic throngs of spectators. The similarity that his visions shared with earthly festival parades came through an abundant array of the images of heathen idols. And yet the lions and bears and leopards and ten-horned monsters of Daniel's visions were not characters in a pagan celebration. These were symbols for the parade of eternity.

Daniel found it ironic that God should choose beasts of the earth to represent the great nations, considering how intensely he had feared such creatures as a child. Even now, as lines creased his brow and grey streaked his beard, a shiver of this old phobia remained.

Daniel recalled the season of his boyhood when this fear had been sufficiently harnessed and bridled, a springtime of long ago when terrible events had forced him to face these and other fears head on. How different his life would have been if not for that spring! If not for that family at the edge of the desert. If not for the boy with the dark, bushy eyebrows. The one with the steel-backed bow and the steel-eyed aim.

Daniel had often wondered what became of this boy. What had happened to his family on the day when God's vengeance turned Jerusalem into a rubbled playground for scorpions?

The seer felt a twinge of melancholy. During his life he'd known many great souls, but their greatness hadn't forestalled the tragedies that befell them. Just as well not to know the fate of this boy.

Then, in the stillness of the Babylonian night, a fresh vision opened before the eyes of Daniel the seer—a vision unlike any other he'd seen. He saw a land with unfamiliar landscapes, a people whose perseverance placed them among the noblest of the earth. Who were these people? Where was this land?

*Far away,* was the Spirit's only reply.

And then Daniel saw the face of their leader. A face with age-lines as distinct as his own. When he noted the eyebrows there was no denying the man's identity. Here was the friend of his boyhood.

Daniel couldn't speak the question on his lips, but the Lord perceived his thoughts and answered, *No. You shall not write this vision. I shall spare this generation of things they cannot understand. This vision shall I save for a new generation.*

The vision came to an end. Tears crested Daniel's eyes. A gentle gratitude settled over his heart. Again the seer's mind reached back to the days of his youth and the first time he had set eyes on this obscure boy now hailed as a king. How old had each of them been then? Eleven? Twelve at the most. It was the year of the last great Passover feast and the beginning of the end of a nation called Judah . . .

# Chapter 1
## PURPLE SILK AND THE
## ROYAL BLUE CLOAK

RAINDROPS FELL LIKE SLEEPY LITTLE CHIMES, MINGLED WITH THE faint echo of singing. In a courtyard below, the Sons of Asaph rehearsed a cheerful psalm of David for tonight's feast in the presence of the king. Prince Daniel, the son of Maaseiah, rested on his elbow, entranced by this mixture of music from man and nature. He gazed out the window toward the Mount of Olives, a view made blurry by the rain's many threads. The voices were so soothing! How he envied these royal singers. Many of them were boys Daniel's age and younger. Musical training had been the focus of their lives ever since they'd learned to talk. What a blessing, thought Daniel, to have every day occupied by song! Later on he'd return to his usual attitude—one which dismissed these boys as a brood of girlish weaklings.

Daniel wouldn't have found much gratification as a singer; he found much more as a prince of the House of David. He felt ashamed, however, that his father, Maaseiah, was only the king's half-brother. Maaseiah's mother had only been King Amon's second wife. If she'd been married first, Daniel's father might have been king instead of governor of Jerusalem. Daniel would have been next in line for the throne. One day Daniel would certainly hold a high position like his father, but this was hardly consoling.

Before Daniel governed anything, he had to endure dreadful days like today, enclosed in a stuffy upper room of the House of

Solomon with all the other young princes and nobles, listening to endless recitations from the Book of the Law. Shaphan, his instructor, was conducting an important examination this morning. Daniel smiled as he noticed that Shaphan had again nodded off. Recently the old scribe had retired as private secretary to the king, turning the post over to his son, Ahikam. This tendency toward narcolepsy was rumored to be the reason.

Daniel found it hard to believe that this teetering pole of skin-dressed bones could be the same lofty Shaphan who'd once identified the oldest known manuscript of the Book of the Law. The sacred scroll had been discovered eleven years before—the very year of Daniel's birth—in a secret niche of the Temple porch. The truths it restored had inspired a sweeping religious restoration. With fire and sword, Josiah, King of Judah, had carried reforms to every province. Yet for all the king's efforts, Daniel knew that abomination still glowed in the land of Judah, ready to reignite at the slightest gust of wind.

Shaphan shook himself and fixed his concentration on the boy now poised before the class. Mishael, the son of one of the king's chancellors, recited the blessings of the twelve tribes of Israel. The old scribe mouthed each holy word as it fell from the pupil's tongue.

Daniel gazed back out the window. He knew he ought to pay better attention. Tonight at the feast a prince might be called upon to quote a particular passage. But Daniel knew if the king chose *anyone*, he would choose his own ten-year-old-brat-of-a-son, Mattaniah. Just like last year, just like the year before.

Earlier that morning, when Mattaniah was asked to complete the examination by reciting the Law of Sacrifices on the Day of Atonement, he glibly refused. Instead, Mattaniah selected his own passage, the one on the keeping of the Passover—the same one he always recited. Daniel took pleasure in noting at least a half dozen mistakes. Since then he'd decided it would be better worth his time to listen to the sweet voices of the Sons of Asaph.

"Daniel, son of Maaseiah!"

Daniel turned his head. Shaphan looked perturbed. This was the second time he had called out Daniel's name. Daniel marched to the front of the room and stood before his instructor. With a punitive look, Shaphan announced the boy's verses.

"Recite for me the laws pertaining to what the children of Israel may and may not eat."

It was a long passage. The chance that Josiah might request it was terribly remote. Nevertheless, Daniel took a deep breath.

"'*And the Lord spake unto Moses and to Aaron, saying unto them, speak unto the children of Israel, saying, These are the beasts which ye shall eat among all the beasts that are on the earth . . .*'"

Daniel continued, declaring the cloven-footed beasts and whatsoever had fins and scales to be worthy of consumption, while the camel, the swine, the hare, the lizard, and a host of other creatures were declared unclean. His wording was exact; his voice was even and strong. Shaphan found no point of criticism. After reciting the final verse, Daniel marched back to his place at the window. He made eye contact only with Prince Mattaniah. Daniel's look was meant to tell his cousin what a spoiled whelp he was. Perhaps the look was also meant to say something to Mattaniah about how unworthy he was of the station in life birth had granted him.

At the same time, while watching Daniel's back, the eyes of most of the other boys silently communicated much the same opinion about Daniel.

A DELUGE OF PILGRIMS PUSHED TOWARD THE GATE OF THE VALLEY of Ben-Hinnon on Jerusalem's southern wall. Caravans and peddlers leaving Judah's capital had thinned to a trickle. The few who sought to exit were, in almost every case, foreign traders. Such men had been making this journey to Jerusalem now for eleven years, not to join in the Passover, but to take advantage of its enormous business opportunities. In years past, camel trains had come all the way from India and China, but of late such caravans were rare in Jerusalem. The thunderclouds of war were resounding in the east.

Amidst the throngs pushing toward the gate, a bearded man led a modest train of six camels, two donkeys, one servant, and three sons. The party had been traveling since sunrise, having spent the night outside Bethlehem. Their cloaks still dripped from the morning downpour. The rain had also left their animals looking muddy and ragged. But as was common in the Promised Land during the spring month of Nisan, the weather had quite suddenly improved. The sun had found a sizable hole in the clouds.

The youngest son rode ahead of his father and brothers. His heel digs into the donkey's withers had inspired it to find gaps in the traffic. The boy looked up at the gate, his eyes radiant with wonder. Sentries carrying long lances paced to and fro on the battlements. A light breeze teased a wide wall banner that displayed the six-pointed star of David. This symbol hadn't been seen in Jerusalem for generations.

His eyes coursed their way along each turret and bastion of the city wall until the granite angled northward up the flowering Kidron Vale. In all his eleven years of life, this was only the fourth time he'd visited his country's celebrated capital. He reveled to know that here his footsteps trod the same ground as the ancient patriarchs and hero-kings.

"Nephi!"

His father's voice shattered the boy's reverie. Nephi's family hadn't followed him to the gate. They were leading their animals off the highway to settle in one of the encampments closer to the Mount of Olives. Limited vacancy in the inns made such encampments common during the great feasts. Nephi's father, whose name was Lehi, sought a place to raise the tents.

The boy spurred his donkey. He caught up with his family just as Lehi had begun bartering with the landlord of one of the campsites.

"Three gerah!" Lehi repeated. "For a patch of ground?"

"Let's move on, Father," suggested Nephi's older brother Laman, looking down from atop his camel. "For three gerah we can afford one of the better rooms."

"Not at this time of year," said the landlord. "The cheapest inn will cost you thrice as much."

"This is an outrage!" Lehi clamored. "I've traveled to Jerusalem at Passover every year for eleven years. I've camped this very spot! Prices have never been so high."

The landlord threw up his hands. "You're free to look elsewhere, but I can't promise I'll have a space when you return." He started to walk away.

"One gerah," Lehi offered.

"Two," said the landlord.

Lehi found the proper weight of silver in his leather purse. "All right, we'll take it. But as one merchant to another, this is little better than thievery."

The landlord pretended indifference as he took the silver and acquainted his patrons with the campground's multiple benefits. Wood and fresh spring water would be carried in for them at dusk and sunrise.

Lehi marveled at how money-grubbing this event had become. At the very first Passover—that is, at the first Passover conducted after King Josiah had resurrected the tradition—twice as many tents had dotted the hillsides and no one had charged rent for a spot of meadow.

At least the spirit of the occasion hadn't yet diminished. There was no shortage of drum flurries and trumpet bellows. Although most of the pilgrims were wet and tired, they joined in with any song. Up and down the roads and throughout the camps wandered jugglers and acrobats, as well as peddlers selling everything from snacks to sacrificial doves.

Lehi had brought his own items for sacrifice, the first fruits of his field: barley, lentils, almonds, and even a snow white lamb, all to be approved by the Levite inspectors. He wished only that he might have brought his entire family to the celebration. An illness had befallen his oldest daughter, Hannah, forcing him to leave her behind with his other daughters and his wife, Sariah. Lemuel, his second son, had also remained home to help. If the Lord felt Lehi was due for a blessing, Lehi prayed it would be the restored health of his daughter upon his return. A similar hope was shared by the entire family.

"Father," asked Nephi after helping to erect the tent, "maybe Hannah would enjoy a gift."

"I plan to return with gifts for everyone," Lehi replied, suspicious that his youngest son might be suggesting this as an excuse to avoid further chores.

"But Father, do you remember? She asked us to find her a measure of silk."

"There isn't much hope of that. War has closed the Silk Road for some time now."

"That's why I should start looking as soon as possible," said Nephi. "If there is any silk, it'll get snatched up before the end of the day."

Lehi sighed. Hannah had indeed expressed this desire. Lehi normally found no reason to afford the prized Asian cloth, but if it could cheer his daughter's heart toward a speedier recovery, he'd make the exception.

"All right," Lehi consented.

"Can I take Sam?"

Nephi's elder brother by two years perked up at the mention of his name. Having tied off the last stake, he approached Nephi and his father, his eyes brimming with familiar eagerness. Although Sam was somewhat small for his age, Nephi could always count on those eyes to fill him with confidence.

"Yes, Sam can go," Lehi replied. He looked around for his servant. "Shamariah, I'd like you to go with them as well."

The servant nodded.

Lehi took three silver bracelets off his wrist. He was about to place the money in Sam's palm, but when he saw the hurt on Nephi's face, he thought better. This was a good opportunity for him to show faith in his youngest son.

"They'll want more than this," said Lehi, slipping the bracelets over Nephi's hand. "But hopefully it'll serve as a down payment. Tell them we'll bring the balance after we've traded our bales. Don't be long. You'll save time by asking around. Meet us at the citadel in three hours—two if you can."

NEPHI, SAM, AND SHAMARIAH STRODE THROUGH THE GATE OF THE Valley and into the market district of Jerusalem. It seemed to Nephi the sun had absorbed every ounce of gold from the sky and heaped it exclusively onto each preceding street. Nephi's donkey had pulled loose its tethers and followed them into the city. Strange how an animal could be so obstinate and yet so attached to its owner. Exasperated, Nephi took its reins and followed Sharmariah and Sam through the narrow, noisy passages of Jerusalem's bazaar.

Merchants sat at the entrances of their cavernous shops, driving away flies with horse switches. Their finest wares were displayed at the edge of the street to attract the greatest number of passers-by. Street peddlers thrust jewelry, linens, spice jars, earthenware and plates of steaming food before the travelers' faces. Shamariah and Sam knew better than to acknowledge them with even a polite refusal. Any word spoken to a peddler might encourage him to follow you the rest of the afternoon. Nephi, on the other hand, felt that if peddlers were bold enough to request a trade, they ought to answer when he asked them where he might obtain silk. Shamariah shooed them off. Any other day the peddlers might have been reluctant to depart, glimpsing the oversized silver bracelets on Nephi's wrist. But this was Passover week. There were plenty of other customers.

A goldsmith on the next street looked up from his tapping and filing long enough to tell them of a nearby clothing shop. The owner had put out word that he would trade valuable byssus fabric for any silk. Whether he'd succeeded or not was unknown. A moment later, Nephi, Sam, and Shamariah found themselves standing before the specified shop.

The shopowner was a portly fellow with bright ruddy cheeks. His two front teeth were missing, causing a slight whistle when he spoke. Nephi wondered if he'd lost them to the fist of some angry customer. On his head sat an Egyptian-style feather cap to hide an obviously receding hairline.

"I strongly suspect," the shopowner began, "that you boys already know what you're looking for."

"We heard you might have some silk," Nephi admitted.

"Silk?" The shopowner eyed his customers carefully. He'd been awaiting this request all day. "I'd have to check," he said coyly. "Mightn't you be happier with something less beautiful? More practical? Something like this?" He indicated some woolen fabric with intricate weavings. "Or perhaps a square of most royal byssus?"

"Well, we'd really—"

Sam interrupted his younger brother. "And how much for the byssus?" Sam suspected the shopowner might be feeling them out, passing judgement on how badly they wanted the silk so he could charge the highest price. Sam's instincts were correct. The shopowner backed off on his finagling.

"Well, honestly, I'm rather ashamed of the quality of this byssus. Ah! But I do happen to have a few measures of the finest silk."

From under the table, the shopowner revealed a neatly folded square of bright purple material. Nephi looked ecstatic. His older brother continued the requisite game, crinkling his nose and scratching his forehead.

"Hmmm," Sam droned. "Do you have any other colors?"

The shopowner looked incensed. "Do you know how rare silk is these days? And how rare it will remain while the war between Babylon and Ashur continues to rage? Be grateful that I have the color I have."

"Very well," Sam sighed. "How much?"

Nephi naively raised the bracelets on his wrist. As the shopowner saw them, his shoulders drooped.

"Not near enough."

"We'll be getting more," Nephi promised. "My father will be trading his wares at the citadel. If I give you what I have, will you hold it for us?"

"I'll be closing early today for the celebration," the shopowner warned. "If you're not back here before then, I'll be forced to sell it again after Passover at full price."

"I understand." Nephi handed over the silver.

"And what *is* the full price?" inquired Sam.

The shopowner put Nephi's bracelets on the scale, although in his profession it would have been embarrassing not to recognize such values at a single glance. "Four times this amount."

"Whatever that total is, I'll double it!"

The voice had called out from behind them. Nephi, Sam, and Shamariah turned to face a gold-lacquered palanquin borne on the backs of four muscle-bound servants. From inside the shadowed cabin of this portable royal chair, a boyish hand reached out and signaled the servants to place the litter on the ground. Daniel, son of Maaseiah, pushed aside the palanquin's embroidered curtains and stepped into the daylight. His sky-blue cloak immediately told everyone that he was a prince of the royal household. Shamariah prostrated himself on the dusty street. Sam and the shopowner were quick to follow. Nephi, however, stood aghast and dropped only after Sam had tugged on his tunic.

The prince paid no mind to Nephi's indiscretion and approached the shopowner's table. After fingering the silk and touching it to

12

his cheek, he informed everyone that they were free to rise.

Daniel spoke to the merchant. "I'll have my attendant pay you directly."

Daniel's attendant produced an ivory coffer and opened it before the shopowner's anxious eyes.

Nephi suddenly remembered the proper etiquette used when addressing royalty. Such modes of address were learned only as trivia and gameplay at the desert's edge where his father had built their estate. Nephi had never spoken to someone of such distinction. As he stepped forward, it struck him how ordinary the prince appeared. Without his royal-blue cloak and jeweled wristbands, he was just another boy. Daniel was even slightly smaller than Nephi. Nephi's eyes may have been brown while Daniel's were bright blue, but overall, Nephi realized the features of royalty were not so different from his own. For a moment he felt terribly silly to have to address this boy with such stuffy rhetoric. Fortunately, he caught himself before the attitude grew dangerous.

"May I find grace in the eyes of my lord, prince, that he may hear the plea of his servant," Nephi chanted.

Daniel glanced at Nephi, slightly amused to hear this country pilgrim use a phrase better suited to the son of a king. "You may speak," he chuckled, turning back to the silk.

Shamariah and Sam became quite nervous. What was Nephi up to?

"My master," Nephi began, "we've been searching for this material since we arrived in Jerusalem. My sister is sick. All she wants is a measure of silk. Surely a prince has many fine things. I'm certain my father would give you whatever you asked of him."

Daniel's attendant continued passing weights of bronze and silver to the shopowner.

Sam stepped forward, "Forgive my little brother. We'll find another gift for my sister."

Nephi stubbornly waited for the prince to respond.

Finally, Daniel replied, "I've also been searching for silk. It's quite precious in Judah these days, even for the house of David. My father, the governor, has asked his staff to be on the lookout. His ceremonial wardrobe needs repairs. Surely you wouldn't want him to attend tonight's feast looking less than his best?"

Nephi crooked an eyebrow. Did this boy actually say his father's appearance was more important than comforting a sick girl? In the quarter of the world where Nephi lived, princes and kings were never important players. In fact, they were targets of ridicule and jest at many supper tables. Today Nephi realized their power could be very real and very unjust.

"Here." Daniel pulled a silver ring with a gold setting off his finger and held it toward Nephi. "This should help as you search out another gift for your sister."

Nephi's hand did not open to accept the ring, but Sam's palm thrust forward in its place. Daniel could feel Nephi's enmity. The prince felt sorely tempted to strike the boy. His fist closed around the ring for just such a task. Then Daniel thought better of it, turned his arm aside from Sam's open palm and dropped the ring onto the dusty street.

The face-off between Daniel and Nephi held the attention of all Daniel's servants. In the meantime, Nephi's donkey had found its way behind the palanquin. The animal noted the richly embroidered curtains, perhaps thinking that since the material smelled of perfume, it might prove as tasty as a desert flower. Just before its first chomp, Shamariah gasped.

Daniel's servants surrounded the beast. Startled by the assault, the donkey bucked. The prince's face paled. In his frantic efforts to back away, he tripped, plopping down on the cobblestones.

Nephi grabbed the donkey's reins, but not before its hooves had found a puddle and splattered mud on every cloak, including one vile spot on the royal blue garment of the prince. After Nephi had spoken a few soothing words to his donkey, it stopped bucking.

"That animal should be destroyed!" Daniel raged. A servant helped the prince to his feet. Shamariah and Sam begged the prince's forgiveness; nevertheless, Daniel further declared, "It *will* be destroyed!" He motioned to one of his servants. "Take it to the stables!"

The servant stepped forward. Nephi clutched the animal's reins. The servant glanced back at his master.

"Take it!" Daniel repeated sharply.

The servant pushed Nephi aside and took control of the donkey, leading the reluctant animal up the street. Daniel snatched the silk from the table and retreated to the safety of his palanquin. The servants lifted the litter back onto their shoulders.

"To the palace!" Daniel directed.

Now that the show was over, the crowd again proceeded to mix and mingle. The royal escort marched down the avenue.

Sam looked at Nephi's face. Sensing his brother's anguish, he opted to leave the scolding to Shamariah. Shamariah obligingly ranted at Nephi about nearly spending Passover in the stocks and how the good name of Nephi's father had been threatened. Nephi heard very few of Shamariah's words. With clenched fists, he watched until the prince's portable chair had completely disappeared. At last, Shamariah and Sam started toward the citadel. With heavy steps, Nephi followed.

Half a block later, Nephi dashed back to the shopowner's booth.

"I want my money back," he declared.

The shopowner grudgingly handed back the bracelets.

Nephi looked in the dust for the silver ring. Now that Prince Daniel was out of sight, Nephi wasn't so ashamed to take it. But the ring was gone! Nephi eyed the shopowner. No, he'd been too busy weighing out the prince's silver and bronze to have taken it. Whoever had snatched up the ring must have been very swift indeed.

Across the street, in the shade of a pottery shop, Nephi spotted a man in a dark black cloak, a type worn by vagabonds and wanderers. His head was veiled under a hood. The man's hand tossed a silver ring into the air and caught it again.

Nephi could feel the man's sinister smile without having to see it. There was something strange about him. Had the man been spying on them? Nephi had no desire to learn his identity. He dashed back up the street to catch Shamariah and his brother.

As the man watched Nephi go, he slipped the ring into a leather pouch on his belt. Stepping cautiously into the open, he looked both ways. Only when he was certain he'd attracted no one else's attention did he scurry off in the direction of Prince Daniel's palanquin.

# Chapter 2
## CONSPIRACY AT PASSOVER

THE KING WAS IN THE GOVERNOR'S HOUSE. SERVANTS FLITTED BACK and forth, meticulous about the arrangement of flowers in wall vases and the symmetrical placement of furniture. Earlier they'd sprinkled fresh sandalwood oil along the way of each hall where the king might walk and placed a pitcher of fresh water on every table just in case, while walking, the king discovered he was thirsty. This visit had been unexpected, otherwise such chores would have been completed hours before Josiah's arrival.

The king's entrance was brisk and his summons of the governor was curt. The two half-brothers and a modest entourage of Judah's dignitaries retired to the governor's councilroom.

Not a moment later, they were joined by a contingent of foreigners. At first sight, the men didn't appear foreign, dressed in simple Hebrew cloaks. But to a keen eye like Daniel's, their features were altogether un-Hebrew and their darting glances revealed that they did not feel at home in Jerusalem.

For over an hour Daniel had been waiting in the councilroom's antechamber. His father had sent for him just before the king's visit was announced. The impromptu meeting had postponed Daniel's audience with his father, but the boy knew better than to run off after he'd been summoned. Daniel would wait until the meeting adjourned. He hoped it would end soon. If not, the first star, the beacon that signaled the beginning of the feast, might appear in the sky for the first time in over a decade without the witness of a ruling son of the house of David.

Daniel shifted nervously on the bench. Folded in his lap was the square of purple silk he'd purchased in the bazaar. His original plan had been to carry the silk to the keeper of the royal wardrobe, but by the time he got back, it was too late in the day to make any repairs. The governor would simply wear another suitable outfit.

Besides, Daniel wanted to present the silk to his father personally, without having to share the credit. He had no idea why his father had called him. Usually such a summons meant a scolding was due. Daniel hoped the silk might soften his father's temper.

Daniel shared the antechamber with the bodyguards of the foreign contingent. When he shifted, several of them looked up. Their eyes looked small and wolfish. Daniel wondered where these men could be from. Not a single word was uttered between them. Talking would have revealed their accent. No one, except for the dignitaries in the councilroom, was supposed to know their identity.

Daniel noticed the hilt of one of their swords. Carved into the metal was the unmistakable image of a spade. Few people in the world yet knew the origin of this image. The symbol was new. Daniel remembered hearing his father remark how strange and unique it was that one of the world's most powerful armies should select as their symbol not a staff or a scourge or an eagle claw, but a golden spade—a symbol for the unearthing and rebuilding of the world. The symbol's designer was the new hero-warrior of the Chaldeans—a prince named Nebuchadnezzar.

Chaldeans! Daniel cried under his breath. The foreigners are emissaries from Babylon!

At the instant of Daniel's deduction, the councilroom doors burst open. Out stepped Josiah, the King of Judah, his tall figure enveloped in his customary blue and gold Passover cloak. On his head sat a coronet, not the usual multi-jeweled crown of David. Such a crown would violate the humility of the House of the Lord, where he would go after this meeting. His triangular face, framed in a sharply-clipped beard, shone almost brighter than the coronet.

Following Josiah out of the room were three Chaldean ambassadors, appropriately servile and well-mannered in the presence of the Jewish king. Josiah's new private secretary, Ahikam, son of Shaphan, was also in attendance. Beside him was Assasiah, the Commander of the Bodyguard. Daniel's father emerged last, looking weary and overly serious as usual.

At the king's appearance, the Chaldean bodyguard knelt. Some final and hushed words were spoken between Josiah and the emissaries, after which they too bowed at the king's feet. Josiah bade them all to rise and dismissed the foreigners without further pomp. Quickly, the men exited the governor's house. Since Daniel never saw them again, he guessed that they left the city just as swiftly.

Daniel watched Josiah and his councilors exchange thoughtful glances. The meeting had apparently been more important than anyone was ready to admit. The thin-faced Ahikam blew a sigh. He appeared glad that the confrontation was over. Assasiah looked pensive. Josiah, on the other hand, looked enthusiastic, almost giddy. He noticed his nephew kneeling beside the bench.

"Daniel! My brother's son!"

The king's motives seemed to be to divert attention away from the exiting Chaldeans and back to himself as he grabbed Daniel by the waist and easily hoisted the eleven-year-old toward the ceiling.

"You look well," Josiah observed.

"Thank you, Your Majesty," said Daniel, slightly embarrassed by the king's actions. "You also look well."

"I am." He set Daniel back on the floor. "You'd better get to the feast, my nephew." Josiah turned to the others. "We'd *all* better get to the feast."

Josiah strode toward the back entrance. His entourage struggled to keep up. Although pushing forty years, Josiah was still this kingdom's symbol of perpetual youth and vigor.

Daniel faced his father. Maaseiah took a moment to recall having summoned his son. When he remembered the reason, his face grew stern.

"Come with me, Daniel." To a servant, Maaseiah directed, "Bring me a towel and a basin of cold water."

Daniel stiffened. A towel and basin could only mean one thing. Reluctantly, Daniel followed his father into the councilroom.

Maaseiah paused before the oaken table. He still appeared somewhat distracted. It wasn't easy to shift his thoughts from the affairs of the kingdom to the affairs of his immediate family, which for the last eleven years had consisted of Daniel alone. At last, Maaseiah's focus rested fully on his son.

In a last effort to cool his father's mood, Daniel raised the square of purple silk. "I found this for you in the market today."

Maaseiah glanced back at the table. At the far end sat an assortment of Chaldean gifts. Among them gleamed a broad pile of silk: blue, wine, yellow, white, black, and purple. Daniel's paltry square dropped back to his side.

The servant entered with a towel and wash basin. Daniel looked up at his father. Maaseiah's face was even and taut. The boy had known this look all of his life. It told Daniel he was first a subject and then a son.

"Do you know the law, Daniel?" Maaseiah asked.

Daniel looked confused. "I can recite—"

"I know you can recite it, but you don't seem to *know* it. My chancellor held audience with a pilgrim trader this afternoon. He claims you seized and condemned one of his beasts because, as the trader's son put it, the animal splashed mud on your cloak. Is this true?"

"No, my father. I mean, yes, but—the donkey was completely out of control! It nearly damaged the curtain on the palanquin. The animal was dangerous!"

Maaseiah stepped forward and backhanded his son across the cheek. Daniel staggered, but he did not fall. The servant, aware of the routine, promptly placed a wetted towel against the boy's face to lessen any swelling. Daniel struggled not to show his anger. Showing anger would only inspire another slap. But the resentment boiled. No other prince in the kingdom received such treatment.

"What you did was unlawful. You know it! You've embarrassed me, Daniel—and during Passover week! Judah has had countless seasons of oppression. Behavior like yours destroys everything your uncle and I are trying to accomplish. How can I maintain the respect of the people when my eleven-year-old son acts like a tyrant? Stealing silk from a sick child!"

"I didn't steal—"

"What has made you so cruel, Daniel?"

With his eyes to the floor, Daniel replied, "I wanted to please you."

Since the death of Daniel's mother shortly after the boy was born, Maaseiah's life had been dedicated solely to the governor-ship. Queen Hamutal and others had often remarked how Daniel's features so resembled his mother. Daniel wondered if his father possessed similar thoughts, especially at moments like this. Such thoughts seemed to ignite an inner rage.

"If you want to please me, then behave like a prince of Judah! Not a sniveling peasant brat!"

"Yes, Father."

Maaseiah recomposed himself. "I have one other matter to dis-cuss with you."

"Yes, Father."

"Were you followed today?"

Daniel looked up, "Pardon me?"

"When you went out into the city, did you notice any strangers trailing the palanquin, trying to learn its destination?"

Daniel feared he'd done something else worthy of a slap. "I— I only went through the Millo, into the clothing district—"

Maaseiah sighed impatiently, "Yes, yes. I believe you. It wouldn't have been anyone I sent to watch you. It would have been someone seeking to discover who rode inside the litter. Whether me, or the king, or another high official."

Daniel shook his head. "I saw no one."

Maaseiah nodded. "I want you to be wary, Daniel. If you see anyone out of the ordinary, report directly to me or Commander Assasiah. There are important events taking place in Judah, Daniel. Your king is befriending very powerful people. People who have very powerful enemies. There are those who would love to confirm this. Jerusalem is rumored to be crawling with spies, especially now, when strangers and foreigners are commonplace. It's unlikely that anyone would harm a young prince, but just the same, I'd like you to have an armed escort when you leave palace grounds. Do you understand?"

"Yes, father."

"That will be all. You are dismissed. I'll meet you at the feast directly."

Daniel hesitated. Then he bowed quickly and left.

\* \* \*

## Daniel and Nephi

THE SETTING SUN PRODUCED A BLOOD-RED REFLECTION ON THE stone wall that separated the palace quarter from the sanctuary of the Lord. In a hasty procession, Daniel and his servants entered the outer courtyard of the Temple. The usual bustle of guests filled the courtyard to capacity. Torches and lamps swung in time to the intermingling choirs.

Daniel's company ascended the steps to the inner courtyard. The boy had seen this courtyard many times before, but he never ceased to wonder at its hugeness. The white-clad priests appeared so insignificant beside the altar of burnt offerings. Daniel watched yet another group approach the glowing sea of flames with the proper items of sacrifice on a great golden dish. As the priests set the oblation in place with a golden shovel, the crucible heat drenched them in sweat. Afterwards, they proceeded to the Brazen Sea—a sacred wash basin resting on the backs of twelve oversized oxen—to be revived and refreshed.

Daniel glanced beyond the altar, into the weakly lit porch of the Temple. The pillars of Boaz and Jachin squared the entrance to the Holy of Holies, where the Ark of the Covenant rested in eternal silence. To every Hebrew boy and girl with the smallest inkling of faith, this place was the permanent dwelling of an Almighty presence. Contemplating it never failed to launch a tingle up Daniel's spine.

The prince approached the royal eating tables, laid out on the opposite side of the courtyard. Under the strict guidelines of the law, no one except the priests should have been allowed to feast on Temple grounds, but King Josiah, the great reformer, without whom the Passover celebration might never have been restored in the first place, permitted himself certain indiscretions which he considered to be minor.

Daniel was greeted enthusiastically by many of the adult court members and mildly by many of the younger ones. Such sentiment had been the lot of Daniel's life. The only good friends Daniel had who were close to his age were Mishael, Hananiah, and Mishael's younger brother Azariah. Each boy was Daniel's cousin by one line or another.

As Daniel took his seat, Mishael called to him across the table, "You're almost too late."

21

"I still got here before the king," Daniel replied.

Everyone of importance was present, except for the king, the queen, and the city governor. The High Priest sat at the far end of the table wearing the shield and twelve gems of the House of Israel as well as the crown, which bore the unspoken name of God.

At the head of the table sat Josiah's sons. Prince Jehoahaz, now twenty-two years old, was bent over his plate, making faces in the golden reflection, as ever utterly fascinated by the mundane. Prince Eliakim, now twenty-four, sat in evident boredom, his elbow on the table, his fist glued to his cheek. Daniel detected Eliakim's eyes roving through the crowd, sizing up each person as if he or she were an entree for the feast. Daniel had never forgotten an observation he'd once overheard the old scribe Shaphan use in describing the king's oldest sons. Jehoahaz, Shaphan said, had a good, bright soul united with a clouded mind, while Eliakim had a bright mind combined with a clouded soul.

Beside Eliakim sat the king's youngest, Mattaniah, bragging incessantly to the only ear obliged to listen, that of Ebed-melech, a Cushite boy who had been given to the prince as his companion and personal slave.

Just as the first star shone out in the firmament, a flourish of trumpets announced the arrival of King Josiah and Queen Hamutal. Servants, court officials, and ministering priests threw themselves to the ground. As the royal hurricane drew nearer, a confused mumbling filled the air, everyone uttering: "I have been held worthy to look upon the countenance of the king!"

Josiah and Hamutal ascended the royal dais. The spacious courtyard became deeply silent, awaiting His Majesty's first words.

At last, Josiah cried, "Rejoice with the Lord!"

The feast began. Serving Levites hurried along the tables with golden plates and pitchers of carefully prepared food and drink. The Sons of Asaph filled the porch of the sanctuary and belted out the first verse of a joyous psalm.

Josiah took his seat beside Hamutal and whispered something in her ear. Daniel watched her blush and scold him teasingly. Though Hamutal had a son in his twenties, she'd worked hard to retain a youthful appearance. Her long auburn hair was worn in the decorative style of Egyptian women, with the forehead clear. Her neck, wrists, and ankles were decked in a marvelous array of gems and chains. Golden varnish glimmered from the nails of her fingers and toes. Apparently, her efforts to remain youthful had been successful since Josiah had years since lost interest in all his other wives and concubines.

Daniel noticed Eliakim observing the king and queen. He thought he saw Eliakim's eyes narrow a little. It was well known that one of the wives with whom Josiah had lost all interest was Josiah's first wife and Eliakim's mother, Zebudah. By tradition only Zebudah should have been allowed in the inner courtyard, but Josiah had ignored the tradition. Seeing Hamutal on the royal dais must have been, for Eliakim, a bitter vision.

Josiah devoured his meal impatiently, not so much because the Passover meal was *supposed* to be eaten impatiently as much as because Josiah was an impatient person in general.

"Are the people eating bitter herbs?" Josiah called down to the High Priest. "Have the doorposts and lintels been sprinkled with twigs of hyssop?"

"They have, Your Majesty," the High Priest replied.

"Then let the readings begin!" declared the king.

Ahikam, the king's private secretary, appeared to have been awaiting this command. He held the ancient scroll in his hands.

"Who will do the reading, Your Majesty?" inquired Ahikam.

"I will hear from my youngest son, Prince Mattaniah."

Daniel rolled his eyes. It was all so predictable.

Ahikam handed Mattaniah the scroll, rolled open to the traditional verses. Nevertheless, if Mattaniah were to glance down at the script even once, it would be viewed as a personal insult to his instructors.

Mattaniah puffed up his chest. "'Observe the month of Abib, and keep the Passover unto the Lord thy God—'"

"No, not that!" the king interrupted. "This year I want to hear the precepts on the waging of war!"

Daniel raised an eyebrow. A hushed murmur arose from the guests. But none was so stricken by the king's request as the young Mattaniah. His face flushed and his eyes darted back and forth looking for assistance. This was one of the rare occasions in his life where no assistance was to be had. He muttered a series of feeble, unintelligible sounds.

Josiah realized his son was at a loss. He showed him neither anger nor pity. "Who knows these precepts and can read them to me?" asked the king.

Daniel deliberately waited for the awkwardness of the moment to fully ripen before he stood and admitted, "I can recite the precepts, Your Majesty."

"Daniel, my young nephew! Very good. Proceed."

Ahikam handed him the scroll. Daniel drew a deep breath and began in measured rhythm: "'*When thou goest out to battle against thine enemies, and seest horses, and chariots, and a people more than thou, be not afraid of them . . .*'"

"Be not afraid of them," repeated the king. He seemed to rejoice that the word of God sounded so near to his own heart.

Daniel recited every burdensome rule to be followed if Judah wished to fight with God's blessing, everything from allowing a betrothed man's return home, to the proper division of the armies. The king listened intently to every word while his subjects were left to wonder why Josiah had demanded such an inappropriate reading. That is, everyone wondered except those who'd attended the meeting in the governor's house.

When Daniel finished, Josiah stood. "So speaks the word of God! Let nothing come between the Lord and me!"

Daniel sat down proudly and looked around. His father had not been present to hear a single verse. How did it happen, Daniel wondered, that whenever he was given an opportunity to shine, his father was off doing the business of the kingdom?

"I'm sorry your father missed that," commented Ahikam as he took back the scroll. "Perhaps I can persuade His Majesty to let you read again later."

"Thank you," replied Daniel. "I'd be forever grateful."

HURRIEDLY LEAVING IN THE MIDDLE OF THE FEAST MAY HAVE BEEN tactless, but Daniel wasn't going to let his father miss his second reading. Two servants accompanied the prince back to the palace quarter and through the spacious doors of the governor's house. Daniel was struck by how quiet the place was. Not a servant in sight. Was it always left so unattended during the great feasts?

"Father!" Daniel cried. His voice echoed through the halls. Daniel's servants poked their heads into different corridors. The governor was nowhere to be found. The prince was ready to conclude that he'd passed his father in the crowd. Maaseiah would be angry to see that his son had left the feast.

A crash sounded at the other end of the house. Daniel looked startled, then ran toward the noise, bounding down the long sandalwood hallway. At the end was the councilroom where he and his father had spoken not an hour before.

"Master Daniel!" called one of his servants. "Wait!"

The warning went unheeded. The servants pursued, but they failed to catch the prince before he reached the antechamber. Daniel skidded to a stop before the open door. The councilroom was dark. All the lamps within had been doused.

"Father?" Daniel's voice was almost a whisper. There came no reply.

The servants caught up to the prince, panting and scolding. Daniel ignored them and approached the open door. It was pitch black inside. The room had windows in the roof, but they had yet to be uncovered since the rainy season was just ending. Daniel couldn't see a thing.

"I'll fetch a lamp," said the first servant. A detachable lamp glowed on the wall at the other end of the hall. Daniel waited in the doorway. As his eyes began to adjust, something took shape on the floor near the far end of the table. A person's body!

Daniel sprang into the darkness. Even before he reached the silent shape, he recognized the cloak. Daniel tried to utter his father's name, but his throat would not release any sound. Under Maaseiah's still hand lay pieces of a broken water basin, the same basin that his father's servant had used to dip the cloth that had soothed Daniel's cheek. Daniel dropped down beside the body. His knees became soaked. At first he thought it was water. Then he realized it was blood.

The second servant entered the councilroom and perceived Daniel kneeling beside the body. The prince's shoulders were trembling.

"Who—who is it?" the servant asked.

Daniel mustered enough control to reply, "The governor."

"God of Mercy!"

The tail-end of the servant's exclamation was drowned out by a deafening scream from the other end of the hallway. The prince and his servant spun toward the open door.

The scream ended. Surely Daniel's first servant was dead, but neither Daniel nor his second servant dared look to discover the murderer. The second servant slunk backwards, deeper into the councilroom darkness.

In an instant, a shadow—a wraith—slipped inside the room. The doors slammed shut, pinching off all light except for a thin crack at the floor. Daniel thought he saw a pair of legs move briskly, soundlessly, off to the right.

His second servant began muttering. "Who's there? NO! PLEASE! I BEG YOU!"

A horrible sound gurgled in the servant's throat. The noise was followed by a rapid succession of thrusts. A body hit the marble floor.

Everything went silent. Daniel refused to breathe. Any instant he expected to feel the cold steel of an assassin's blade as it slashed his throat. But the doorway opened and the wraith's silhouette stood against the square of outer light. Daniel could see only the man's back and the black hood that covered his head. If the man turned at this instant, Daniel knew he would be discovered. As the prince scooted under the table, his legs made a slight shuffle, of no more volume than a spider's steps, but the assassin had ears tuned to such noises. He whipped around. The black hood fell away from his head. The white of his grinning teeth seemed to shoot a beam of illumination back into the room, exposing the spot where Daniel groveled.

The sight of the assassin's face made the prince gasp. This man was no stranger to crime. Numerous past offenses had been punished by the mutilation of his features. One ear had been severed. The entire cartilage of his nose had been carved away, leaving a wretched and blackened scar with gaping holes for breathing. He lacked both small fingers on either hand, but this didn't seem to enfeeble his grip on a double-edged dagger.

Daniel slid the rest of the way under the table. The doorway shut again. Blackness returned. Had the assassin fled into the hallway?

Or was he even now gliding toward his victim like a demon-ghost?

Daniel listened. He listened hard. The viper was coming, but from which direction? How could he escape its strike? Daniel couldn't hear so much as the scrape of the killer's toe against the floor or the flutter of his cloak.

But he felt something. Was it a wisp of wind on his cheek? A soft exhale from the holes that were once this man's nostrils?

Daniel burst upward, his palms pressing the bottom of the table. Normally it would have taken a sizable adult to turn the heavy table on its side, but the terrified prince somehow managed it with equal ease. The assassin shrieked in anguish as the rim smashed down on his knee. He swung the blade. Daniel felt the dagger's tip slash a strand of his hair. He leaped toward the doorway.

Despite the injury to his knee, the assassin vaulted over the table, his phantom eyes blazing. Daniel threw open the door and stumbled into the antechamber, slamming it again on the killer's arm. Still, the dagger did not drop from his grip.

Daniel bolted down the sandalwood hallway. The assassin, favoring a limp, did well to keep up until the prince veered into a side foyer. The killer lost his balance and fell against the wall, his shoulder shattering a flower vase. Breathless, Daniel slipped into the gallery and then into a storage hall beyond. Either side of this hallway was lined with closets. Daniel already knew which one he would hide in—the same one he had often used to elude the eunuchs and chamberlains during a game of hide and seek. The floorboards inside the end closet on the right were loose. Underneath the boards was a vault of sorts, the purpose for which only King Solomon might have remembered. Daniel threw back the closet's curtain and fell inside. Even as his fingers tore up the floorboards, he heard the curtains of every closet down the line being tossed aside.

Daniel dropped into the vault, sending a rodent or two scurrying into crevices. When the curtain on Daniel's closet was thrown back, the boy had yet to replace the final floorboard. He held it in place with his hand. The normally hawk-eyed killer failed to notice the gap in the floor where the prince's manicured fingertips protruded. He went on to the next hallway.

Daniel's breathing remained erratic, mixed with stifled sobs. His cloak, still moist with his father's blood, stuck to his legs. Daniel struggled to replace the last floorboard, his arm trembling. He sank to his knees. How he hated his father! He hated his strictness. His discipline. His callousness. Mostly Daniel hated him for dying before his son could earn his love.

"What will become of me?" whispered the boy under his breath. If only this were a dream. Could he make it so by falling asleep? Daniel shut his eyes, sighing deeply. Yes. Only a dream. Just a sleeping vision.

"Prince Daniel!" shouted a voice.

Daniel opened his eyes. He felt vibrations in the palace stone—the march of many sandals.

"Prince Daniel! Are you here?"

Daniel recognized the voice. Assasiah! The Commander of the Bodyguard!

"Assasiah!" Daniel cried.

The footsteps entered the storage hall. "Daniel! Where are you?"

"I'm here!"

The floorboards over Daniel's head were torn up again. Assasiah's massive hand gripped the nape of Daniel's cloak, hoisting him out of the vault. Daniel latched onto his rescuer's waist. His sobs released with full force.

But the commander took hold of the boy's shoulders. "What has happened?" he demanded. "My guards reported screaming."

"My father is dead!" cried Daniel. "In the councilroom!"

"Go and see!" Assasiah commanded a pair of guards.

"There was a man in a black robe," the boy continued. "His face was marred—"

"Search the house!" Assasiah ordered the rest of his men, except for two. He turned back to Daniel. "We must get you out of here. No assassin would attempt such an act alone. If you're the only witness, they'll try to kill you at the first opportunity. Are you the only witness?"

"I think so. He stabbed both my servants."

"We must inform the king!" said Assasiah. "He must hear the details from your own lips. First we have to get you someplace safe." The commander thought a moment. "The tunnel!" He faced the two remaining guards. "Take him to the pool of Siloam.

28

Traverse the underground passage through the rock and meet us at the city's outer wall. I'll bring the king. Hurry! Protect the prince with your very lives!"

WHILE CELEBRATION ECHOED THROUGH THE NIGHT, DANIEL AND HIS armed escort moved swiftly away from the palace district, keeping to the shadows. Daniel was so delirious with grief, he depended entirely on the guards to lead him. Upon reaching the ladder at the top of the steep entrance, he couldn't remember a single step of the journey.

Daniel and the guards descended the ladder. The rungs were slick from dripping water. At the bottom, Daniel plunged into water as high as his chest. The century-old passage had been designed as an overflow channel for copious winter rains. This year the water was especially deep and especially cold. The three figures, with the aid of a single lamp, waded into the spectral gloom. The narrow tunnel with its arched roof wound and curved relentlessly. The mustiness aggravated a cold suffered by one of the guards. His coughs reverberated through the tunnel.

The water, shoulder-deep in places, made the going terribly slow. Just beyond the place where King Hezekiah's inscription marked the meeting point of the miners who bored from either end, Daniel stumbled, slipping under the water's surface. After a guard helped him to his feet, the prince folded his arms across his breast and shivered uncontrollably. Why had Assasiah chosen such an awkward place to meet the king? Surely he could have thought of a less treacherous rendezvous point. Daniel's head felt light. His bowels ached. He expected any moment to lose his dinner.

The final turn toward the opposite entrance drew nearer. Lights danced on the stone wall ahead—the reflected torches of King Josiah and his bodyguard. Daniel heard the snort of a camel.

A camel?

It seemed odd that the king would bring camels rather than steeds. Daniel proceeded around the corner. One guard walked fore and the other aft as they emerged from the passageway.

Someone shouted. The lead guard reached for his sword but he was given no time to unsheathe it. The rear guard tried to flee back into the tunnel, but he made it less than a dozen ells before shrieking his final cry.

As for Daniel, the boy stood in perfect cataplexy, unable to move, unable to comprehend. Grinning down on him was a noseless face with a severed ear and a cloak whose color blended into the night.

The assassin grabbed Daniel's hair and yanked him toward the dagger's tip. The blade set tight against the boy's throat, drawing a trickle of blood.

"Stop Zaavan!" Assasiah, the commander of the king's body-guard stepped through the other men. "You heard our orders!"

"Letting him live is bad advice," said Zaavan in his high-pitched but thirsty voice.

"I won't have innocent royal blood on my hands," Assasiah insisted.

Zaavan grudgingly let him go. Daniel's eyes looked up at Assasiah's face, a face he'd seen nearly every day of his life. A face he'd always trusted.

"Strip him of his robes and bracelets," Assasiah commanded. "He'll have no need of such finery where he's going."

"With such finery on him he might fetch us a better price," suggested one of the men. Daniel immediately guessed that these rogues with their camels and desert burnooses were not part of the royal bodyguard.

"Don't be a fool!" Assasiah scolded. "No one must know who he is. The sea Arabs at Ezion-geber will pay dearly just for a young Hebrew slave!"

Zaavan had told Assasiah that these men so hastily hired to take Daniel into the wilderness would have to be tossed into the dungeon with their tongues cut out the moment they returned. Suggestions like the one he'd just heard convinced Assasiah that Zaavan had been right.

But before anyone could lay their hands on the stricken prince, before they could strip off his wet royal garments and divide his property like wolves, the boy collapsed on the stony bank. Something snapped in Daniel's mind. The prince faded into a kind of dream-like awareness. His mind returned to the glorious inner courtyard of the Temple. The king listened with a heart full of pride as the boy continued reciting from the ancient scroll. The voices of the Sons of Asaph resounded like a choir from the presence of God.

# Chapter 3
## AT THE DESERT'S EDGE

NEPHI SKEWED HIS EYES TOWARD THE ROCKY RIDGE. THE SUN had just settled into the west, turning the cliffs deep purple and making any movement in the shadows indiscernible. Nephi sighed. The light had faded too much. He knelt again and set his fingers against the dirt, feeling the lip of the footprint. It was a lion's print, he was certain of it. A leopard's foot was smaller. A wolf's was differently shaped. In fact, the tracks made it clear there were *two* lions. Possibly three. Only someone with skills like his father's cousin Ishmael would know for sure.

Just before Nephi had left for Jerusalem with his father and brothers to attend the Passover festivities, the old men who gossiped under the ancient terebinth tree in the village claimed to have seen three lions in the overlooking hills. No one believed them, of course. Lions hadn't been seen in this part of the desert for over thirty years. Failing eyesight was blamed for the mirage. Nephi looked forward to confirming the old men's sighting.

If he'd discovered the footprints earlier in the day, he might have glued his eyes to the ridge all afternoon. Those shadowy crags were the obvious place for lions to watch and wait until dark. Such activity for his mind would have been a welcome diversion. As it was, he'd spent all day shepherding his father's flock of sheep under the hot sun, while his soul wandered beneath a cloud of deep depression. Even the bow and quiver of arrows Nephi had brought into the hills for target practice remained untouched beside the boulder.

A Levite physician from Beersheba had visited the estate the day before to see if he could discover a reason for the enduring sickness that afflicted Nephi's older sister, Hannah. The Levite spent the night reciting prayers and administering treatments. A mustard poultice was applied to her chest. She guzzled a full pitcher of barley gruel as well as an expensive elixir of herbs and myrrh, but for all the Levite's efforts, Hannah's fever remained high, her eyes grew cloudier, and her voice sank to a whisper.

Toward morning, the physician absolved himself of all blame and turned the matter over to the Lord. He accepted payment and rode away shortly after sunrise. Nephi's exhausted mother, Sariah, collapsed in tears. She was still crying when Nephi left the house to perform his usual chore of grazing the sheep.

Nephi returned to the boulder and retrieved his bow. He slipped an arrow out of the quiver and balanced it on the string. The boy's teeth clenched. It would be a foolish lion who tried to attack his sheep this day, Nephi thought. Then he lowered his bow and sat back against the boulder.

All day long, his mind had flirted with the concept of exchanging his own life for that of his sister's. Did God ever grant such requests? Laman said the Babylonians believed it. He said the Hittites did, too. There seemed to be no precepts in his own religion allowing such substitutions. Maybe it was merely a precept his father had overlooked.

The idea made sense to him. Hannah had so much more to offer the world. She'd been recently betrothed to the son of a local landowner. The wedding was to have taken place that summer. Her fiance had visited her every day since she became ill. Hannah's wedding would have been the first in the family. Laman might have married sooner, but his mind was too caught up in the family business. Hannah had a spirit about her that no other child in the household possessed. She had a unique talent for helping people see how wrong they were without making them feel defensive and ashamed. Only Hannah could make Nephi's father laugh at will.

Nephi loved her. She'd spent long hours telling him stories about distant lands—beautiful palaces, strange-looking animals, and funny customs. Her stories were mostly fiction and rumor since she'd never ventured outside of the land of Jerusalem, but Nephi loved them just the same. Once Hannah had taken the

32

blame when Nephi forgot to tie the old nanny goat and it chewed up Lemuel's sandals. She had stood in *his* place. Why couldn't he stand in hers?

A thought struck Nephi—maybe that was why the Lord had brought the lions to this part of the desert. Maybe God *meant* them to kill Nephi so Hannah could get well and the balance of life could continue as before. The exchange would be more than fair.

As the youngest son, Nephi felt he had little to offer the world. Laman would take over his father's estate and business dealings. He had the head for it. Sam would likely run the estate along with Laman. He was the one purported to be the hardest worker. Lemuel was the one everybody looked up to as religious. When Father was traveling, the family turned to Lemuel to solve any matter of the Law. Nephi, on the other hand, on days he wasn't grinding away the morning with the family tutor, tended the sheep. He hadn't even been included in the harvest. While each of his brothers and most of the servants were out in the fields laughing and singing the harvest songs, Nephi was stuck in the hills with the sheep. The sheep and his bow.

Nephi glared at the ridge again. From its steep inclines, the breeze carried the tune of a *bulbul*. There couldn't be lions up there. It was said such birds wouldn't sing if danger was near. Nephi looked around. Every sheep in the fold was staring at him. *Hasn't the sun gone down?* Nephi imagined them to be asking. *Shouldn't we have started for home an hour ago?*

Nephi glanced back into the valley where the silver-gray terraces of the olive groves marked the borders of his father's estate. A person approached over the crest of the hill. Nephi had been anticipating someone's approach all day. This was how he would learn of his sister's death. Someone would come to him in the lonely hills. Perhaps that's why he'd stayed so late. His mind was set. This was how he intended to be informed.

It was Shamariah. Would his family have such grave news delivered by a servant?

"Nephi!" Shamariah cried. "Why haven't you come home? Your father is worried."

"I forgot the time," Nephi replied. "And how . . . how is

Hannah?" He tried to make the question sound casual, but the effort failed.

Shamariah turned away. "She's doing well."

"Really?" said Nephi, grasping at any straw of hope.

"Well," said Shamariah, his conscience pricked by Nephi's enthusiasm, "at least she's doing no worse."

Nephi's shoulders drooped. Had he really hoped to hear the worst? The anticipation of Hannah's death burned at his guts like lye. Every time Nephi's hopes that she might recover were crushed, his soul was stirred up to a new comprehension of pain.

Shamariah began flapping his cloak at the sheep to get them to follow. "Come, Nephi. Supper is waiting."

The sheep weren't enticed in the least by Shamariah's cue. Only when Nephi flapped his cloak did the flock begin to move toward home.

NEPHI ENTERED THE DINING HALL OF HIS FATHER'S HOUSE JUST AS Lehi began the prayer on the meal. Apparently, they couldn't wait for the youngest son any longer. After all, darkness already covered the sky. Not that this was a usual and routine meal in Lehi's household. Nephi's mother, Sariah, was not in attendance. She continued her lonely vigil beside Hannah's couch in the back bedroom, interrupted only when it was time to nurse her fourteen-month-old daughter, Orpah. Nephi stood in the archway and waited patiently for Lehi to conclude the prayer. Hearing his father's voice always soothed Nephi. It lifted his spirit and renewed his confidence that everything would be all right, even as tragedy lurked.

Nephi stood in the archway, his head bowed. He opened his eyes a slit and saw the meal—boiled lentils, barley cakes, green almonds and goat milk. No meat. Obviously his mother had not directed the cooking today. She liked to serve meat during harvest days to strengthen her hard-working children.

In spite of their long labor, everyone at the table was neatly groomed. But fresh clothing couldn't disguise the gloom on their faces. After the prayer, eating commenced slowly.

"You grazed the sheep rather late, my youngest son," Lehi commented.

Nephi hurriedly washed his hands and face in the wash basin and said, "I'm sorry. I saw lion tracks today. There was more than one."

Everyone perked up, grateful someone had finally introduced a new subject of conversation.

"Lion tracks?" Lemuel repeated. "And how would you know lion tracks, little brother?"

"Ishmael described them for me once."

"Are there lions, Father?" asked Nephi's sister, Zeruah. She was only five and looked a little frightened.

"I think you listen to the old men in the village too much," said Laman and popped an almond into his mouth.

"You'll have to show us these tracks," said Lehi.

"Perhaps we should send for Ishmael to confirm the tracks," Sam suggested.

"Ishmael is hunting," reminded Laman.

"If everyone would just take my word for it, we could save time and organize a hunting party first thing in the morning," said Nephi.

"No one would believe a boy," said Lemuel.

Nephi bristled. "Those who've seen me shoot my bow don't see me as just a boy."

Lemuel snapped back. "After what happened in Jerusalem with the governor's son, do you think you should be treated as anything other than a child?"

"Enough," said Lehi. "Nephi has already been chastened enough for that. When I think of the tragedy in the governor's house that day, I regret to have burdened his final hours over a matter so trivial as a pilgrim's donkey. We'll worry about Nephi's lions tomorrow." He motioned his youngest son to sit and eat.

Even as Nephi took his place, he could hear raindrops on the roof. By morning the tracks would be gone.

Beside Nephi sat his nine-year-old sister, Leah, who held little Orpah on her lap and gave her a barley cake. The infant appeared more interested in making crumbs than eating them. Nephi swept away her stray morsels and grabbed the lentil bowl.

"By the way," said Laman, "I spoke with some fellow caravaneers this afternoon. They had news from Jerusalem. The governor's murderer was found. It was his chamberlain. The commander of the bodyguard had him beheaded yesterday morning at the Gate of Potsherds."

"Laman," Lehi scolded, "save such descriptions for a place other than a meal which God had blessed."

Lemuel spoke harshly. "Anyone who conspires against this kingdom will be cut down like grain before the sickle of the Lord. In our lifetimes we will see Judah crush all its enemies."

Lemuel's tone of voice was familiar. When Nephi was younger, Lemuel's tone was quite frightening.

Laman mocked his brother's fanaticism. "I hope God will spare Egypt at least until summer, after I've traded our bales in Noph."

Lemuel stood up, shaking his finger. "Egypt will be the *first* to feel the fire of God's vengeance!"

Laman chuckled and turned back to his meal.

Nephi had often heard neighbors remark to his parents how blessed they were to have such a disciplined and forthright son like Lemuel. Lately Nephi had begun to wonder if his manner was more like sanctimony.

"Remember, Lemuel," said Lehi, "the Lord is God of all nations. Not just Judah."

"And that's why God has raised up our great King Josiah," Lemuel declared. "So that every kingdom and ruler may know the power of the one true God." Lemuel seemed to have entirely missed his father's point.

"Do they know what happened to the governor's son?" Nephi asked Laman.

"The rumor is the same. He also was killed."

"Just as well," said Lemuel. "From what I've heard, he'd have grown up to become a worse tyrant than Manasseh."

Nephi began to nod at Lemuel's statement, but one look from his father told Nephi his nod was inappropriate. Lehi put a stop to the ill-mannered conversation by requesting Laman to give him an account of the day's harvest. The rest of the children finished their meals in silence, their minds again consumed by the prevailing depression. After the meal had ended, Lehi asked Nephi to take food to his mother and Hannah. Nephi considered asking if Leah or Sam could take in the food. He hadn't seen his sister in two days. She'd looked horrible then. If she looked worse now, Nephi didn't think he could bear it. But Lehi looked at him squarely to make sure the request was promptly obeyed. Reluctantly, Nephi gathered up the lentils, cakes, and a bowl of warm broth. He walked slowly toward the back room, hesitating at the door. At last, he entered.

The room reeked of vinegar, myrrh, and other medicinals. A single lamp burned at the foot of Hannah's bed, bathing the room in soft orange. The purr of raindrops on the roof mingled with the tinkle of water in an earthenware bowl as Sariah squeezed the excess out of a rag and laid it across Hannah's forehead. More rags had been draped over Hannah's shoulders and neck. This had been the routine of Sariah's watch since the fever began. Though evidence was lacking on whether it helped, such activity had to be more worthwhile than sitting helplessly idle while her daughter's life faded away.

Nephi avoided glancing at Hannah's face, looking instead at his mother. Sariah's features were pale and the curls of her long dark hair tumbled disorderedly down her back. Her tired eyes told Nephi that if she continued this vigil much longer, her condition would shortly resemble Hannah's. Despite her exhaustion, Sariah found an endearing smile for her youngest son. Her eyes involuntarily moistened.

"I've brought you supper, Mother," said Nephi, stating the obvious.

"Bring it here, Nephi."

Nephi stepped closer. Sariah requested him to set the food on the floor. She drew Nephi in for a long embrace. His mother didn't seem to expect to be hugged in return. In fact, her embrace prevented him from doing so by pinning his arms. Sariah kissed Nephi's cheek and laid her head on his shoulder, using this opportunity to finally rest her eyes. In the position his mother placed him, Nephi had no choice but to gaze down at his sister.

Hannah slept, though not peacefully. Her breaths were short and infrequent. Her eyes had sunken deeper into their sockets and her lips were blistered and cracking. Her cheeks, once so pleasantly round that her father had described them as having been fashioned smooth on a potter's wheel, were now engraved with a bluish hollow. The girl of fifteen resembled a woman of fifty. Sariah touched her daughter's swollen hand.

"Hannah?" she said softly.

Hannah gasped a long breath and her eyelids fluttered open.

"You must eat now," Sariah instructed.

"I'm . . . I can't," responded Hannah weakly.

But her mother had already drawn the wooden spoon from the lentil broth and held it to her lips. "You must eat a little."

Before Hannah sipped, she focused on Nephi. Seeing her little brother gave Hannah's features their first signs of true life that day. Her eyes sparkled like mother-of-pearl as her hand grasped out to touch him.

"Nephi," she whispered tenderly.

Nephi knelt and took her hand, then he placed it gently back on her bed as if he feared the limb might break if it hung there. "Are you feeling better?"

"I am because you came."

Sariah again pushed the spoon toward her daughter's mouth. "Come now," she coaxed. "There's not much this time." But in fact, the bowl was full to the rim and Sariah was determined that Hannah would consume every drop.

Leah appeared in the doorway carrying little Orpah. The baby was crying. When Orpah recognized her mother, both arms reached out and the tantrum heightened dramatically. All these days of limited maternal attention weren't sitting well with the infant.

"I think she's hungry," guessed Leah. "But she won't eat the cakes."

Sariah sighed and turned to Nephi. "Will you start feeding Hannah?"

"All right," Nephi replied uncertainly.

Carefully, Sariah placed the brimming spoon in Nephi's fingers. She promised her oldest daughter she'd be right back and departed to nurse Orpah in her own room.

Nephi and his sister were alone, nevertheless he found it difficult to look at her. Instead, he concentrated on the quivering spoon as he tried to settle the broth against her lips. When she made no effort to raise her head and accept it, Nephi looked mournful. Hannah's eyes continued to sparkle for her brother.

"You have to help me a little," said Nephi.

Hannah gestured for him to take the spoon away. "In a moment."

Nephi lowered the spoon and looked down, stirring the broth. "What's wrong, little brother?" Hannah asked.

"Nothing."

"Why haven't you been in to see me?"

"The harvest," Nephi answered. "I helped bundle the barley last night."

On the shelf beside the bed, Nephi noticed the trinket he and Sam had selected for her in the Jerusalem market. Sam had guessed it went around the ankle. Nephi took it in his hand and shook it. It made a pretty chime. Hannah had acted pleased when he'd brought it in to her, but Nephi knew she had been looking forward to the feel of silk on her cheek. Nephi set the trinket back on the shelf.

"Nephi," said Hannah, her voice a little stronger, "lay your head on my lap the way you did when you were little."

Though hesitant about such a childish gesture, Nephi found himself doing precisely as requested. Besides, with his head turned away like this she couldn't see his escaping tear. Hannah stroked her brother's hair. Nephi shut his eyes tightly, cutting off the images this setting brought back. One of his earliest memories was of Hannah rocking him to sleep this way. When he was five, Nephi had fallen into the spring below the olive trees. Laman had fished him out, but it was Hannah who held him and stroked his hair while the fear and the water dried away.

"I saw you in a dream today," Hannah proclaimed.

Nephi turned toward her. Dreams were not trivial matters at the desert's edge. Lehi had often guided his family by dreams. Such guidance had always been correct.

"What happened in your dream?" Nephi asked.

"You were older," Hannah replied. "You spoke to a great gathering —as great a gathering as I've ever seen. Men, women, children. Some were not even Israelites. You taught them the word of God. Everyone listened. Many had their mouths open in awe. There was a wonderful power about you, Nephi. That power came into me. My heart filled with fire."

Nephi speculated on its meaning. He couldn't imagine anything he could possibly say to such a crowd. Telling Nephi the dream had stolen much of Hannah's energy. She closed her eyes.

"Hannah? Are you all right?"

"Yes," she whispered weakly.

Nephi felt his stomach twist into painful knots again. He laid his head back down on her lap. "I'm frightened, Hannah."

"Why should you be frightened?"

Nephi faltered. Speaking of it somehow made the reason for his fears more inevitable. "I don't know," he replied.

Hannah smiled. "Don't worry, little Nephi."

Any other time, the addition of 'little' would have offended Nephi. But today, the epithet suited him perfectly.

"I won't if you say so," Nephi lied.

Hannah stroked Nephi's hair one final time. "I'll never leave you. Not forever," she assured him.

"You promise?" Nephi's voice cracked.

"I promise," said Hannah.

Her hand stopped moving. She fell back asleep.

Later that evening, Hannah slipped into a delirium from which she never returned. In the loneliest hours of night, while the palm of her father rested firmly on her forehead, as if determined to prevent his oldest daughter's life-force from escaping, Hannah's spirit slipped through his fingers and returned to her God.

ISHMAEL GUIDED HIS CAMEL ON A STEADY NORTHWARD TREK. A clammy northern breeze gently fanned the thick mist that hung over the barrenness. The sun was a feeble white circle in the extreme of the sky. Despite the weather, Ishmael knew precisely where he was. A man of the desert knew his proximity solely by the color of the sand and the coarseness of its grains. Ishmael had heard stories—and he was inclined to believe them—which claimed that old Arabs who had gone blind could guide caravans across the desert by a sense of smell. Even the sand's odor along the different roads was distinct.

In truth, the mist comforted Ishmael. These were dangerous paths in normal weather, suited only to smugglers who tried to avoid the taxes levied on the main roads or to bandits who lay in wait to rob them. The unwritten law of the desert stated that bandits must not attack a lone man with one camel, but the mist eased his mind all the same. Besides, these were the best hunting grounds for mountain goat and oryx at this time of year. The meat, salted and dried, made good jerky for travel in the wilderness. The hides and horns would be sold to his cousin Lehi, whose son, Laman, would trade them in Egypt. Here and there he set a few live traps as well. Egyptian priests thought that burning a live oryx in the name of their god, Set, restored order to the world. Ishmael didn't believe such rituals—not wholly anyway—but the income he received through selling such animals sustained his family through the winter.

Ishmael hummed a certain tune in his head, one that blended with the rocking pace of his beast. The lyrics spoke of warriors and gold. Most desert songs did. Then, all at once, Ishmael yanked the halter rope tied to a ring in his camel's nostril. The beast snorted and stopped. Ishmael peered into the drifting mist. Something was out there. A dark outline on the sand. A dead animal perhaps?

Ishmael's feet thumped the camel's neck. It lurched forward, trotting slowly. As soon as Ishmael recognized the shape, he shook the halter rope. The camel knelt on its foreknees, then settled on its belly. Ishmael dismounted and approached the shape, but not before he'd pulled his long-knife out of a sheathe behind the camel's shoulder.

The shape was dead all right. But it wasn't an animal. It was a man. As soon as Ishmael drew close enough to stand over the body, he saw other corpses off in the mist. Four. Seven. Over a dozen men, all of them slaughtered with blades, their blood consumed by the thirsty earth. The men had been dead two days— maybe three. Vultures busily pecked at the flesh, unflustered by Ishmael's appearance.

Bandits, Ishmael concluded with certainty. Every corpse had been stripped of all personal belongings. A few, with fatal wounds in the head, had even been stripped of their cloaks. The smell and swarming of flies caused Ishmael to pull the veil on his burnoose more tightly over his nose and mouth.

Foolish smugglers, thought Ishmael. What experienced caravaneer didn't know the hazards of this road? No one with a load of goods traveled these paths unless his train was guarded by a hundred armed men. Where had these people been headed? Ishmael gleaned from the camels' hoofprints that the train had been traveling south, likely toward Ezion-geber or Kadesh-barnea. Now bandits had taken their bales, their beasts, and their lives. Horse prints disappeared toward the mist-blurred cliffs in the east, the same direction from whence they came, leading the train of newly acquired luxuries. And so ended the story.

Or perhaps not.

Ishmael spun around, his eyes searching the steeper, western cliffs. A rock had fallen. It bounced three times and carried other stones with it. The echo reverberated. The rock could have been set in motion by an animal, perhaps a leopard who wished to join in the feast before the vultures finished it all by themselves. But Ishmael didn't think so.

Any other day, Ishmael would have mounted his beast and fled, but something compelled him to investigate. He didn't have to lead his camel far along the cliff-line before he found evidence of a human presence. Someone had climbed here. The displaced limestone made the trail obvious.

Again, Ishmael was tempted to ride off. Any other man of the desert would have. The source of this noise could only bring trouble. A bandit would try and carve out Ishmael's heart. An injured caravaneer might present such a burden, he'd spell doom for both of them. The desert had no patience for curiosity or compassion.

Yet an unnatural curiosity gnawed at Ishmael's flesh like a pestiferous flea. Cursing himself, Ishmael began to climb. The mist thinned with his ascent. He reached a ledge that careened toward a shallow cave. His long-knife still firmly in his grip, Ishmael stepped toward the opening. There was shuffling inside.

"Who's in there?" he demanded. "Show yourself!"

The shuffling stopped, but no one emerged. Cautiously, Ishmael ducked his head inside the shadow.

A boy, as frightened as a cornered jackal, scrambled and scraped at the back of the cavity, desperate to find some other route of escape. His tunic was in rags. Only the whites of his eyes had been spared a thick layer of dirt and grime. Blood had dried in his hair. The boy had been left for dead, Ishmael concluded.

"Easy, boy," coaxed Ishmael. "I won't hurt you." He set down the long-knife to prove it.

The boy molded himself into the deepest corner of the cave, hyperventilating and hiding his face in his arms. His breathing turned into a low whine. Nothing Ishmael could say would ease this boy's conviction that death was imminent.

"I'll bet you're hungry," said Ishmael. "Likely you're more thirsty than hungry, but my water-skins are with the camel. I do have some dates."

He removed his pouch and poured the dried fruit into his palm. Holding it toward the boy, he said, "Well? Don't make me stand here with my hand out forever."

The boy kept his face buried, but at least the whining stopped. Ishmael tossed him a date. It hit his shoulder and bounced inside the fold of his arms. One of the boy's dust-blackened hands managed to find it. He stared at the shriveled glob as if he wasn't sure what to do with it. At last his teeth sank into the moist flesh. He chewed once, then twice, then swallowed it down in a single gulp, looking up for more.

"Go on. Take them all," Ishmael invited.

The boy searched Ishmael's eyes. Did this man really intend to let him live? Leaning forward, he greedily snatched up all Ishmael's dates. After downing three at once, his throat managed to utter the words, "Can I . . . have water?"

Ishmael nodded. "But I haven't enough to waste so promise me you won't slobber it around like a camel."

"Promise I . . . I won't."

"What's your name, boy?"

The boy's expression blanked. His eyes strained. He looked at the ground, his lips trying to form something and then failing. "Uh—I—"

"What's that?" asked Ishmael.

The boy looked up, minutely shaking his head. In a graveled and faltering voice he replied, "I can't . . . I don't remember."

# Chapter 4
## FORGETTING AND
## REMEMBERING

D ID YOU SEE HIM YET?" WHISPERED SHEMIMA.

"How can I when you keep blocking the doorway?" grumbled Abisha.

"He's absolutely the most beautiful creature I've seen in all my life," sighed Shereen.

"All nine years of it, eh?" said Jumanah.

"No one's handsomer than Nephi," defended Nadira.

"Better decide that after you've seen him," said Shemima.

Their mother, Mocheleth, broke up the gathering in the entranceway of the room where the mystery boy slumbered. "How is he supposed to sleep when you're all gaping and gossiping? Don't any of you have chores? Come now. Get away from there."

The daughters of Ishmael, aged seven to fifteen, sneaked a last peek at the boy brought home by their father in the middle of the night and went about their business.

Mocheleth returned to the breakfast table. "So what do you intend to do with him?" she asked her husband.

Ishmael dipped his bread in a bowl of honey. "I'll present the matter before the elders the next time I go into the village."

"Oh, yes. The *elders.*" Mocheleth spoke the word distastefully. "Those old winebibbers will talk, scratch their beards, drink a little more wine, talk some more, and finally turn the matter back over to you where it started. If you intend to bring another child into this household, adding to the two sons and five daughters I've already borne you, I've a right to be the first one to know about it."

Ishmael tried ignore his ranting spouse and finish breakfast. He knew Mocheleth was not an ungracious woman. She simply wanted to know what would be expected. If the routine of her life had to adjust for the needs of a third son, she wanted to be prepared, especially since her husband spent half his nights in a given year under the desert stars.

"Perhaps there will be nothing to know about," said Ishmael patiently. "Perhaps he'll begin to remember who he is and where he is from and I'll take him home to his family."

"Assuming, of course, his entire family wasn't killed by the bandits," said Mocheleth.

"Yes, assuming that."

"I can't believe he remembers nothing. You're sure he remembers nothing?"

"I was with him almost two days. He remembers nothing. Not even his mother's face, I'll wager. I've heard of this condition before. It's not the first time the sun has drunk a person's memory. The delirium may last a few days or . . ."

"Or?"

"I heard tell of a Philistine in Gaza whose memory never *did* return. He left his first wife and married another. Much younger and prettier. Sometimes this delirium can have its advantages." Ishmael suppressed a grin.

Mocheleth picked up the milk pitcher. "Husband, I ought to crack this over your head!"

Mocheleth noticed the guest boy standing outside his room. Embarrassed, she set down the pitcher.

Ishmael greeted him cheerfully. "Well, look who's up to swipe half my breakfast."

The boy glanced around at Ishmael's home—uncut stone walls, dirt floor. The morning sun illuminated the table where Ishmael and Mocheleth sat. Ishmael's eleven-year-old daughter, Shemima, peered through the window. When the boy saw her, the girl disappeared amidst a flurry of giggling.

"As you can tell," said Ishmael, "we don't entertain guests very often. How do you feel?"

"I feel all right," the boy replied, but in fact he was still quite weary.

45

"My youngest son's garments fit you well."

The boy looked himself over. He had been half-asleep when they arrived the night before and he could only vaguely recall having been dressed in these clothes.

"Don't worry," assured Ishmael. "Amnor wouldn't mind. Besides, he and my oldest son, Gad, have been hired out for the harvest. I don't expect them home before the Sabbath."

"Come eat some bread and honey," Mocheleth invited.

"I must wash my hands," stated the boy.

Ishmael felt embarrassed. The rites of the Law of Moses were not strict disciplines in his home. Ishmael's blood ran Israelite, but like most men of the desert, he was not overly religious. When Ishmael *did* offer sacrifice, it was upon self-erected altars, rather than exclusively at the House of the Lord as ordered by the king. The long arm of Josiah's reforms hadn't reached quite this deep into the wilderness.

"You'll have to wash in the wadi. It's not far. About a hundred paces."

For an instant, washing in a muddy stream seemed distasteful to the boy. He remembered no reason why it should be, so he nodded and left the house.

"At least we know he's Jewish," commented Mocheleth after he was gone.

In the stone-fenced yard of Ishmael's home, four of his daughters were busily engaged in chores, stoking the fire of the clay oven for bread baking, and filling goatskin bags with curdled milk to be fist-punched into butter. Work ceased when the boy stepped into the yard. All eyes bearing down on him made the boy feel uncomfortable. He gulped out an awkward "shalom" and aimed his steps toward the stream.

Jumanah, Ishmael's oldest daughter and the one least intrigued by this stranger four years her junior, cupped her hand under Shereen's chin and closed her sister's gaping mouth.

"He's gone now," Jumanah teased.

But Shemima, a much more determined female, quickly tied off the goatskin bag and proceeded to follow him. Seven-year-old Nadira did the same.

"Shemima! Nadira!" scolded Jumanah in a harsh whisper. "You'll get us all into trouble!" But since Shereen had also joined her sisters, Jumanah decided she'd better tag along, just to keep things from getting out of hand.

Abisha was washing clothes in the wadi when she noticed the guest boy approaching. She brushed the mud off her garments and straightened her headcloth.

The boy knelt at the water's edge and began washing his hands. It seemed to him he should be saying something as he washed, but he couldn't recall the words. All at once the feel of cool water on his skin brought back the cravings he'd felt while alone on the desert. Although he'd practically gorged himself on water the night before, he touched his lips to the stream and sucked in long and deep, his eyes closed in dreamy satisfaction.

A girl's laughter broke his spell. He raised his head.

"We *do* have a well," laughed Shemima. She was perched on the boulder above him. "You don't have to drink in the mud."

The boy arose and wiped his mouth.

"I'm Shemima. What's your name?" Ishmael had made all his daughters perfectly aware of the boy's amnesia, but Shemima enjoyed seeing males put at an immediate disadvantage. That is, whenever the infrequent opportunity presented itself.

"Don't be rude, Shemima," said Jumanah.

"Don't you even remember where you're from?" Shemima asked.

He shook his head.

"So you could be from anywhere!" Shemima concluded. "Persia or Greece—or even China!"

"Don't be ridiculous," said Abisha. "People from China have yellow skin and pointed ears and six fingers."

"I'm afraid I really don't know where I'm from," the boy replied.

"What *do* you remember?" asked Shereen.

"The first thing . . . is your father's face. Nothing before that."

"Then how do you remember how to talk?" asked Nadira.

"I'm not sure."

"So as far as you're concerned," continued Shemima, "we're the first girls you've ever met."

"I guess so."

Shemima jumped down from the boulder and confronted the boy. "Do you think we're pretty?"

Except for a brief giggle from Shereen, all the girls were pin-drop silent, awaiting his answer. None of them had been around males enough to know if they were attractive. Their brothers, of course, didn't count.

"Uh—sure. You're all . . . you're all very pretty."

"Then you want to kiss me, right?"

The boy's eyes widened. "Huh?"

Shemima nudged even closer. After all, this was the only way she knew to prove if he was telling the truth. "If I'm pretty, then you should want to kiss me."

"And me too!" cried Shereen.

The boy tried to back away. "I don't think it's proper."

"I knew it," mourned Abisha. "He's the son of a Levite."

Shemima followed him, moving in even closer. "Is that true? Are you the son of a priest?"

"I—I don't know. I don't think so."

"Then we'd all like a turn at being kissed."

Shy little Nadira let out a shriek and took off for home. The boy fell backwards in the stream. "I can't!" His voice cracked on the last word.

Shemima turned to Abisha and Shereen. "Together we could hold him down."

The boy looked sincerely terrified.

Jumanah threw up her hands. "I'll have no part of this." Although she fully intended to stick around and watch.

Nadira had reached the top of the gully. "There's a rider coming!" she shouted back.

The announcement startled the girls. As the sound of galloping hoofs grew louder they dashed up the gully. Shemima paid the boy a final ravenous glance, tempted to pucker her lips and pounce before he knew what hit him, but Nadira shouted that the horseman was their oldest brother, Gad.

Only after Shemima had started running up the rise did the guest boy feel it was safe to climb out of the water. He resolved never again to venture out alone.

Ishmael and Mocheleth had also emerged from the house to greet the rider.

"I've come home to deliver bad tidings," said Gad before dismounting. "I just heard the news yesterday myself. Hannah has died. Lehi and his family are in mourning."

LEHI MADE THE FUNERAL ARRANGEMENTS THE DAY HANNAH DIED. It was the most painful thing he'd ever done. The burial procession was filled with much lamenting, the loudest coming from a hired troop of professional mourners. Hannah's body was laid to rest in a private chamber of the family tomb, her only companions the skeletons of Lehi's mother and father, grandmother and grandfather, great-grandmother and great-grandfather, and a great aunt.

Lehi's ancestors had not lived at the edge of the desert for many generations. Lehi's great-grandfather had been a landowner in the northern kingdom of Israel before the warlords of Assyria ransacked the land and carried off her most distinguished citizens to unknown corners of the world. Lehi's great-grandfather was said to have been something of a prophet. As the story went, his southward migration had been inspired by a vision. He sold his lands in Ephraim, much to the disdain of friends and neighbors, and purchased a barren piece of real estate at the southern edge of the land of Judah. It was only a few years later when the Assyrian storm arrived and the northern kingdom vanished into history.

At present, Lehi's estate was the most profitable in the district. The last two years had been particularly fruitful, especially since Laman had been willing to carry the estate's increasing surplus as far north as Damascus and as far south as Memphis—or Noph—on the Nile, thus eliminating the middle-men in the Jewish trade city of Hebron.

Having enjoyed such ease and prosperity for so many years, Hannah's death came as a staggering blow. The family had been unprepared for such pain. The seven days required by custom for uninterrupted mourning were badly needed. Lehi, Sariah, the five oldest children, and their faithful servant Shamariah, sat day after day on the floor of the main room, named the Hall of Joseph after Lehi's great-grandfather. The males had torn their garments in certain places. Sariah, enveloped in coarse linen, dipped her hands in a bowl of ashes from time to time and strewed them over her shoulders.

Day after day the house resonated with high-trilled cries. Smiling or laughing was forbidden. Throughout each day visitors arrived from the village and neighboring estates, partaking of the food and drink prepared in abundance and offering up their sincerest condolences. Mourning was interrupted only when the youngest children needed parental attention or when Dagan, the estate's bailiff, arrived after dark to give a brief accounting of the day's harvest.

For father Lehi, it was a time of lonely anguish and bitter reflection. On the first day of mourning, Sariah often heard him longingly whisper the question "Why?" to his God.

"Why take Hannah?" he would ask. "The flower of my family. As pure as spring rains. Have I offended Thee, Lord? Have I not kept Thy Law all my days? Have I not taught Thy Laws to my children? What have I done to deserve such a curse?"

On the second day, Lehi seemed angry and distant and spoke nothing at all. Sariah moved once to touch his hand, but Lehi shrank away from her and turned his face toward the wall.

On the third day, Lehi cried his most bitter tears. But by nightfall, his countenance had changed. His spirit had relented. Lehi whispered to his wife, "When, my sweetest Sariah, did I begin to stray from my God?"

She offered him her hand again. This time Lehi took it and held on tightly.

"You're the most faithful man I know," Sariah replied.

Lehi shook his head. "When I was young, maybe. Before my father died. I think I now know one reason Hannah may have been taken from us, my wife. To help me remember."

Lehi's eyes welled up with tears. Sariah curled her arms about her husband's shoulders.

On the fourth day, Lehi sat silently. All day, his gaze moved from one of his children to another. At last, he said to Sariah, "They don't miss a thing. None of them."

"What do you mean, my husband?"

"They know that in this home, the estate is first and God is second."

"That's not what you've taught them."

"It's the example I've set."

After another hour of silence, he pointed out old Shamariah across the room. "How long has Shamariah been with us?"

Sariah thought a moment. "A long time. Since Lemuel was born."

"Seventeen years. By law he should have been released with his portion ten years ago. How many bondmen and bondwomen have remained in our service beyond the lawful seven years?"

Sariah was somewhat confused. This law of emancipation was known to her vaguely, but no one in all of Judah and Benjamin, from the king to the smallest farmer, was known to adhere to it, nor would many bondmen think to request it. "I doubt Shamariah would ever leave us after all this time."

"Perhaps today he wouldn't, but back then he might have. Many of the others might have left as well, as it was their right, but the choice was never given to them."

Laman sat close enough to overhear his father. Lehi watched his oldest son's expression grow uneasy. Laman's concerns could be deduced easily enough. The expense of releasing so many men and women all at once would put half the estate out of business. Lehi made no further mention of the matter that day.

On the fifth day, Lehi spoke again, but in much quieter tones so only Sariah could hear.

"I've taught my children much about God's laws," he began, "but very little about His love. They know how to fear Him, but not how to love Him."

"We've done the best that we could," said Sariah.

"I don't think so," Lehi responded. "Children don't focus their solemn thoughts on that which they fear. Look at Laman. My passion for building up this estate has seized his heart. I'm afraid this estate has become his god, just as Moloch and Baal become gods to the heathen."

Sariah was not blind. She also felt many of her husband's concerns. But her nature inclined her toward defending her children. "Laman is still young. Sometimes the Lord's spirit is forced to wait. Perhaps after he marries, he will follow Lemuel's example."

"Lemuel causes me as much distress or more," said Lehi. "He fears and respects the Lord, but he understands nothing of His mercy. Nothing of His patience. He knows the laws and commandments by rote, but cares nothing for God's motives in designing them."

Lehi spent most of the sixth day in prayer. His words may have been the most fervent and humble he'd ever uttered. He pled for forgiveness. He asked for no other blessing. Only to know how he might make things right. That evening, though his body had been physically dormant for the past six days, his muscles felt oddly exhausted, as if he'd spent the entire day in the fields. Perhaps it was an exhaustion of the soul. Rarely had his spirit been so exercised. Though his house was now empty of guests and his family lay fast asleep, Lehi wandered to the table in the Hall of Joseph and sat in the light of the ever-burning lamp. His gaze turned toward the window.

The view through this window had filled Lehi with wonder all the days of his life. Tonight the undulating hills and mountain chains toward the north were lost in moonlight. When he was a child, barely eight or nine years old, that same northern sky had been darkened by a fierce cloud of dust. A horde of Scythian horsemen had invaded the country of the Lord on a trail of murder and rapine that extended beyond the borders of Egypt. The men had drawn close enough for Lehi to note their pig-tailed hair, wide mouths, and merciless eyes before his father snatched him away from the window and fled with his mother and sister into the protecting arms of the wilderness of Judah. Little remained of their livestock and grain when they returned, but the house, and this view from the window, had been spared. Lehi had found that one of the Scythian's curved swords had been carelessly left behind in the field. Now quite rusted, it still hung on the wall where his father had placed it as a reminder of God's mercy.

Lehi had seen many things through this little porthole. Caravans with over five hundred nodding camels had passed along the road northwest of his property and continued down into the land of Simeon and the Wilderness of Zin. The magnificent coaches of foreign princes had trodden by as well, preceded by runners and heralds and fairy-tale figures riding horses with purple saddle-cloths and blinding gold bridles. But nothing Lehi had seen from this window prepared him for what he was about to see.

Lehi's weariness had deadened all the feeling in his limbs. His mind emptied. Sleep crept inside the lids of his eyes. One instant he was awake. The next, his chin had dropped onto his chest.

This sleep had scarcely lasted the tenth part of an hour when Lehi snapped back to full consciousness. His senses were incredibly clear, fresh, and alert, as if he'd rested the full night. He did not doubt that he was entirely the master of reality and truth within and without when something began happening outside.

The moon and stars no longer cast a glimmer on the landscape. The world had darkened. But a shape was forming! It hovered over the hills, looming nearer and nearer until it filled his whole frame of vision through the window. A cauldron! A seething black pot whose glowing contents slapped his face with hot breath. Lehi gasped. Its proximity to his home—its immensity! The roof should have ignited like straw! The very foundation of the house should have melted under its fervency. But the only sure evidence of its temperature was the sweat on Lehi's brow. Lehi couldn't breathe. His heart beat wildly.

And then the Voice came.

It was a voice he'd heard before, but only as a vague and brief whisper or as a hollow, distant call, like a boulder rolling down the side of a mountain. Tonight, it came with profound clarity, filling the room with gentle mellowness. Every crack in the wall, every fissure of wood, became filled with its presence, equally and simultaneously. Yet he could pinpoint no source for the Voice. It arose and diffused everywhere at the same time, as if it had been there all along, submerged by the preoccupied traffic of the busy world.

"Lehi," said the Voice.

Lehi discovered he'd fallen to his knees. Instinct told him he should also avert his eyes, but they were fixed upward—he could not shake them. Neither, he supposed, should he have been able to loose his tongue and speak, but after one feeble choke he heard himself reply, "Here am I, Lord."

"Rise and look."

Gathering his feeble legs beneath him, Lehi directed his gaze back at the boiling cauldron suspended outside his window. An increase of courage entered his soul. A portion of the Voice seemed to have penetrated his flesh and filled every limb and fingertip to capacity. With his frame thus supported, Lehi watched as the edge of the cauldron inclined toward him from the north and spilled over. A massive wave of glowing liquid metal spurted up and washed around the corners of his house, continuing in a southward stream. Lehi's land—in fact, the entire countryside—burst into flame, rooted up, and melted into a twisted, blackened waste. That is, all but Lehi's home. The dwelling place of his family remained intact.

The Voice spoke again, and for the first time, it seemed to come from a distinct location, close to Lehi's ear.

"What seest thou?"

Lehi replied, "I see a seething pot, spilling forth destruction."

"From which direction is its course?"

"From the north."

"Thou hast seen well. Out of the north an evil shall break forth upon all the inhabitants of the land. If thou wilt hearken unto my voice from this day, thou and thy seed shall be spared. Remember my warning. Remember my words—and listen."

That final word—*listen*—hovered exultingly in the air, like the prick of a harp string. Before the vision closed, before the fire and cauldron receded back into the oblivion from which they came and before the moon and stars returned to hang in the firmament over a newly burgeoning landscape, Lehi opened his arms wide. Gratitude filled his heart to bursting and soaked his cheek in free-falling tears. His mind had lost nothing of its tense alertness. He knew this had been no illusion, no dream, no enchantment, but an experience as intimate and true and real as he himself.

All at once, Lehi felt as weak and fragile as an infant. The Voice withdrew, but slowly. He was not left cold. Nevertheless, his body collapsed and Lehi faded again into distant sleep.

THE DAUGHTERS OF ISHMAEL HAD DECIDED TO START CALLING HIM Jophy until such time as he remembered his real name. The boy knew the name meant "beautiful" and he was embarrassed every time he heard it, but the tag caught on and soon Ishmael, his wife and two sons were using the name as well.

It wasn't until late afternoon on the seventh and final day of official mourning that Ishmael's family arrived at Lehi's estate. Jophy rode pillion on the horse with Ishmael's thirteen-year-old son, Amnor. As they drew nearer to the main house, Amnor bragged that the structure's cedarwood beams had been shipped all the way from Lebanon. The stones had been individually cut and the gardens had flowers that grew only along the Nile. Amnor was quite proud of his father's rich cousin Lehi and he expected Jophy to be equally impressed. Jophy was not. For an instant Jophy seemed to recall walking among gardens much more colorful and plush. The memory triggered a stab of pain. He pushed the pain back, somewhere far away. And then with regret, he desperately tried to recover it, but it was too late. The memory was gone.

Frustration surged in Jophy. This wasn't the first time he'd suppressed memories just as they tried to surface. The previous night, a face had flashed in his mind. A terrible face with dreadful scars. He awakened with a scream. Mocheleth came and held his trembling body. At first, such motherly attention seemed so unfamiliar, the boy felt foolish. Then he clung to her gown like a sailor who clings to the mast in a raging storm. Mocheleth held him until the trembling stopped, until he fell back to sleep.

When Ishmael announced that the family would be traveling to his cousin's estate, Jophy had felt a rush of excitement. Only a vague awareness remained in his mind to convince him that anything at all existed in this world besides harsh desert. An idea nagged at him. He wondered if the best way to trigger the return of his memory would be to see new sights, hear new sounds, and smell new smells. But on the morning of departure, as everyone started mounting the camels and horses, Jophy's stomach grew queasy. He wanted to blame the animals. Beasts of any shape or size made him terribly nervous. But it was more than that.

Jophy yearned to know his identity—he really *did*—but the fact was, something inside had decided it was better *not* to know. Perhaps this "something" was right. Perhaps it was best if he never found out.

Servants took Ishmael's train of camels and horses to be hobbled and fed. The family was led inside Lehi's home and into the Hall of Joseph. Father Lehi arose and embraced his cousin. Sariah went immediately to Mocheleth. Ishmael's arrival on this final day of mourning lifted the spirits of Lehi's family more than Ishmael could know. Their children had played together all of their lives. Gad and Lemuel were best friends, as were Amnor and Sam. But no friendship had been quite as close as the one between the oldest daughters, Hannah and Jumanah. Jumanah had not taken the news of Hannah's death well. When she stepped into the hall, it finally hit her that Hannah was truly gone. She was the first in Ishmael's family to add fresh tears to the pool that had already fallen.

Nephi looked around nervously for little Nadira. He didn't need any of her pokes and giggles today. Over the past year, Ishmael's youngest daughter had made no effort to hide her overwhelming crush on Nephi. Though Nephi had tried everything—lizards, frogs, even spiders—he couldn't seem to shake her interest.

Ishmael's daughters settled down on the floor with Nephi's sisters. Nephi heard giggling from his sister, Leah. However inappropriate the sound may have been, it cheered Nephi's soul. There would be laughter again in this house. And then Nephi noticed that the girls were sneaking glances at the new boy Ishmael had brought. Ishmael was presently introducing him to Lehi and explaining, in hushed tones, the traumatic circumstances which had brought the boy into his life. Nephi heard only snippets of the conversation. Something about a caravan being ambushed as well as the phrases "half-starved" and "doesn't remember his own name."

Nephi noticed that even little Nadira had joined in the reverie, pointing her finger and covering her mouth so no more giggles could escape. He felt unexpectedly jealous.

Nephi glanced again at the stranger. *Yes*, he supposed. A girl might find him handsome, although Nephi was certainly no expert on the matter.

He found himself staring hard at the boy. His light brown hair. His blue eyes. There was something about that face which bothered Nephi. Something about his . . .

Nephi leaped to his feet, his mouth hanging wide, his eyes as large as walnuts. Almost everyone in the room turned to look at him. Nephi had been silent and still most of the last seven days. Such sudden movement from Nephi was noteworthy.

Jophy couldn't help but notice Nephi glaring at him. But why? He certainly didn't recognize Nephi.

As Nephi leaped across the room to tug on his father's sleeve, his brother Sam also began staring at the boy with a strange sense of recognition.

"Father," Nephi interrupted.

"In a moment, Nephi." Lehi turned back to Ishmael.

"No!" said Nephi. "I have to talk to you *now*!"

Lehi considered Nephi carefully. His youngest son showing such insistence was rare. Lehi allowed himself to be dragged into the adjoining room.

"What is it?" Lehi demanded.

"That boy," Nephi began. "I know him."

"From where?"

"Don't you realize, Father?" Nephi struggled to keep his voice a whisper. "It's *him*!"

"Him *who*?"

"The governor's son! I swear by my life! That boy is Daniel the Prince!"

# Chapter 5
# A ROYAL HOUSEGUEST

THE BOY WHOSE NAME WAS NOW PURPORTED TO BE DANIEL BECAME exceedingly curious when Lehi reentered the room with his youngest son and paid him a bewildered, even mildly frightened glance. Lehi then proceeded to approach person after person to whisper something frantic in their ears. Whatever might have been the message he whispered, it enticed each person to likewise glance in Daniel's direction. All had the same agitated expression. Lehi, Ishmael, Nephi, Sam, Shamariah, Laman, and Lemuel gathered at the doorway and made a hasty exit.

The party sought the privacy of the family sanctuary situated east of the main house. It was an unkempt, roofless structure that hadn't been used particularly for religious ceremonies since before Laman was born, not since Josiah had issued the decree forbidding formal worship at any place outside the Temple. Nowadays it was only used for special occasions, such as when Lehi or Laman entered into a solemn business contract with a neighbor or tenant farmer and swore the customary oath.

There among the old stones that had once belonged to an altar, Lehi proceeded to interrogate Sam and Shamariah, seeking to confirm Nephi's claim.

"I'm not sure about it," said Shamariah. "This *could* be the same boy. My eyes have dimmed a bit over the years."

"Well, *I'm* sure," Sam declared. "That boy in there is Prince Daniel. There's no doubt in my mind."

No one else in the room could claim to have ever met or seen the prince. Lehi had no choice but to trust his two youngest sons.

"How is it that such a prominent figure from the house of David came to be starving and helpless in the wilderness?" asked Ishmael.

To Lemuel the answer was as clear as a bell. "There's a conspiracy in the kingdom! The chamberlain didn't murder the governor at all. Someone else committed the crime. Someone who wants to destroy King Josiah. We have to spread the word!"

"Don't be a fool," said Laman. "If the wrong people heard about this first, our entire household could be destroyed."

"Laman is right," said Lehi. "Every moment this boy dwells among us, our families are in grave danger. I suspect the prince knew his father's killer. They sent him off so he wouldn't talk. In the port cities of the south he could be sold as a slave. Among the spice traders, he would have little chance of ever returning to his homeland."

"Perhaps, then, it is some incantation that has taken his memory," suggested the superstitious Ishmael.

Lehi brushed off the suggestion. "I've never heard of such an incantation. But whatever the cause, his loss of memory may be the best thing that could have happened to him. It will prevent anyone besides the seven of us from knowing his true identity. This will give us time to go directly to the king. Each of us must swear to keep the matter private."

Everyone present took the oath.

"Ishmael and I will leave at first light," Lehi declared.

"I would also like to go along," requested Lemuel.

"What about Prince Daniel?" asked Nephi.

"For now his name is Jophy," said Lehi. "Don't even mention his real name. Such information might trigger something in his mind."

Laman agreed with his father. "If this boy is half as spoiled and thoughtless as I've heard, who knows what vagabonds he'd spill his guts to in order to coerce them to take him back to Jerusalem?"

"Where will he stay?" asked Sam.

"If I'm headed to Jerusalem," said Ishmael, "I'd prefer he did not stay with my family."

"He should stay here," Lehi suggested.

"Here?" balked Nephi.

Lehi nodded. "If he's here, no one will ask questions. They'll assume he's an itinerant hired on for the harvest."

For Nephi this was disturbing news. The grudge he felt over Hannah's death still boiled. All week, he'd sought some object on which to vent his anger, some person on whom he could sufficiently place blame. Now this object—this person—had been provided. Wasn't this Daniel the same person who'd snatched away Hannah's last chance for a moment's happiness? Perhaps the feel of silk would have brought color back to her cheek. Perhaps the thought of living to see it made into a veil or shawl would have given her a reason to keep fighting. Now, no one would ever know.

And it was because of him.

That evening Lehi told Sariah he'd be traveling to Jerusalem in the morning with Lemuel and Ishmael. The boy, Jophy, was to remain on the estate.

"Laman will introduce him to Dagan in the morning for field work."

Lehi felt uncomfortable with this statement even as he said it. Could harvesting barley be appropriate work for a blood member of the house of David? It wasn't unreasonable to think Lehi could be beheaded for subjecting a prince to such labor.

He decided on a more congenial option. "On the other hand, I'll tell Laman to have him help Nephi with the flocks."

Sariah studied her husband's face. She sensed this was no ordinary agitation.

"Will he sleep with the other workers?" she asked.

"No," Lehi replied. "He must sleep in the main house. Treat him well. Treat him as one of our own."

Sariah nodded. She desperately wanted an explanation. Who was this boy? What had he done? How did all this inspire a trip to Jerusalem? Lehi shook his head slightly, a sign to Sariah that, for the time being, she must hold her questions.

Lehi wished desperately that he could tell her. Certainly, his wife was the most trustworthy of all of them. But there was no reason for more people to know, and more importantly, Lehi was bound by an oath.

"There's nothing to worry about," Lehi told Sariah. Lehi also seemed to be reassuring himself. "We will place our trust in God—absolutely in God."

# Daniel and Nephi

\* \* \*

WHEN NEPHI AWOKE THE NEXT MORNING, HIS FATHER, HIS BROTHER, and Ishmael were gone. Nephi wandered outside and looked into the stables. His father had taken horses instead of camels. This would hasten the journey, but it also added risk. Though Lehi had much wealth, he hadn't yet attained official status as one of Judah's noblemen and only the noblest of families were allowed to ride horses in and around the nation's capital. It was said that desert pilgrims who arrived on horseback sometimes had their steeds confiscated. His father must have decided that the increased speed made it worth the risk.

Nephi noticed Amnor and Gad at the other end of the stable. They were preparing their camels for the day's journey home with their mother and sisters. Nephi retrieved his bow and quiver from their usual place with the other tools. As he turned to leave the stables, he nearly ran smack into his brother Sam.

"Have you seen Laman yet?" asked Sam excitedly.

"No."

"Then I'll be the one to tell you. A servant from Elijah's estate rode through this morning. Elijah lost sixteen sheep two nights ago. Lions! They're sure of it. You were right."

"I told you they were lion tracks!" cried Nephi.

"They're rounding up volunteers from every estate to join in the hunt."

"Thanks for telling me, Sam."

Nephi rushed back toward the main house. Laman just had to let him join the hunt. With Ishmael gone to Jerusalem, Nephi considered himself one of the better trackers in the district. Besides, he'd discovered the paw prints before anyone else.

Nephi met his oldest brother outside the front door. At Laman's side stood the prince. Daniel's hair hadn't yet been straightened and his eyes still squinted at the daylight. Laman wore a satisfied smile. He seemed to enjoy having awakened a prince at such an early hour. In Laman's opinion, all royalty slept until noon.

"You're to take Jophy with you into the hills today," Laman instructed.

"What about the hunt?" Nephi pleaded.

Laman became impatient. "Now you want to go off and hunt lions? Someone must graze the sheep. You think I should do it? Or Dagan, perhaps? This is *your* job, Nephi. We've no one else to spare."

Nephi looked at Daniel. "Why do *I* have to watch him? I thought he was supposed to work in the fields."

"Father's orders," said Laman.

"He doesn't even have a water-skin. Did anyone make him a lunch?"

"Mother always packs you enough for two. Remember, if you see strangers approaching, you're to flee home immediately. Forget about the flock. We've much more to fear from strangers than lions."

Laman glanced quickly at Daniel. Surely the prince would find such instructions odd, but they needed to be said. Laman walked past the two boys and went about his business.

The boys stared at one another: Daniel with moderate shyness, Nephi with obvious disdain.

"Good morning," said Daniel. "I'm glad to finally talk to you. Your mother thinks you and I are about the same age."

Nephi scanned Daniel once from head to toe. "Looking at you, I'd say I was a little older."

He marched past Daniel, offering him no signal to follow. Daniel caught up as Nephi opened the sheepcote to release the flock.

"Have I offended you somehow?" Daniel asked.

Nephi pretended not to have heard the question. He sauntered down the path, flapping his robe. The sheep began to follow.

"What makes you ask that?" Nephi finally replied.

Daniel walked beside Nephi. "Your manner. The way you're acting. The way *everyone* is acting."

"Oh? And how is everyone acting?"

"As if they know something about me and what they know isn't pleasant."

"What do you think it is that we know?"

"I'm not blind. I noticed when you pulled your father aside yesterday. I noticed when everyone left the house to speak privately. Ever since then, all of you have treated me differently."

"Differently?"

"How often does your father give up his bed to a stranger?"

"My father is very gracious."

"Yet he put his own cousin in guest quarters. Why did Ishmael and your father decide to leave so suddenly?"

Nephi shrugged.

Daniel pursued the matter further. "And why am I staying here instead of returning with Amnor and Gad?"

"How should I know?" blurted Nephi. "Why don't you ask Laman these questions?"

The remainder of the their walk past the olive groves and into the hills was silent except for the bleating of sheep. Nephi's reaction had only heightened Daniel's suspicions. Something was up. Did they know who he was? Why would they refuse to tell him? Could his identity be so terrible? Maybe he was a criminal sent out into the desert to die. Maybe he was a spy or a traitor. Maybe Lehi and Ishmael had gone for the authorities.

Later in the morning, Nephi settled the flock on the same grassy hilltop where he'd grazed them the day before Hannah's death. The spring grasses here were plentiful, and besides, Nephi had already built several targets for his arrows against the sandy incline about forty paces to the east. The targets consisted of three separate circles of rocks. Two of them were large and the other was quite small. Nephi continued to ignore Daniel and strung his bow.

Daniel watched him curiously. "Nice bow," he said.

Nephi eyed Daniel warily. "Thanks. It's old."

Nephi's bow stood up to his elbow. It was of Egyptian make, encased in leather and birch bark and composed of birch wood and ibex horn with a backing of ox sinews for added elasticity. The bow had been given to him by Sam, who'd never had much of a passion for archery. In its day, the weapon might have been used in battle. Even now, its trajectory was impressive, but a portion of its original strength had waned.

"Laman promised me I could travel with him to Noph in a few weeks to trade for a new one," Nephi added.

"Are you any good with it?"

Nephi huffed. "I've never met anyone my age who was better. This autumn I plan to compete with the adults at Hebron."

Nephi's display of pride gave Daniel an idea. "Tell you what—
if I can shoot an arrow with more accuracy than you, will you tell
me everything I want to know?"

"Everything about what?"

"About who I am. I feel certain there are things you're not saying."

Nephi stepped toward him with a grin. "Let me get this straight.
Are you challenging me to a contest?"

Daniel casually scanned Nephi's display of targets against the
sandy incline, pointing out the smallest circle of stones. "If my
arrow lands nearer to the center of that target than yours, will you
tell me who you think I am and why your father has gone to
Jerusalem?"

Nephi drew his thick brows together suspiciously. "How much
practice have you had?"

"In all honesty," Daniel replied, "I can't recall ever having
touched such an instrument."

Nephi laughed, but he couldn't mask his nervousness. This had
all the elements of a fool's wager. How much archery training
might a prince of Judah be given? There was a good chance he'd
been given much. But if he couldn't remember who he was, how
could he possibly remember such training? Maybe Prince Daniel
was experiencing a kind of instinctive recollection which gave
him confidence. But all this didn't matter. Nephi had sworn an
oath.

"I can't," said Nephi.

"Why not?"

"Because I can't."

"Because you're afraid you would lose?"

"Of course not," Nephi scowled. "I just *can't.*"

Daniel sighed. "I understand." His voice oozed with sarcasm.
"If I stood the chance of being humiliated by a total stranger, I
probably wouldn't accept such a challenge either."

"Humiliated!" Nephi leaned nose to nose with the prince. "If I
were bit by a scorpion and kicked in the head by a horse, I could
*still* shoot better than you!"

"I'm sure that you could," replied Daniel calmly. He sat down
on the ground and got comfortable. "It's obvious you're not a
coward. You're probably refusing my challenge because you're

afraid you might hurt my tender feelings. Am I right?"

Nephi boiled. Here he was, Daniel the prince, just begging to be slammed in his place. The prince may not have remembered his name, but his arrogance hadn't subsided one iota. How often would Nephi have a chance to humble and shame someone who deserved it so badly?

"Get up," Nephi seethed. "I accept your challenge."

Daniel hopped to his feet, beaming with enthusiasm. "And if the arrow I shoot lands closer to the center, you'll tell me everything?"

"I'll tell you everything," Nephi agreed through his teeth.

"Swear by your life?"

Nephi hesitated. This was a much stronger oath than the one he'd taken with his father. Nevertheless he heard himself say, "I swear by my life."

Nephi thrust his bow toward Daniel.

"No, no," the prince insisted. "You may go first."

Nephi paid Daniel a final scowl and retrieved an arrow from his quiver. He chose one with a bronze tip. Normally he would never use this arrow to shoot into the dirt, preferring instead one of the cheaper-quality iron-tips. But the bronze-tipped arrow was longer and straighter. Nephi slipped the drawing ring over his finger and balanced the projectile onto the string. With his sandal, he drew a line in the dirt. After setting his toes at the base of this line, he pulled the arrow back to his ear. Nephi's temper still burned, but this did not concern him. From experience, Nephi knew that when he was angry, he tended to shoot better.

Daniel watched the blood pumping in the vein on Nephi's neck as Nephi released the string. The bow let out a twang. The wind whistled through the arrow's feathers. With a thump, the bronze tip pierced the dirt. Nephi sprang forward to verify its point of impact. Daniel could tell from where he stood that the arrow had imbedded the ground exactly between the stones on the lower curve of the circular target. Not a bulls-eye, but considering the distance and size of the target, the shot was undeniably impressive.

Nephi spun around to see Daniel's reaction. Did the prince look intimidated? Not really. Daniel's nonchalance sent a shiver of doubt through Nephi. The prince reached out for the bow with a patronizing wriggle of his fingers. Nephi handed it over.

Daniel chose Nephi's only other bronze-tipped arrow. *If he breaks it,* thought Nephi, *I'll see to it that he buys me another one if it's the last thing I do.* Daniel also borrowed Nephi's drawing ring. Before pulling back the string, he squinted at the target.

Nephi reminded himself that there was nothing to fear. He knew only one or two people in the district who could readily beat that shot and these people had been archers for fifteen or twenty years. Still, he held his breath.

And then Daniel began walking forward, keeping his eyes focused on the target.

Nephi dropped his arms. "What are you doing?"

"I think I'd do better if I stood closer," Daniel replied.

Nephi marched after him. "If you stood closer? Are you crazy? You can't do that! I've already drawn the line!"

"You drew your own line. Not mine." Daniel continued until he was a mere three paces from the target.

Nephi stood to the side of him, continuing to protest. "You're cheating! How could you possibly think—?!"

"Quiet!" scolded Daniel. "I'm trying to aim."

Flabbergasted, Nephi watched as Daniel drew back the string and let the arrow fly. Of course, it stuck directly in the center of Nephi's tiny circle of rocks.

"That doesn't count!" Nephi raved. "It's not fair! You have to stand where *I* was standing. Those are the rules! Any buffoon knows that!"

"We agreed to no such rule," defended Daniel. "Only that my arrow would land closer to the center of the target. Therefore, I win."

"You cheated!"

"I didn't. Tell you what. In our next contest, if it'll make you feel better, I'll let you make the rules."

Nephi couldn't believe what he was hearing. Did Daniel actually believe such a con game would bind Nephi to his oath?

Daniel must have sensed that he'd overplayed things a bit, because he resorted to a different approach.

"Nephi, listen to me. You don't know what it's like not knowing

66

who you are. Not knowing your own name. Where you come from. You must tell me who I am. I command it!"

Daniel grew quiet. He listened to the echo of his own words. Words so familiar. Words that came so easily to his tongue. Were they words he frequently spoke or words that were frequently spoken *to* him?

As if he could read Daniel's mind, Nephi decided he should convince Daniel of the latter. It would be a valuable lesson for this sniveling prince. One day Daniel would thank Nephi for teaching him such a wonderful lesson in humility.

"Okay," Nephi began. "You win. I'll tell you who you are. You, Jophy, are a slave. You've been a slave all your life. Your parents were slaves, your grandparents were slaves, and your great-grandparents were slaves!"

Daniel shrank away from Nephi. Something about this proclamation didn't sound quite right.

"No. This can't be true. If I'm a slave, what was I doing out in the desert?"

"Uh, well . . ." Nephi perked up as a response popped into his mind. "Because you were being taken to another city to be sold. Your caravan was attacked and you were the only survivor."

"How would you know all this?" Daniel demanded.

"Because we saw you in Jerusalem over Passover. You were . . . well, being a slave. Doing slave sorts of things."

Daniel presented his boldest challenge. "If I'm a slave, then why would your father allow me to sleep in his bed? I don't think so, Nephi. Your story doesn't make sense."

Nephi was not to be defeated. "You slept in my father's bed because you're a *royal* slave. My father didn't want to be accused of mistreating royal property. Men have rotted in dungeons for lesser crimes."

"A royal slave?" repeated Daniel.

"Yes. In fact you were owned by the king himself."

Daniel became lost in thought. Images started flashing in his mind. A man in royal robes. Was he a king? A beautiful garden. A palace garden? The setting in which Nephi placed him was somehow familiar. Could he be right? Daniel grew faint. He barely caught himself before collapsing. Nephi's words were starting to ring true!

"What was my name?" Daniel begged.

"Well, frankly, we don't know yet. We're going to stick with Jophy for now. All we know for certain is that we saw you in Jerusalem. You were one of the slaves of King Josiah. That's one reason my father went to Jerusalem. To find out your real name. The second reason was to buy you."

"To buy me?"

"Yes," Nephi continued. "We kind of like you. We think you'll make a good worker. In fact, if everything turns out right, the plan is to make you my personal servant. Isn't that exciting? You'll be working for me!"

Nephi grinned widely and watched for Daniel's reaction. Daniel the prince did not look particularly thrilled.

# Chapter 6
## THE HALL OF JUDGEMENT

I F YOUR HORSES ARE TO BE RETURNED," SAID THE GUARD AT THE Gate of the Valley of Ben-Hinnom, "then it will be by the word of the king. Since you're seeking his audience, maybe you'll get a chance to ask him personally."

A hearty laugh broke out from the ranks of the other guards in hearing distance. How foolish for these strangers to try and bring steeds into Jerusalem. Had they kept themselves in the desert all of their lives?

"Where might we find King Josiah at this time of day?" Lehi inquired.

"You're out of luck if you want to see His Majesty today. The Egyptian ambassador is here. He wants to speak with the king too. I've a feeling the king's ministers will give him priority."

The guards laughed again. Lehi ignored their taunts. He continued through the gate on foot with Ishmael and Lemuel. The arrival of the Egyptian ambassador was no secret. Word of his presence in Judah had been mentioned to Lehi by every traveler within a day's ride of the city. Nearly as many visitors bustled through Jerusalem's narrow streets today as at Passover. A mood of intensity prevailed in Judah's capital, an air of excitement most ardently expressed by those horsemen who had been allowed to retain their steeds since they had arrived in the unmistakable robes of nobility. These men— various city mayors, influential family heads, and blood relatives to the house of David—rode by swiftly with little concern for the pedestrians they might trample, shouting to one another "The kingdom of David!" with their fists raised to the sky.

All of the horsemen were headed in one direction. Most pedestrians were headed this way as well. The gathering place was the royal palace quarter, or more specifically, the throne room of King Josiah and the spacious Hall of Judgement which sprawled before it. The proclamation had spread like wildfire that King Josiah would meet the Egyptian ambassador in public for all Jerusalem to hear and consider.

Lehi, Lemuel, and Ishmael flowed with the excited crowd. The guard at the gate was right. Any chance of meeting with the king this afternoon seemed remote. Nevertheless, they had to try. After all, it was the only reason they were here.

Lemuel found the excitement contagious. "What do you suppose all this means?" he asked his father.

Lehi shook his head. In all his days he'd never observed such an anxious mood among the citizenry of Judah. Instinct told him it could only mean one thing. The people of God were preparing for war.

Outside the Hall of Judgement, the rambunctious crowd was tightly condensed. Lemuel urged Ishmael and his father to fight their way inside the hall, even as far as the edge of the throne room. A detachment of the king's guard prevented them from pressing in any further. Inside the throne room, a much more ordered crowd presented itself. The quiet within was so deep and pregnant that even a cough seemed to carry the weight of sin.

Lemuel caught his breath as he saw, looming above the heads of the guards, the eminent figure of King Josiah. The monarch of Judah looked down from the gold and ivory throne of Solomon. The royal chair jutted upward from a dais built half as high as the room. Josiah's hands lay with royal immobility on the throne's widely curved arms. Wrapped in his royal robes, the king looked like a bright blue flame in a great golden lamp, a controlled flame that looked as though it might prefer to break loose and burn without restraint rather than shine with a steady light. On the steps beneath the throne sat Josiah's eldest sons, Eliakim and Jehoahaz, between the two golden heraldic lions of Judah.

To the right and left of Solomon's throne stood the chief dignitaries of the state. Those who filled high military posts displayed a considerably more brilliant appearance than those who held civil offices. In spite of the afternoon's thick shroud of humidity, Josiah's generals were adorned in full armor. The place designated for the commander-in-chief of the army had once belonged to Maaseiah, Daniel's father and the late governor of Jerusalem. Today, that place was occupied by the newly promoted Assasiah. Beside Assasiah stood the man purported to be Josiah's fiercest general, Elnathan, son of Achbor.

Upon the benches of the throne room sat every chief priest from all the Levitical orders, as well as the great and petty princes from across the kingdom.

Attention was now drawn to the throne. Ahikam, the king's private secretary, had just finished introducing the ambassador of Pharaoh into Josiah's presence.

The Egyptian was a tall man with a high headdress, the ribbons of which hung down low on either side. His cape gleamed in seven different colors and the back of his transparent upper garment displayed a yellow, winged sun on a delicate blue background. His hands were filled with two eternal symbols of Egypt—a fan of peacock feathers in his left and a long golden staff in his right. In a toneless chant, he began to speak. Although the ambassador knew Hebrew fluently, he'd been instructed by his superiors to communicate strictly in the pure language of the Nile while in the presence of the Jewish king. Therefore, an interpreter was present to offer an immediate translation.

"The King of the Upper and the Nether Lands, the Son of the Gods, who loves his Fathers, the Father of the Gods, who loves his Sons, the Chosen of Path, to whom Ra has given strength and Amon his living image, Necho the Son of Ra and of Osiris-Psammetichus, who comes forth in true kindness, the greatest power ever to have appeared on any throne, the Lord of the Diadem of the Serpent and Vulture, the Possessor of the golden Horus necklace, which endows men with life and happiness . . ." After inhaling, the Egyptian concluded with: ". . . speaks thus unto thee, O King of Judah."

His flowery introduction was followed by still more sentences of tortuous splendor. Lehi strained to understand. Over and over echoed phrases like "the Bearer of Beauty," "He who tarries in the Ship That Never Decays," and "His Serenity before Whom the Hearts of Men Grovel."

Lemuel found it disturbing that so many titles were employed for the sole glorification of one man, Pharaoh of Egypt. After all, the ambassador didn't grant the king of Judah or his God any titles of dignity whatsoever.

The ambassador wasn't *trying* to offend anyone. He merely spoke with overwhelming conviction that nothing in this world could surpass the universal greatness, wisdom, and beauty of Egypt, beyond whose borders existed nothing but melancholy shadows. Uniquely by virtue of his presence, armed with a message from Pharaoh, the ambassador brought to the other nations of the earth a kind of redemptive power that breathed life into the miserable specters who inhabited them.

The ambassador continued, "I report unto you, Josiah the King, not by compulsion, but as a matter of courtesy, of the existence of uncountable ships in a mighty fleet, a fleet that strikes terror even into the divine rulers of the sea. This fleet lies ready to sail in a channel of the Father of all Rivers, whose banks are swollen every year by tears of joy shed by the nine supreme divinities. Manned by invincible warriors, this fleet will set out under the exalted guidance of the sacred flagship on the next new moon. Innumerable war chariots will accompany the fleet along the shores of the Philistines until it sets anchor in the great bay by Mount Carmel. From there, His Magnificence to Whom the Gods Smilingly Pay Homage will illumine the countryside as he marches across Israel's plain to join with the Assyrian princes at Haran who now wander homeless in the earth. Pharaoh Necho—may he live, prosper, and be healthy—together with the Assyrian princes, will then save the world from the terrible scourge engendered by the corrupt and impotent gods of Babylon."

Save the world? Rescue Assyria? Lehi raised an eyebrow at such proclamations. It was true that word had reached every caravan from Greece to Sheba telling of the total annihilation of the Assyrian capital at Nineveh by Nebuchadnezzar's forces and the subsequent escape of a portion of the Assyrian army to Haran, about a hundred and fifty leagues north of Jerusalem. But Egypt should have felt nothing but glee at Assyria's destruction.

Pharaoh Necho's motives were quite clear. The balance of world power was in flux. If Necho could defeat Babylon, the entire known world would fall under Egyptian dominion. Assyria would be his. Babylon would be his. And, as Josiah was keenly aware, the newly independent nation of Judah would also be his.

The king listened to the Egyptian ambassador in wrathful silence. Months ago, when Josiah realized he'd be forced to choose sides in this new world order, he swiftly selected Babylon. Not because he felt any particular love for the Chaldeans—one day he fully expected to see his secret treaty with Nebuchadnezzar broken. Perhaps Josiah would lead Judah's army to the banks of the Euphrates himself. But for now, Egypt presented him with a most convenient opportunity. He didn't even have to go to them. They were coming to him.

The long-awaited moment had arrived. Josiah would now begin the glorious campaign of subjecting all the nations of the earth to the will of the Lord Adonai. How appropriate to begin with Egypt, the land of their fathers' bondage.

When Josiah had made his decision to oppose Pharoah, it was met with raging dissent from his inner circle. Some of his advisors had business interests with Egypt, as did most Jewish traders and merchants, including Lehi. Judah's economy had grown to love things Egyptian with unparalleled passion. To Josiah, this was just one more yoke which had to be broken.

The ambassador concluded his address by issuing a request— actually it sounded more like a threat. He called for Josiah to order all Jewish settlements en route to provide Necho's army with ample provisions. Josiah was then asked to vow to Egypt an oath of obedience.

The king remained silent, motionless except for a dance of his fingers on the throne's golden arm. The stiff Egyptian began showing signs of uneasiness. Josiah summoned his secretary. Ahikam stepped forward.

"Tell the ambassador that when he has offered up in the name of Pharaoh the seven morning sacrifices which he has hitherto omitted, I will present my answer, not to him, but to Pharaoh."

The Egyptian's eyes widened. His hands trembled. His mouth opened to request clarification, but Josiah took no further notice of him. The ambassador was dismissed. As the embarrassed Egyptian withdrew with his attendants, he touched the ground with his fingertips, an act he hadn't considered consonant with Egypt's dignity when he first entered.

As soon as Pharaoh's representative left the hall, the assembly erupted with an unprecedented roar of approval, but the blue flame in its golden lamp shot erect and the clamor was hushed.

"Now is the hour of the kingdom of the new David!" Josiah announced. "The kingdom of the God of Jacob, and the kingdom of the triumphant law! Judah is strengthened! Israel is reborn! Nothing can withstand the avenging lightning of God!"

Josiah's thunderous voice inflamed the crowd to an ear-rending chant. "The kingdom of David! The kingdom of David!"

Lemuel became swept up in the chant as well, thrusting his fists to the ceiling in rhythmic accompaniment. Even Ishmael tried his hand at hooting this new watch-cry.

Only Lehi resisted the intoxication. Many questions sprang to his mind. What of his vision of a few nights before? In his vision the cauldron of destruction was poured out from the north. Egypt was to the south. In spite of the clamor which might have prevented him from hearing his own voice, Lehi prayed inwardly to hear the voice of God. Did this campaign against the Land of Bondage really possess the blessing of Adonai? Would God truly allow this genera-tion of hoodwinkers to rebuild the kingdom of David? Did Josiah act according to the will of God or the will of his own heart?

Suddenly, the tumult died away. The assembly began to notice that the old scribe and former royal secretary, Shaphan, had been strug-gling for a hearing. Lehi recognized Shaphan at once. He deeply revered this old man. Lehi remembered well Shaphan's role in the recovery of the manuscript of the law. Lehi's heart filled with antici-pation. Perhaps someone would finally make sense of this madness.

"I, too," began Shaphan in a weary voice, "add my praises to our glorious king. There has never been a better one in all of Israel and Judah. Few here assembled remember the days of his fathers, Amon and Manasseh, when abominations were allowed to run rampant." He faced the throne, directing the remainder of his remarks to Josiah. "O great King, from the day when you were a little child, no older than your youngest son, Mattaniah, have I loved you and served as your teacher. Therefore, I beg you, O great King, incline your ear towards me one final time. You have peace before you. Peace for many years to come. Why do you wish to break the peace which is yours, when there is no necessity? Why do you wish to shorten those years? Why, my King?"

Shaphan's voice trailed off. He'd begun to sob and his hands raised to cover his face. Shaphan's son, Ahikam, helped the old scribe back into his seat. To the crowd, Shaphan's words were no more than the ramblings of a fragile old man—an out-of-touch generation.

Josiah sat with his brow furrowed in deep lines. Cries broke out again in the assembly. The king quieted the hall again and pointed toward the back of the room.

There, along the far wall of the Hall of Judgement, Lehi noticed a bench where a half-dozen men sat in contemplative calm. Lehi knew their identity by the untanned and pungent animal hides wrapped about their bodies as a symbol of mock humility. This was the bench of the prophets. Such men were customarily invited to these events as witnesses for God. They weren't often called upon to comment. But Josiah, once again eager to set an example of piety and obligate God's support, invited them to speak.

"Has word come from the Lord?" he asked them.

All heads turned to the bench of the prophets. Instantly, one of the unbathed, shaggily-dressed figures detached himself from the others, outstretched his hands and dropped onto his knees, staring upward as if directly into the face of Jehovah. He didn't want to miss a single word as it came to him directly from the Lord's lips.

"Word has come!" he cried. "And a vision!"

The man's entire frame began shaking, as if caught in the grip of an epileptic convulsion. His tongue wagged out of the corner of his mouth and a line of spittle dangled from his chin. The convulsion persisted a good half minute until at last he regained his composure and pronounced his prophecy.

"The waves of the Nile roll through the desert! Prancing in its flood are the horses of the Egyptian warriors. Mud! Corruption! Wreckage! The Father of Rivers is consumed by the desert sands. And in the midst of its waters is consumed the Egyptian warriors!"

Such an appropriate vision! It sprang to mind Moses as he commanded the waters of the Red Sea to consume the army of Pharoah Ramses nine centuries before. A roar of applause followed the prophecy. Contentedly, the prophet strutted back to his seat.

Josiah appeared to hear this pronouncement without emotion. His eyes searched the bench for another prophet to step forward. When none did, he repeated his invitation, only this time he directed it to one specific man.

"What says the prophet from Anathoth?"

Attention was fixed on the figure at the farthest end of the bench. This person appeared distinct from the others. Partly because of his exceptional height and thinness, but primarily because his garb was a simple tunic—not a robe of repellent skins. Lehi did not recognize this man, but only because Lehi was not a current resident of Jerusalem.

Jeremiah of Anathoth had already developed quite an unsavory reputation among the local citizens. Whenever he appeared on the pulpit of the Temple's outer courtyard, his words had been condemnatory, bleak, and depressing. He declared that the people had forgotten God, that they'd become vain, fat and wicked, and that the Lord was preparing to take vengeance. In light of the renewed religious temperament inspired by Josiah, this message seemed sadly outdated. It seemed much more worthwhile to listen to the other prophets—the ones who spoke of comfort and happiness and victory over all Judah's enemies. Yet it was the disparity of Jeremiah's message that had captured Josiah's attention. Every time Jeremiah spoke, Josiah tried to have a scribe on hand. Because of the king's favor, Jeremiah had been allowed to continue his mission unhindered, despite the hatred he inspired in the hearts of Temple officials.

Jeremiah reluctantly accepted the king's invitation to step forward. His chin was cocked to the side and his eyes were downcast in shyness. The other prophets glared at him with distaste. As far as they were concerned, Jeremiah was not one of them. The king may have liked him, but that didn't mean he'd get *their* respect.

Jeremiah could feel the contempt from the other prophets; nevertheless, he felt compelled to speak, if only briefly. At first his voice was weak and faltering, but as he continued, its tone took on a quality that left Lehi in awe.

"My beloved King," Jeremiah began, "I have received no word from the Lord on this matter and no vision. I do not know whether the Lord Sebaoth supports this campaign or not. The Lord seems content to allow Judah to play out the course of its own destiny for the sake of some future chain of events. I know only the visions that I have heretofore been granted. I know that the wine cup of fury has been consumed by all the nations of the earth. And I know that out of the north an evil shall break forth upon all the inhabitants of this land like a river of molten iron from a seething pot. And it is because my people have turned their hearts far from me, saith the Lord."

Jeremiah lowered his head and returned to his place on the bench. A discontented murmur rolled through the crowd. How dare this man tarnish the spirit of the occasion! This was not a time for injuring morale, it was a time to bolster it at any cost!

Jeremiah's words filled Josiah with fleeting uncertainty. Why would the Lord refuse to speak on this matter? The events set in motion this day might well culminate into the most important era of all time! Could the Lord really be so uncommitted?

Attempting to restore the proper mood, one of the lesser generals on the stand stepped forward and cried, "Then according to this man's word, let the first nation to drink of the wine cup of fury be Egypt, the land of our fathers' bondage!"

The words had their proper effect. Frenzied cheering again filled the hall. The king's confidence seemed restored. He rose out of his throne, cried something inaudible over the yelling, and waved his good-byes, disappearing behind the throne and through a private exit.

The assembly began to break up. Men embraced each other, cruel oaths were taken, covenants were made, blood-brotherhood was sworn. The prophets on the bench filtered into the crowd, seeking coveted attention by shouting prophecies of doom on Egypt and victory for the kingdom of the new David. Only one prophet failed to join in the celebration. Jeremiah of Anathoth remained alone beside the bench. His headcloth had worked loose and patiently he tried to rewrap it in the midst of all the hoopla.

Lehi fought his way through to where Jeremiah stood. He approached Jeremiah from behind and set his hand on the tall man's shoulder. Jeremiah turned with a start, expecting that only someone who wished to rebuke him would desire his attention. Instead, Jeremiah found a man whose eyes gleamed with respect. Lehi struggled to find the words. At last, he announced, "I, too, have seen the seething pot. I have felt the heat from the wave of molten metal which brings destruction from the north. I know the judgements of God are upon this people and upon this land."

At first Jeremiah could only stare back in disbelief. He searched Lehi's face for telltale signs of deceit. He'd known so much false friendship in his life. Then Jeremiah's features filled with warmth. He grasped Lehi's shoulders like a lonely child who'd at last found a friend in this world.

"I am Jeremiah," he said. And then Jeremiah felt strange. For in the sacred fraternity to which he and this man belonged, there seemed little need for names.

"I am Lehi. This is my cousin, Ishmael. And my—" Lehi looked around for his son. "There he is. My son, Lemuel."

Lemuel nodded, but kept his distance. Disapproval marked his brow. Like everyone else, he'd found Jeremiah's speech inappropriate and offensive. Lemuel hoped no one of importance noted the kind of company his father kept.

Lehi searched Jeremiah's penetrating eyes, as if they might light the way to all knowledge.

"When," Lehi asked, "will this destruction come? Has the Lord revealed it to you?"

Jeremiah shook his head. "The Lord has not revealed it. But it's coming soon. I feel it. Much sooner than anyone will readily accept. The people must prepare."

"We must prepare ourselves," added Lehi.

Jeremiah smiled. His penetrating eyes now gleamed a heavenly twinkle. "May peace be with you always, Lehi. You've lifted a great burden from my heart. I thought . . . I was alone."

"Peace be unto you, Jeremiah of Anathoth," responded Lehi. "Neither of us was ever alone. Nor will we ever be."

AFTER FOUR DAYS OF BEGGING, PLEADING, AND EVEN BRIBING A doorkeeper, Lehi was at last admitted into the House of Solomon on Mount Moriah, but since he was unwilling to state the reason for his visit, no one took him seriously. The king had been in closed session with his generals since the assembly had concluded. He had no time for idle chat with pilgrims. What could a desert trader possibly know that would interest the king in a time of war preparations? Lehi, Ishmael, and Lemuel took up residence at a local inn, determined to stay until their message was delivered.

On the third day, Lehi finally found himself in the presence of the king's secretary, Ahikam.

"Please," Lehi implored. "The message I have to deliver may be vital to the welfare of the kingdom. You have to trust me. The king alone must hear what I have to say."

"Yes, yes," said Ahikam impatiently. "The chancellor has already informed me of your insistent conditions. But His Majesty is extremely busy—"

"Then I'll come back later today," Lehi insisted. "I'll come back tomorrow. I'll come back the next day and the next. I cannot leave Jerusalem until I've delivered my message to him."

Lehi was tempted to tell Ahikam that his message concerned the king's nephew and the governor's death, but an impression repeated in his mind that even such scanty hints should be reserved for the ears of Josiah. Lehi's instincts told him this conspiracy could only have been successful if it had involved someone at the very top. Maybe the man responsible happened to be the very man whom Lehi now addressed.

Ahikam sighed. "Very well. I'll speak with His Majesty tonight. Return first thing in the morning and I'll see what I can do."

Precisely as directed, Lehi showed up the next morning. He brought Ishmael and Lemuel along to further support his facts. Upon arriving at the palace, another of the king's secretaries reported that Ahikam was not in attendance. He'd left Jerusalem to conduct some royal business, but had left word that Lehi and his party should be brought to one of the king's council chambers. Lehi and the others followed the escort. When they entered the chamber, it was empty. They waited alone with the king's sentries.

After nearly an hour, a man draped in royal garments finally strutted through the doorway, but he was not the king. Accompanying this man were several bodyguards and secretaries. He took his place in the ornamented chair at the front of the room. One of the secretaries introduced him to the three guests.

"His Eminence, Prince Eliakim, son of Josiah!"

The youthful Eliakim kicked back in his chair and laced his fingers on his stomach. Eliakim did not possess the muscular stature of his father. Though he was in his mid-twenties, Eliakim's frame still presented the gawkiness of a teenager. His eyes bulged slightly and his chin was pointed. His manner showed the same impatience Lehi had met with all week. Obviously, Eliakim was also very busy. Apart from all the war preparations, Eliakim had recently undertaken the project of building a summer palace for himself on the Mount of Olives.

Lehi, Ishmael, and Lemuel knelt. Eliakim directed them to stand, desiring to waste as little time as possible. "I'm told your name is Lehi. I'm told you have a message to deliver."

Lehi looked confused. "We must deliver this message to the king."

"The king left Jerusalem this morning," stated Eliakim. "He won't return for several weeks. His Majesty has ridden forth to gather in the armies of every tribe and family for the noble cause to which our glorious nation will soon be engaged. Anything you would tell my father, you can certainly tell me."

"But this is a matter of national security," said Lehi.

Eliakim looked insulted. He appeared on the verge of losing his temper. "I'm Josiah's eldest son and the successor to the throne of David. I will lead one of my father's largest armies. Any matter of national security is my business as much as it is my father's. I *command* you to tell me your message."

Lehi looked at Ishmael and then at Lemuel. Ishmael shook his head, having no advice for his cousin. Lemuel's expression seemed to say, *What are you waiting for, Father?*

After all, this was the king's eldest son. They wouldn't be able to meet with Josiah for weeks—if ever! They couldn't wait that long. The message had to be delivered. If the king himself wasn't available to hear it, could there exist a better second choice?

Lehi relented. "All right. But I request that you clear the room of all who don't need to be here."

Eliakim agreed and dismissed all but his first secretary and two bodyguards. This desert trader had indeed peaked Eliakim's curiosity. Perhaps this wouldn't end up to be such a waste of his morning after all.

"Speak," Eliakim repeated.

"Daniel, the son of Governor Maaseiah, is alive."

Eliakim tried to mask his surprise, but he wasn't very successful. Leaning forward, he directed Lehi to continue.

"My cousin, Ishmael, found him wandering alone in the wilderness, half-starved and nearly dehydrated. He was part of a caravan headed south. The caravan was ransacked by bandits. Prince Daniel was the only survivor."

"And where is this boy now?"

"At my estate, which sits at the edge of the desert near Hebron. But I'm grieved to inform you, his mind was affected by these events."

"How was it affected?"

"He doesn't remember anything. He doesn't know how he came to be in the place where he was found. Nor does he remember anyone from his past. He doesn't even recall his own name."

"Then how do you know this is Daniel, son of Maaseiah?"

"Two of my sons confirmed his identity. They had occasion to meet the prince a few weeks before he came to us. It was during the week of Passover—the day of Maaseiah's murder."

It occurred to Lehi as he listened to himself that this whole thing sounded terribly absurd. He wished he'd brought Nephi or Sam to back up the claim.

Eliakim started to laugh. "Oh, my dear fellow. I can tell by the urgency in your voice that you've spoken sincerely, but I sadly regret to inform you that Daniel, the son of Maaseiah, is dead. He was buried on the same day as his father. I helped place his small body in the sepulchre myself. Excuse my ill-timed laughter. For a brief instant I actually believed what you were saying could be true. I was prepared to toss aside everything I'd seen with my own two eyes. That's how dearly I miss my cousin and my uncle." Eliakim's eyes moistened. He looked away.

Lehi started to stammer. "I—I don't know what to say. I'm— I'm *so* sorry. I desperately beg your forgiveness."

"Don't worry," consoled Eliakim. "I'm not offended by your message. The brief instant of hope I gained from your words was more refreshing than you'll ever know. It invigorated me and reinforced my determination toward the cause which sits before the great nation of Judah. For that, I thank you."

"I don't know how my sons could have made such a mistake."

"Young boys are prone to mistakes. I can understand. I'm not so far removed from those reckless years myself. But please, I'd be honored if you'd allow my personal escort to take you to the gates of the city."

"We have no horses," said Ishmael.

Ishmael's statement added to Lehi's embarrassment. Nevertheless, he explained, "Our horses were confiscated at the Gate of the Valley."

"Your beasts will be returned," Eliakim declared. He looked to one of his guards for confirmation. The guard nodded.

Eliakim indicated his secretary. "Please give my servant clear directions on the location of your estate near Hebron. I'm sure my father will wish to compensate your family for any inconvenience you might have suffered."

"Oh, no. That won't be necessary," said Lehi.

"I insist," said Eliakim. "Your mission here was certainly inspired by an unprecedented loyalty toward the house of David. If all the men in this kingdom possessed such loyalty, our enemies would crumble to dust in our very presence."

As the guards led the three desert pilgrims toward the door, Eliakim further stated, "I hope you soon discover the true identity of your houseguest. His family, if they're still alive, must feel quite desperate."

"Thank you," said Lehi, "for your tolerance and your patience. We apologize again. I still can't understand how—"

"I'll hear no more of it," said Eliakim, rising from his chair. "If you wish to apologize for taking up our valuable time this morning, you may do so through your continued obedience to the house of David."

Lemuel bowed. "It was an honor to meet you, Prince Eliakim."

Lehi, Ishmael, and Lemuel were led from the council chamber. Eliakim's secretary escorted them from the palace. The guard did what was necessary to release their horses.

Eliakim remained in the chamber alone with a single bodyguard. He returned to his chair. The prince's face had blanched. His breathing had quickened—as if he'd been bitten by some potentially fatal insect.

The change was so dramatic that Eliakim's bodyguard asked, "Are you all right, Your Eminence?"

"Yes," he tersely replied. "Why shouldn't I be? Where is General Assasiah?"

"He'll be leaving Jerusalem shortly to help recruit—"

"Find him!" Eliakim commanded. He struggled to calm himself. "I mean, inform him that he must postpone his trip. An emergency has arisen."

The bodyguard looked a bit perplexed.

Eliakim lost his temper. "What are you waiting for? Go! I must speak with Assasiah at once!"

# Chapter 7
## MASTERS AND SLAVES

THE MID-MORNING SKY WAS SOUPY GREY, COMPLETELY VEILING the sun. Nephi stealthily led Daniel through the marsh gully near the spring. There was just enough dry ground to avoid sinking in mud, but each tall blade of grass tickled the boys' legs with a cool drip of dew. The morning before, Daniel had made the mistake of laughing out loud, scaring off a covey of red-legged partridges before Nephi had crept close enough to unleash the pebbles in his sling. Nephi glanced back at Daniel and noticed the prince again struggling to maintain a straight face. Nephi narrowed his eyes threateningly.

"Sorry," Daniel whispered. "I don't know why my legs are so ticklish."

Nephi widened his eyes, tensing every muscle in his face. Couldn't this boy stay quiet?

Daniel put his hand over his mouth. He had no desire to clean the stables again as Nephi had made him do yesterday.

The two boys continued toward the spring, bypassing several vacant nests in the grass. The red-legged residents couldn't be far away. At last they began hearing a faint guttural chirp. The noise was less than ten steps ahead. Nephi loaded the pebbles in his sling.

With one more step, there arose a flash of blue feathers. Three partridges took to the air. Nephi let the pebbles fly. One bird was struck. It spun back toward the earth, splashing into the waters of the spring.

"Got him!" cried Daniel.

With a sweep of his hand, Nephi directed Daniel to fetch the fallen partridge. Daniel cringed. Could wading through marsh mud be considered remotely civilized?

"Well, what are you waiting for?" asked Nephi. "Go get the bird!"

Reluctantly, Daniel shook off his sandals and gathered up his cloak. He tip-toed to the edge of the spring and glanced back at Nephi before entering the water, his face full of pain.

"Hurry!" urged Nephi.

One more step and Daniel was ankle-deep in ooze.

Nephi smiled. Having a personal slave wasn't half bad. He didn't feel the least bit guilty. Well, maybe he felt a *little* guilty, but he hoped such feelings would pass. *Think of the great lesson he's learning,* Nephi told himself. Sariah had scolded him the day before when she saw Jophy doing all Nephi's chores. Nephi wished he could have told her who the boy was. Then she'd understand— maybe even approve. Then again, maybe not. One thing for certain, Laman sure got a big kick out of seeing Daniel work a few blisters into his palms. His oldest brother didn't seem the least bit nervous about the repercussions of forcing a prince to perform manual labor.

As Nephi watched Daniel wade further out into the spring—into water so deep he didn't bother to hold up his cloak any longer— he found himself beginning to appreciate his slave for something more. These days in the hills could get awfully monotonous. Nephi had never had many companions, except for Sam, who lately had begun to enjoy hanging out with boys a few years older—maybe for the same reasons Nephi had enjoyed hanging out with him. Some of the estate's tenant farmers had children, but they always seemed too old or too young for Nephi.

Nephi jarred himself. Had he forgotten who this boy was? This was Daniel! The obnoxious prince! Nephi only needed to think on the dying face of his sister one instant to reaffirm that he and this boy could never be friends.

Daniel, the partridge now in hand, had started to make his way back. Everything below his shoulders was drenched. Everything below his knees was black with mud.

"Let's go, let's go!" urged Nephi. "We have to get back to the flock before a predator comes along. Setting my coat on the rock only fools the sheep for about an hour. Then they figure it out and start looking for me."

Daniel and Nephi heard the whinny of a donkey. Dagan, the long-bearded bailiff of Lehi's estate, looked down on them from the rise overlooking the marsh. He appeared anxious.

"Nephi!" he cried. "Come home at once. Your father has returned from Jerusalem."

FROM THE MOMENT LEHI HAD GUIDED HIS STEED OUT THROUGH THE Gate of the Valley and begun the homeward trek with Ishmael and Lemuel, his heart felt stricken with regret. A coldness had gripped his soul. A nagging tormented his mind.

That night, camped north of Hebron, he confided his feelings to Ishmael. "I fear I've made a grave, grave error."

"How so?" wondered Ishmael.

"The promptings of the Spirit were clear. I denied those promptings. Ishmael, what have I done?"

"I don't understand."

"Only Josiah was to have heard our message. I knew this with every fiber of my being, yet I allowed myself to be drawn in by Prince Eliakim's persuasions."

"You had no choice," Ishmael contended. "If you had defied the prince, he'd have cast us all in prison. Who knows when the king may return to Jerusalem? Organizing the armies of every tribe might keep him away for weeks."

"No!" Lehi shook his head, shutting his eyes tightly. "No argument can change the truth. The Lord gave me a warning. Barely a week ago he told me if I hearkened unto His voice from that day forward, I and my seed would be spared." A terrified look seized Lehi's face. "I've failed, Ishmael! How many times must I fail before I finally understand? Now I've marked my own family for destruction!"

Nothing Ishmael could say comforted his cousin. Lehi left the camp, wandering past the fires of the other travelers and into a nearby field where some boulders concealed him from view. Alone in this place, Lehi spent most of the night pleading for God's mercy, pleading for instruction—for some shred of insight that might save his family from doom and also save the life of Prince Daniel. Lehi knew, as sure as he knew an unseasonal south-westerly wind had followed them from Jerusalem's gate, that some evil force was close on their heels, a force unleashed by the word of Josiah's black-hearted son. Lehi gazed off toward the hills of the north.

How close was this force? He couldn't know for sure. He only knew that it was coming.

An answer to his supplications came to him the next morning, on the final leg of his journey home.

*Egypt.*

The word resounded in his head like waves against a cliff. Safety for Daniel lay beyond the borders of the Land of Bondage. In return for providing Daniel with swift passage across the desert, security would be granted to Lehi's family. But even as this promise entered his mind, he doubted. Lehi crushed the doubt as he would crush a glowing ember underfoot.

The moment he arrived at his estate, Lehi summoned his oldest son, Laman. He also sent for Nephi and Daniel. Nephi left the marsh where he and Daniel had been hunting and rushed directly home. Daniel stayed outside while Nephi went inside and found his father and Laman in the Hall of Joseph, arguing heatedly.

"Father," ranted Laman, "what am I supposed to trade in Egypt if I leave as soon as tomorrow? We haven't even begun harvesting wheat—to say nothing of pressing olives. Oil is our most valuable commodity in Noph."

"We can trade wool and textiles," suggested Lehi.

"We've hardly enough to make it worth the trip."

Lehi took his oldest son by the shoulders. "Laman, please. Can you be ready to leave in the morning?"

Laman sighed. "I suppose. It'll be a much smaller caravan than the one I'd planned."

"You must believe the word of God," Lehi proclaimed. "We have to trust the Lord on this matter."

Nephi watched a wisp of impudence cross his older brother's face, as if hearing his father mention the Lord in conjunction with business left a pickled taste in his mouth.

Laman noticed Nephi in the doorway. "Pack your stuff, little brother. It looks like you'll be trading for that new bow of yours a little sooner than you'd expected."

"We're going to Egypt?" asked Nephi excitedly.

"You'll be leaving first thing in the morning," his father confirmed.

"That's great!" Nephi cried.

Lehi approached his youngest son. "You'll be taking Jophy with you."

Nephi whitened. "We're taking the prince?"

Lehi gestured for Nephi to lower his voice. Laman closed the door.

"But why?" demanded Nephi. "This was supposed to be *my* trip. I've looked forward to it all winter."

Lehi looked his son in the eye. "Listen to me carefully, Nephi. If Prince Daniel doesn't go with you to Egypt, he will be killed. Our entire family will be destroyed with him. This much I know. The Lord has revealed it to me."

Nephi's eyes widened. Rarely had his father spoken so directly. "If Laman and I take him with us, will the family be safe?"

"I have faith that this is so," Lehi replied. "But even if it's not, in God's eyes we will still have done the noble thing. Remember my son, when we pursue a noble cause, the noblest change may only be that which takes place in our hearts."

Nephi had heard this saying from his father before. He'd never really understood it and today was no exception. Still, he knew that hearing these words meant the matter was closed. Prince Daniel would travel with them to Noph.

NEPHI FOUND IT DIFFICULT TO SLEEP THAT NIGHT. THE LONG DAY OF preparations should have guaranteed an easy slumber, but his mind raced with so many thoughts, he couldn't keep track of them all. He'd never been to Egypt, so tomorrow began a great adventure. All those years of learning Egyptian from tutors hired by his father might finally pay off. At the same time, it wasn't an adventure he'd imagined having to share with anyone but Laman. All of Nephi's life, he'd held Laman in the highest respect, even if that respect was coupled with a dash of fear. He looked forward to becoming a little closer to his oldest brother. Hopefully, Prince Daniel wouldn't steal all the attention.

Nephi glanced over at Daniel. The prince snored softly on his bed at the other end of the room. Daniel had been sleeping in Nephi's room ever since his second day on the estate. It was his mother's idea. Somehow, Sariah got it into her head that Jophy might be "good" for Nephi. A new friend—one who could talk with her son late into the night—might help Nephi forget about Hannah's death. Mothers. They could sure get some weird ideas.

An unusually high wind whistled and moaned through the thin window slits near the ceiling, adding to Nephi's insomnia. Mighty gusts roiled the desert dust. Some of the dust found its way through the window slits. Perhaps that's why Nephi's throat felt so dry. He reached for the water pitcher at the head of his bed. Empty. Wasn't Daniel supposed to have filled it? Nephi was sorely tempted to wake the prince and send him out to the well. He'd have done it too, if his father hadn't scolded him for an hour that afternoon after he heard how Nephi had treated Daniel like a slave.

Nephi was finding it difficult to work up enough spit to swallow. Unhappily, he climbed out of bed and carried the pitcher toward the front door. He pushed the door forward a little. A heavy gust whipped it open the rest of the way. Indeed, the full intensity of the wind could only be appreciated while staring out the open door. Every reed on the date palms bent in one direction. Branches and brush tumbled across the yard. Ishmael had often said that winds coming off the desert carried the voices of souls who'd perished there. Every victim since time began seemed to be howling in anguish tonight. The well, barely visible through dust and darkness, looked impossibly far away.

Nephi heard a noise behind him. He jumped with a start and spun around to face Prince Daniel.

"Don't *ever* come up on someone like that!" scolded Nephi.

"What are you doing, Master Nephi?"

"I thought I told you not to call me that anymore—at least not in the house."

"Sorry."

"I was going to get some water but—"

Nephi stopped talking to listen. He perceived that the wind carried not only the voices of the dead, but the frightened neighs of every horse in the stables.

"The wind seems to be upsetting them," suggested Daniel.

"They've never acted so upset by wind before," said Nephi. He stepped out the door.

"Where are you going?" asked Daniel.

"To check the stables. I can fill the pitcher on the way back."

"Would you like me to come along?"

Nephi was already too far away for Daniel's voice to carry. Sheltering his face with his sleeve, Nephi forged blindly toward the stables. Last year a fox had sought refuge in the stables from a similar storm. The little beggar had gotten away. Nephi hoped it was back. A fox hide would fetch a nice price in Noph.

As Nephi passed the well and reached the brink of the stable's north entrance, a feeling of dread settled over him. Nephi recalled all the warnings his father and oldest brother had recently issued—warnings about strangers, about conspirators, about assassins lying in wait.

How stupid not to have awakened someone else! How stupid not to have asked Daniel to accompany him! Nephi looked back at the house. Daniel appeared to have gone inside. Too dark to tell. Nephi turned back toward the stables. A sheltered oil lamp glowed a tiny flame near the corner where he kept his bow. Reaching that light seemed a much more sober option than wandering back through the darkness. Besides, he would be able to arm himself.

Nephi entered the stables. The horses and donkeys continued their frantic display, darting back and forth, kicking at the gates of their stalls. The cause of commotion seemed to be centralized outside the west entrance, where the goat pen was situated. From the place where the lamp balanced in the groove of the stone column, Nephi hoped he could spot the intruder and still leave himself plenty of time to load a bronze-tipped arrow if necessary.

He walked toward the lamp, directing his eyes toward the goat pen. His feet stepped carefully, fearing he might startle whoever or whatever was out there. Upon reaching the lamp, Nephi raised it up. As the light increased, Nephi began to sense a presence in the goat pen, something other than goats. All the goats seemed to be gathered in a tight cluster at the far end. He raised the lamp higher. There was movement. An outline became visible. The shape was *enormous*!

Fierce yellow eyes turned into the lamplight. The beast raised its head, its teeth red with blood from the goat carcass upon which it fed. Nephi heard an ungodly roar. For an instant the sound stifled the screaming of the wind. Even the earth seemed to tremble.

Nephi dropped the lamp and water pitcher. He dove toward his bow and quiver of arrows. The lion took flight, hurling itself over the goat pen wall. Four hundred pounds of feline landed in the center of the stables. The beast continued toward Nephi at full speed, its jaws extended so wide the boy thought he could see all the way into its stomach. Nephi wasn't even given enough time to *draw* an arrow, to say nothing of placing it on the string and aiming. He could only raise his arms across his face as a fragile defense. *End my life quickly,* his spirit requested, *with as little pain as possible.*

"NEEEPHIII!"

The scream had come from the south entrance. There stood Daniel. His right hand gripped the curved Scythian sword which had hung on Lehi's wall. The lion skidded to a halt, startled and bewildered. Its claws could have finished off Nephi from where it stood, but instead, the beast sought escape. It began running, but not back toward the goat pen where escape was guaranteed. In its confusion, the lion aimed itself toward the south entrance, where Daniel stood with his rusty weapon.

The prince hadn't anticipated this turn of events. He'd drawn attention from Nephi only to turn the tides of destruction on himself! The lion had seen Daniel now. It knew that this boy was the only thing that stood between itself and freedom. Again, the cat revealed its fangs.

At this instant, a glint of Daniel's memory returned. He'd seen this image before—a terrible charging beast with blood-dripping fangs—but only in his earliest childhood nightmares. Tonight the nightmares had come true. All of Daniel's irrational fears about four-legged creatures stood justified in one sweeping instant.

Daniel swung the sword. At the same time, he closed his eyes and dropped to both knees, preferring not to know if, or where, the sword struck its target. His arm felt the impact. The sword had hit something. Daniel felt a blast of the lion's breath as it released a roar of pain. Upon opening his eyes, he saw that the lion's snout was badly cut and bleeding. The lion's paw delivered a blow to Daniel's shoulder. The prince toppled end over end, finally crashing against the stable's stone wall. Daniel's vision had blurred. His eyes focused two seconds later, but only in time to see the four-hundred pound feline again lunging for his throat.

A bronze-tipped arrow pierced the flesh beneath the lion's mane. Another anguished roar echoed through the stables. The lion's front legs collapsed. It rolled once. The beast looked like it might attempt one final vengeful lunge when another arrow split the air. This one found a vital spot behind the front shoulder. The mighty animal did not cry out again. It collided with a stone column and rolled onto its back, flailing and convulsing. After half a minute, the lion sucked its final breath and lay still.

Daniel saw that his feet and the lion's snout were separated by less than five steps. Nephi stepped in front of Daniel and approached the unmoving carcass, another iron-tipped arrow loaded and ready in his bow in case the cat showed any sign of life.

Within a minute, Lehi's entire household arrived in the stables, awakened by the lion's roars. They surrounded the two boys and the dead cat.

Daniel's shoulder had been dislocated. Shamariah was called upon to pull it back into place. Nephi stayed at Daniel's side while the old servant performed the excruciating operation. Daniel gritted his teeth, suppressing any groans. The shoulder popped into joint.

"It'll smart for a few days," said Shamariah, "but after that, you should be good as new."

Ishmael watched Daniel's eyes closely to see if the incident had jarred some significant bit of memory. It became clear as Daniel apologized for having torn his borrowed tunic, he still remembered nothing. A prince would never have concerned himself over the condition of a ragged, homespun garment.

"Well," said Laman, stepping away from the lion's carcass, "this one is number three. The hunting party claims to have killed the other two near the south ridge yesterday morning."

Nephi met Daniel's eyes.

"You saved my life," said the prince.

"If you hadn't called out when you did," Nephi responded, "I wouldn't have been around to save it."

Lehi overheard the two boys and knelt beside them.

"An interesting predicament," he said thoughtfully. "Alone, either one of you would have perished. But together, you've managed to slay the king of beasts."

# Chapter 8
# THE ROAD TO EGYPT

As Lehi watched his sons and the prince ride into the desert, he felt a great burden lifted from his shoulders. God had spoken. He had obeyed. A pattern was established. A pattern he hoped to follow for the rest of his life.

Ishmael traveled with the caravan as far south as Beersheba, at which point he detoured toward his wilderness home, anxious to reunite with his family. Laman guided the camels along the Brook of Besor, hoping to put enough distance behind them the first day to assure his arrival at Raphia by the following night. The season was still relatively cool, so their usual midday rest was cut short. Along the Way of the Sea into Egypt, temperatures were expected to be much more severe and a good portion of their traveling might have to be undertaken after dark.

Laman mourned the size of his caravan: a mere twelve camels. Other than Prince Daniel and his brother Nephi, he'd brought along only four other servants.

Daniel was content to ride atop the second camel with Nephi. It was gadfly season and the painful bites of these insects made the dromedaries a little jumpy. Nephi's confidence at the reins was encouraging to the prince.

Nephi actually enjoyed having a passenger. It offered him a captive audience as he told the prince all he knew about life in the wilderness.

Laman watched distastefully as Daniel guzzled the last drops in his water-skin and asked Nephi for some of his. This wasn't so disturbing while they traveled beside the wadi, which still flowed a thin trickle, but it was a habit that needed to be broken before they crossed the Sinai. Laman's experience as a caravaneer over the last two or three years had seasoned him to be mercilessly intolerant of weakness. Complainers received no sympathy from Laman. After all, the long-distance caravaneers who traveled the Silk and Incense Roads wouldn't bat an eye at the idea of leaving a sick or insolent man behind to die. Laman admired such implacability.

The travelers pitched their tents that first night outside the walls of Sharuhen on the border of the land of the Philistines. Their campsite wasn't much to speak of, but it had a nearby well. This place marked the party's last chance to fill their water-skins before crossing a long and monotonous trail to the caravanserai at Raphia near the Mediterranean coast.

After Daniel had finished topping off his water-skin at the well, Laman snatched it away, spilling half the liquid into the dust.

Handing it back, he declared, "This is all you will drink until we reach Raphia. You must learn to conserve. If you don't, your habits will endanger us all."

Laman hesitated before turning away, perhaps remembering the identity of the person he spoke with. Laman bit his cheeks in resolve. Prince or no prince, there were rules for traveling on the desert, and those rules had to be obeyed. Besides, it was looking like this boy might never get his memory back anyway.

As Laman walked off, Daniel looked to Nephi for reassurance. Nephi shrugged in helplessness. "I suggest you take a big drink from the well tonight and then another one in the morning."

As darkness settled over the landscape, Laman appeared to relax somewhat. Everyone gathered around the fire to enjoy a meal of roast mutton and dried figs. Laman brought along a couple of duck's eggs, strictly for himself. He chipped away a small corner of the shell and sucked the yolk down his throat, sighing with deep satisfaction after he'd swallowed.

"We did well today," Laman declared, leaning back to take in the night sky. "We should reach Raphia tomorrow afternoon. Then I'll feel like I'm truly home."

"You don't feel at home on your father's estate?" asked Daniel.

"Of course I do, but it's not the same. At the estate I'm always subject to someone else's laws. Those of my family, my religion, my nation—the list seems endless. In wilderness stations like

Raphia, there are no such restrictions, no laws to bind men down and do their thinking for them. Raphia is owned by the caravaneers. Oh, I know the territory is claimed by Egypt, but there are no more Egyptians in Raphia at any given time than there are Philistines or Phoenicians or Greeks or Jews. Even the Egyptians that *are* there would first consider themselves citizens of the nation of traders before they would call themselves Egyptians. Nowhere on earth is a man more free than he is inside a wilderness caravanserai."

A shooting star cut the sky. Laman gasped in amazement as the streak flickered out.

"The universe is filled with so many wonders," he continued. "How arrogant to think that one culture or people holds all the answers. In the company of traders, ideas from every corner of the world can come together fearlessly, so that everyone can ponder, consider, adopt, and improve. Even God Himself comes to a place like Raphia from time to time, although if He wishes to speak, He soon finds He must wait His turn—just like everyone else."

Nephi was shocked. At home Laman sometimes felt given to reveal snatches of his personal philosophies, but never in such poetic detail and conviction.

"You sound almost . . . blasphemous," said Nephi.

"Blasphemous?" repeated Laman. "To me, blasphemy is when a person declares his way of life, his view of God, and his interpretation of the cosmos to be the only true one. A caravaneer always avoids such rigid opinions. He's above such bickering. One needs only to listen to the sermons of an Egyptian priest or a Chaldean soothsayer for a moment to realize that his gods possess knowledge and beauty which, in ways, exceed our own."

Even something deep in Daniel's psyche cringed at this attitude. "Are you saying you believe in the heathen gods?"

"I neither believe nor disbelieve. All I know is, I've seen fascinating visions in the company of traders. Enough to convince me that powers exist and miracles occur in many lands and many religions. All men, in essence, worship the same gods. They merely call them by different names and emphasize different laws. The Jews certainly emphasize more than their fair share of laws."

"But these are the laws which God gave to Moses," said Nephi.

"Please," begged Laman, "don't start talking like Lemuel—so

94

wrapped up in his own view of truth he can't see beyond his own nose. I've got higher hopes for you, little brother. I think you'll make a great caravaneer."

Daniel appeared absorbed in concentration. At last he proclaimed, "A stone is not a bird. A leaf is not a fish."

Laman raised his eyebrows. "Pardon me?"

"Truth must be universal," said Daniel. "It can't be one thing in one nation and another thing in another nation. Truth can't take on one form today and another form tomorrow. There can only exist one truth—or the word itself has no meaning."

Laman was a bit taken back by this eleven-year-old's attempt at wisdom. Nevertheless, he found Daniel's views stimulating. It always invigorated Laman to discuss deep and complicated things. Conversations about truth were much more entertaining than truth itself.

"You may be right," said Laman. "Perhaps the word 'truth' has no real meaning. I like that idea. I like it a lot." Laman nodded and drifted into his own thoughts, drinking in the stars.

After the fire had burned down to glowing coals and the crickets began to lose their voices, Nephi and Daniel retired to their tent. They lay awake together for some time without speaking.

Finally, Nephi declared, "I don't think I want to be a caravaneer."

"Why not?" asked Daniel.

"I don't think I'd want to see the world the way Laman does. Seems like it would get awfully old after a while—always learning and learning and learning and never figuring anything out."

LATE THE FOLLOWING AFTERNOON, AS THEY STRODE THROUGH THE gates of Raphia, Laman's caravan of twelve camels and seven persons presented a singular color—dusty, trail-worn, sand-grimed grey. It had been a hard day's ride along a bleak and tedious trail. Toward midday, as the caravan descended toward the sea, the sun began to deliver its promised oppression. The wind also picked up, ceasing to blow only as the walls of Raphia took shape on the horizon.

Nephi could feel the dust through his hair, between his toes, in his ears—even stuck in the grooves of his teeth. It comforted him somewhat to see that most of the other traders and travelers looked equally filthy. They passed hundreds of faces along the city thoroughfare—faces from all the nations of the earth. Every face displayed features distinctly its own and yet, to Nephi, they possessed one similar quality. Like the varied rock formations of the Sinai, each countenance bore lines custom-cut by the desert wind.

Traffic was heavier than normal in Raphia. Tents had been erected from one end of the courtyard to the other. Rumors of a northbound Egyptian war machine had launched more than the usual number of merchants along the desert roads, all hoping to find profitable opportunities along the Nile. Traders were well aware that no army could travel on an empty stomach and also that every warrior needed adequate clothing and weapons.

After relieving the camels of their bales, Laman ordered the boys to water every beast at the troughs. Daniel welcomed such an order. He'd drained the final drop from his water-skin almost four hours before. Though the camels hadn't received water in over two days, the prince felt ready to challenge any one of them in a drinking contest.

A pool sat at the northern end of Raphia's courtyard. Drinking space at the troughs was hotly contested between the animals of the various caravans. Nephi and Daniel waited for a half an hour before finding an open space. Their camels wasted no time immersing their snake-like snouts in the sun-warmed liquid. They drank slowly and deliberately for nearly twenty minutes, at last raising their heads to shake the residue from their pendulous lips.

Nephi went with his older brother to pay the innkeeper while Daniel approached the pool. Before stepping onto the platform, he removed his shoes. The smooth stonework felt good under his toes. All around the pool's edge, a short containment wall presented plaques with the carved images of Egyptian, Canaanite, and Philistine gods. It was a newer structure, built shortly after Egypt had reclaimed Raphia from the Assyrians. Daniel knelt at the pool's edge and took a deep breath. For the first time he realized that water had a distinct smell—a glorious smell.

He dunked his head in the pool. When he came out, the dirt from his face and hands had created a cloud in the water. He swung back his hair, grateful when the rivulets ran down his spine.

Several voices started laughing. A pack of shabbily-clad youths stood a short way down the containment wall. Daniel guessed they were locals. Perhaps boys Daniel's age were rare sights among the endless caravans. Dunking his head had amused them. It must have also made the prince appear vulnerable, because one of the boys approached.

"Bronze?" the boy requested, his hands outstretched. "Silver?" He'd guessed Daniel's nationality from his manner and dress, but clearly Hebrew was not the boy's first language.

Daniel shook his head. "I have none."

The prince found it odd that the boy wore a grin instead of a meek frown, as seemed fitting to a beggar. When the boy glanced back at his eager friends, Daniel realized he intended some sort of mischief.

"Bread?" the boy asked. "Food?"

"We may have some to spare. You'll have to ask my master."

But the boy had already drawn close enough to snatch what he really wanted—Daniel's sandals. Daniel made no attempt to stop him. He merely watched in idle curiosity as the boy dashed away with the footwear dangling from his fist.

After reaching his friends, the boy turned back to taunt Daniel, displaying his prize. "Very nice!" he shouted. "Thank you!"

Nephi's arms clasped around the boy's neck from behind. He'd watched the whole incident from where he stood beside the camel troughs. Within seconds he'd wrestled the boy to the ground. The other boys appeared as though they might offer help to their friend, but Nephi was considerably larger than any one of them. The idea was quickly dismissed.

Nephi didn't merely take the sandals back to Daniel, he took the whole boy, forcing him to walk ahead with his arm twisted painfully behind his back.

Upon reaching Daniel, Nephi commanded the boy to return the shoes.

Uncertainly, Daniel raised his hand to accept. The boy dropped the sandals on the ground. Nephi angrily bent the boy's arm higher.

"No, don't," Daniel said to Nephi.

The prince leaned over and lifted the shoes. He handed them back. The boy looked surprised. Nephi let go of his arm. The boy rolled the sandals over in his hand, unsure of what to make of the gift. Then the boy noticed Daniel glancing down at his bare feet.

After several backward steps, the boy flung both sandals into the pool. He ran off laughing and taunting with his gang. Daniel watched as the boy and his friends slipped through a gap in the courtyard wall and disappeared.

"I could have told you the gift would insult him," said Nephi. "Why did you want to give him your sandals?"

"I don't know," said Daniel.

"If you *really* wanted him to have them," explained Nephi, "you should have left them at the pool's edge, as if they'd been forgotten. That way, his pride wouldn't have been injured. He wouldn't accept them now if they were offered on a golden platter."

The prince sighed. "I have much to learn."

Nephi was struck by Daniel's sincerity. He thought back on the Prince Daniel he remembered from the Jerusalem bazaar, the one who outbid him for a patch of silk. Nephi hoped that if God ever returned Daniel's memory, a small piece of Jophy would remain.

Daniel's shoes floated out in the middle of the pool. Nephi waded in to fetch them. On the way back he heard the sweet call of a female voice.

"Come out of there, boy," the woman purred. "Come with me and I will give you and your companion a proper bath."

She couldn't have been much older than Nephi's sister, Hannah, before she died. The maiden's shimmering black hair had a narrow streak of gray, combed high and decked with jewels. She might have been the most outwardly beautiful creature Nephi and Daniel had ever seen—so much so that they felt inclined to avert their eyes, for she wore a robe which was almost transparent, embroidered with silver stars and golden staffs of grain.

In averting his vision, Nephi noticed dozens of similarly-clad women making their way among the tents, flirting with the men and dancing to the tune of lutes and clapping hands. Nephi's nose was hit by a waft of incense and spice. In the fading light of day, Raphia had taken on the appearance of a festival.

"Come!" urged the maiden, the golden bracelets on her wrists jingling as she beckoned.

"W-w-we need to get back to our tents," said Nephi.

"Nonsense! Your tents aren't going anywhere." She came closer. "I see that you are men of Judah?"

Neither boy had ever been called a man before. The sound of it was flattering and yet frightening.

"That's right," said Daniel.

"I could tell by your accents. Come. There are no silly customs and laws in Raphia to keep you from enjoying yourself. You've had a difficult day. Many more difficult days are likely to come. Tonight, you must refresh yourselves."

She tried to give the boys a star-cake. Nephi hid his hands behind his back in horror. He immediately recognized these cakes as symbols of heathen worship.

"We worship the one God of Abraham, Isaac, and Jacob," cried Nephi.

The girl frowned, lowering the cakes. "There is no cause for bigotry here—especially from ones so young. Many men of Judah have passed through Raphia and partaken of the blessings of Ashtoreth, the Queen of Heaven."

"We don't believe in Ashtoreth," proclaimed Daniel.

The girl heaved a weary sigh. Fortunately, experience had taught her that such prudish views could usually be overcome with gentle persuasion.

"Then I should be allowed to open your minds and hearts. Ashtoreth takes nothing from the divine male gods of the earth. How could the Lord Adonai rule in heaven without His female counterpart, the divine Queen? It is Ashtoreth who fulfills the most secret prayers of women, forming milk in our breasts and an even sweeter milk in our frequently sad hearts."

"You speak abomination," Nephi declared.

The girl noticed a bright blush on each boy's cheeks, even if they tried to look away. She giggled. "Don't be silly. Abomination can never be so comforting, so pleasurable, and so beautiful."

Teasingly, the girl tried to step around them so the boys couldn't avoid seeing her.

Laman walked up to the poolside.

"There you both are." Laman noted the girl. "What's going on here?"

"I was merely offering your companions the goodness and hospitality of Raphia with a star-cake and a fresh bath," the maiden replied.

"They have work to do. You've detained them."

"I meant no harm."

The girl handed her star-cake to Laman instead. Laman looked down at the food. He accepted it graciously, picking off a seed with his fingernail and setting it on his tongue.

"Don't you think these boys might be a little young for your 'goodness and hospitality?'" asked Laman flirtatiously.

"If they're old enough to ride with a caravan—"

Laman finished the statement for her. "—then they're old enough to partake of the joys of Ashtoreth. Yes, yes. I know. But it might do well for you to be aware, these boy don't have any bronze or silver. I assume that you charge for your 'baths?'"

The girl nodded.

Laman smiled at her widely. He turned to Nephi and Daniel, speaking harshly. Did he think this tone of voice would impress the maiden?

"Take the camels back to camp! Make sure the servants feed them. Afterwards, have them hobbled in the space I reserved in the arcade. I want you both to build a fire. By then, I should be back, but if I'm not, eat supper without me."

Laman placed his arm around the girl. She smiled back at him. Laman aimed her toward the stone staircase that led to the caravanserai's private upper rooms. He sent Nephi a quick wink, as if his younger brother should approve, almost admire the thing he was about to do.

Laman noted the look of concern in Nephi's face—the look of pleading. He whispered something in the girl's ear. She continued up the stairs alone and waited at the top.

Laman stepped back to Nephi. "Don't look so glum, little brother. Life is like a precious flower. Enjoy its color and fragrance today. By tomorrow, it may have wilted. In a year or two, you'll understand. Until then, let this be a secret between us."

Laman grinned wryly and turned away. No words came to Nephi's heart. As he watched his oldest brother ascend the stairs, he could feel himself shaking.

When Laman reached the upper story with the girl, he leaned over the balustrade, shouting with mock anger. "What are you boys waiting for? Go!"

Daniel and Nephi returned to the troughs where the camels had finished drinking. The prince noticed a tear had streaked Nephi's cheek.

"Are you going to be all right?" he asked.

"Yes," Nephi replied. He wiped the tear swiftly away. "Let's get the animals back to camp."

In the space of one evening, by a muddy well in a dusty foreign place, Nephi had deeply changed his views of two persons—a boy he'd once looked on as an enemy and a brother he'd once looked up to as a man.

DAGAN LOOKED FORWARD TO HIS BED.

Today he'd overseen the first day of harvest for Lehi's wheat crop. He and the other hired workers, along with the remainder of Lehi's children, had spent the afternoon and evening threshing wheat. Grains were separated by tossing them into the air so the breeze might carry away the lighter chaff. The grizzled bailiff wondered if he was getting old before his time. Such work had never been quite so exhausting. Dagan could feel the wheat dust in his beard. The dust also stuck to his back and chest where the rivulets of sweat had run.

After paying his final farewell to Lehi and the others at the granary, Dagan descended the hill where he lived alone in a comfortable one-room stone shanty along the wadi. There, his most prized possessions awaited him—a thick woolen blanket and a duck-feather pillow. Could a man really ask for more in this life?

The bailiff brought no lamp or torch to light the way. He'd walked this path so often that he knew the exact position of every rut and stone. It bothered him though, as he neared his house, to see that the familiar glow of lamplight did not illumine the outer edges of his front door.

Strange. He'd thought that filling his table lamp with oil had become as habitual to his daily routine as waking up. In all honesty, he couldn't remember if he'd done so that morning or not. More evidence of his increasing age.

Dagan stepped up to the door. It fell open under the touch of his hand.

Now he was certain the place had been intruded. Those mischievous hirelings! Every year they seemed to be less and less trustworthy. Well, nothing to do but take an inventory at first light to see what had been stolen. Hopefully, his duck-feather pillow was not part of the booty.

Dagan entered the darkened house and made his way across the dirt floor, toward the opposite wall. In the center of the room, he came to a halt. He listened. Dagan knew he was not alone. The sound of breathing was all around him.

One of the shadows lunged out of the darkness. A hand gripped Dagan's throat and pushed him back until he fell against the wall beside the open window. The hand's grip was so powerful, Dagan could neither speak nor breath. With squinted eyes, he tried to perceive the face of his assailant. Starlight reflected through the window, providing him with his only source of light. Dagan discerned enough to know that his attacker's face was hideously deformed. The man's nose and ears had been severed off!

"Tell me," the assailant demanded in a high, thirsty voice, "where is the prince?" He relaxed his grip enough for Dagan to reply.

Dagan gasped for breath. "Prince? What prince?"

"Daniel, the son of Maaseiah!"

"I don't know what you're talking about. I've never met such a person."

The noseless attacker took a moment to think. Then he asked, "Where is the guest boy? The one who has lost his memory?"

"Jophy? Why, Jophy is gone."

"Gone? Gone where?"

"He has ridden with Master Laman into Egypt."

"Egypt! Why has he been taken to Egypt?"

"The Master has bales to trade in Noph."

"How long ago did they leave?"

Dagan's knees gave out. It was all Zaavan could do to hold him up by the throat.

*"Please,"* Dagan begged. "I'm but a poor servant. I have nothing to give you."

Dagan felt the sharp point of a dagger directed into his stomach.

Hysterically, Zaavan repeated his question. "I did not ask you for gold! I asked you how long ago did they leave?"

"Not two days ago," Dagan replied.

He was asked no more questions.

The next morning Lehi's humble bailiff was found in his house with a knife wound in the belly. There was evidence to suggest that Dagan did not die right away. Somehow he'd managed to crawl across the room and reach the top of his bed. His head and face were nestled in the softness of his duck-feather pillow.

# Chapter 9
## IN THE LAND OF A THOUSAND GODS

For seven endless days and nights Laman's caravan forged its journey along the road known to traders as the Way of the Sea, resting only during the hottest hours under the sun and the coldest hours under the stars.

Nephi told Daniel that people who spend long periods on the desert sometimes see false visions on the landscape. The prince was skeptical on this point until the afternoon of the seventh day. In the shadows of the distant rock formations he thought he perceived a pair of following eyes. At sunset he could have sworn a giant dagger pierced the earth at the horizon line, sending a wide wave of blood crawling toward them across the sand. Daniel shut his eyes tightly to convince himself the vision wasn't real.

On the eighth day, the caravan passed beneath the frontier fortresses of the Land of Egypt. On the ninth, their camels crossed the region of Set only to be tormented a good part of the afternoon by flies. Pulling their burnooses tighter over their faces didn't help much. The insects clustered black upon their backs and heads.

On the eleventh day, under a bright azure sky, they at last reached the outlying settlements of Egypt's mother city. Foreigners may have pronounced it as Noph or Mennuphi or Memphis, but to the priests who devoted their lives to serving local deities, the place was known solemnly as "Ha-Ko-Ptah" or the "dwelling place of the spirit of Ptah." The temple of Ptah was the city's main attraction, rivaled only by the pyramids in the region toward the setting sun known as the "Western City of the Dead."

The boatmen who carried their animals and provisions from the east shore to the west shore of the Nile sang melodies that claimed the gods had built Noph the day after the world was created and would support it until the day the world was destroyed.

All of Egypt seemed intoxicated with celebration. Citizens dressed in their most colorful garb. On every corner, dancers twirled while minstrels chanted praises to Pharaoh. Tonight was the first night of the new moon and tomorrow, Pharaoh Necho, the living deity of Egypt, would sail up the Nile in a freshly purchased fleet of Corinthian triremes, gathering warriors and mercenaries along every inch of the delta, until Necho's army, two-hundred thousand strong, marched into the heart of Asia where he would save the world from the evil forces of Babylon. A spectacular farewell parade had been scheduled that evening.

As Laman's caravan wound toward the center of town, Nephi experienced a peculiar crawling in his soul. Even Daniel, who possessed no specific memories of his heritage, felt an instinctive discomfort in this place. Neither boy had ever ventured so far from Jerusalem's gates. Incorporations of stone were rare sights in Judah, but in Noph, idols and images dotted the countryside as commonly as weeds. In every direction sprang flowering chapels and shining shrines dedicated to mammals and birds, fishes and reptiles. Nephi started to understand the saying that Israel had a natural aversion for the people of other lands. Not an aversion born out of haughtiness, although that was how it was often manifested, but an aversion born out of a simple longing for truth and order over confusion and spectacle.

At the same time, Nephi realized that the saying was double-edged. For the people of other lands, there also seemed to be a natural aversion for Israel. Nephi saw it in the hostile faces of everyone who noticed their caravan and divined its origin.

Laman seemed unaffected by the local sentiment. From atop his camel he offered the boys a colorful lecture on the meaning and significance of every landmark. His descriptions carried all the pride and piety of an Egyptian believer. Before the bustling chapel of Bastet, Egypt's cat-headed goddess of love and marital fidelity, his speech attracted the ears of several bystanders, but when he remarked in passing that he knew more about the Egyptian religion than most Egyptians, people looked offended and moved on.

In the handsomely paved square between the great temple of Ptah and Noph's market district, Laman left the boys to shop for Nephi's new bow. One of their servants knew the location of the weapons and tools district and agreed to escort them.

"Be back at the square before sunset," Laman instructed. He and the other servants guided the camel train toward the nearby exchange district to complete the business of the trip.

Nephi and Daniel gazed into the courtyard of the temple of Ptah. Burning incense hazed their view. The boys couldn't go in, of course, for fear of defiling themselves, but they could walk along the outer hall of columns, which to them was the most interesting aspect of the temple anyway.

Each of the thousand columns was festooned with living flowers: pink and scarlet, hyacinth and emerald, lavender and gold. Nephi reached up to feel the hieroglyphic grooves. Abruptly, he backed away, looking in both directions. Could touching a column somehow be viewed as sacrilegious or disrespectful? He felt relieved to see an Egyptian boy doing exactly the same thing.

Daniel and Nephi couldn't read the sacred writings, but neither could most Egyptians. Nevertheless, the endless sequences of pictures held them spellbound. Each column immortalized some aspect of Egyptian life: the deeds of the gods, a sacrificial feast, a violent land battle, a procession of captives, even the hippopotamus hunts of Pharaoh.

Daniel and Nephi followed with the local citizens who walked along these columns every day to gladden their hearts. At the other end of the square, the people diverged into the various market streets. The air at the edge of the bazaar was so thick with pollen from innumerable flower stalls that their eyes began to water.

Down the first street, Nubian slaves squatted in long rows plucking feathers from plump geese, ducks, fowls, pigeons, snipe, and moorhens. As Nephi listened to their joyful work songs, he remembered that similar labors were once performed in this country by his own ancestors.

The poultry market all by itself appeared as large as the entire lower section of Jerusalem. Beyond it lay open cook houses, eating places, and beer shops. The sweet odor of roast pork was mixed with the tang of fermented barley. As appropriate to their Israelite upbringing, Daniel and Nephi held their breaths as long as possible. What a relief to reach the avenue of the joiners and cabinet-makers where the noble smells of sap and sawdust permeated the air.

Soon they reached the riverfront and the sprawling fish market. Long stalls were strewn with silver scales and splashed with cold reddish-blue blood. Choppers were driven into the bulging bodies of Nile pike and other great river fishes. The pieces were then tossed onto scales where a man croaked out the price with a hoarse voice and nimbly wrapped each sample in fig leaves.

Noph's fish merchants had devised a rather unique way to dispose of unwanted fins, heads, and entrails. Parallel to the river, a pit had been dug and reinforced with stone walls. Daniel watched a man dump in a bowl of fish guts. A cacophony of splashing and snarling rose out of the pit. The prince couldn't resist the temptation to peek inside. At the bottom of the pit, four full-sized crocodiles wallowed in the muck, looking only moderately satisfied by the fishermen's waste. The instant Daniel's head appeared, one leaped up on its tail and bit the air with a hollow snap. Although the pit had a depth twice Daniel's height and a roof of crossed wooden poles, the prince gasped and leaped backwards.

At last, they entered the avenue of the toolmakers. The very first shop boasted a wall display of fine bows. Wide-eyed with anticipation, Nephi entered the shop and began fingering the selection. The shop owner, a well-dressed man with thin silver hair, looked on nervously. It didn't take Nephi long to deduce the class of customers catered to by this shop. Its bows had been fashioned from the finest and rarest materials. Most were embroidered with gold or silver and inlaid with gems.

Nephi found one particular bow so striking, he had to lift it off the wall. The weapon felt heavy, and yet so sturdy and balanced in his grip.

"I've never seen anything like it," Nephi told Daniel.

The shop owner approached. "Very expensive," he said in Egyptian, hoping such words would fend off the young browsers. In his judgement, these boys were not of the type or class to afford his wares.

"How was it made?" Nephi asked in the shopowner's native tongue.

"Imported from Sidon," replied the shop owner. "The backing is Damascus steel. Please—!" He took back the bow and replaced it on the wall.

Nephi felt somewhat offended, but the shop owner was right. The silver he'd been allotted wouldn't even cover such a weapon's down payment.

Nephi and Daniel were alarmed to discover that nearly every other archery outlet in the district presented barren walls. They learned that every toolmaker in Noph had been commissioned to fashion armaments for Pharaoh's forces. New weapons were snatched up by the state wherever they were found. The boys located a few used bows here and there, but the quality of the articles wouldn't have stood up to the one Nephi already owned. Nephi had truly chosen a bad week to go bow-shopping in Egypt.

NEPHI AND DANIEL ARRIVED BACK AT THE SQUARE JUST AS THE SETTING sun had touched the pinnacle of the step-pyramid on the western desert. The evening's festivities were underway. The avenue along the square was lined with thousands of eager faces, all awaiting the first spectacles of the parade. Each person carried some form of light, whether a lamp or torch.

The boys were ready to give up all hope of locating Laman when he emerged from the masses. He'd been watching for the boys from the steps of the Hall of Columns.

"It's not the best week for Jewish traders either," Laman told Nephi after hearing about the boys' troubles finding a bow. "Every citizen in Noph has heard how King Josiah insulted the Egyptian ambassador. My buyers threatened to pay me only half-price for my bales! *Half!* I reminded them of our contract and threatened to exchange our oil in Damascus from now on. They backed down. What a relief to learn that the language of trade is still louder than the language of politics."

Approaching music filled the square. The first spectacle of the parade marched along the avenue: a band of court musicians blowing flutes and pipes, strumming hand harps and lutes, and beating little drums.

The harmonies were enchanting, almost hypnotic. Nephi closed his eyes and breathed in the music. As he opened them again, the musicians crossed before him. Nephi sensed something disturbing about them, but it took a moment for it to register. When it hit him, his stomach lurched into his throat.

Yet it was Daniel who cried, "They're all blind! Every one of them!"

Where the musician's eyes should have been sank burnt-out cavernous sockets. Gentle tappings with a stick guided the players, as if they were sheep. Nephi and Daniel were horrified.

Laman explained. "The Egyptians believe that by blinding their minstrels, it forces them to develop a keener sense of hearing. To us, it may seem cruel, but you have to admit, they turn out some of the finest players ever heard."

Behind the band marched two thousand warriors of Pharaoh's army, arrayed in full armor, their lips and nails brightly painted and their hair stiffly lacquered. Now and then, someone from the crowd would recognize a son or husband or father and raise up a cheer, but none of the soldiers ever turned to acknowledge his name. Their eyes remained fixed in the forward position. Their chins were as rigid as their shields.

After the warriors, marched the priests of Ptah. Their steps were short and sprightly. Each wore a short kilt with a lion's tail extending out from behind. Some wore woven wigs embroidered with pearls while others displayed towering headdresses. Those of the highest orders had their heads completely shaven. Daniel and Nephi watched more and more bald-headed men approach in the flickering light.

In the distance, surrounded by a vivid red glow, swayed an object which seemed to be the focus of the whole procession. It was a boat of some sort, borne along on two golden poles by no less than nineteen priests. The keel ended in a gazelle's head and the bow concluded with a large golden *ankh*, the Egyptian sign of life. Atop the cabin-shrine in the center of the boat stood something of human-form enveloped in mummy wrappings. Whatever it was, it had been dead for centuries—maybe millennia.

The masses bowed to the mummy as it passed. Nephi tensed with fear. How could he kneel to this heathen thing? To do so would be a direct mockery of God's second law from Mount Sinai. As the boat loomed closer, Nephi realized he and Daniel were the only ones still standing. Even Laman had dropped to his knees.

An anxious murmur started to awaken around Daniel and Nephi. Laman reached up to grab the boys' shoulders and forcefully yanked them to the ground.

"Don't be stupid!" Laman exclaimed. "*Everyone* bows to Ptah on the sacred barque. There is no worse insult in this city. The people would tear us apart like wolves!"

In case they'd failed to understand, Laman continued to hold them down while the boat passed along the avenue.

Next in the procession arrived the *living* god of Egypt. Pharaoh Necho rode upon a palanquin that resembled a fiery war chariot. If ever there existed a moment when the ruler of Egypt so resembled a god, it was now. The ten thousand lights of the square reflected off Necho's golden armor while he sat as unmoving as the mummy of Ptah. Alongside Pharaoh's chariot marched numerous counselors who continually fell out of formation so they might devotedly kiss the chariot's golden rim and afterwards, writhe blissfully, and trip back into place.

Nephi noted two tall cages to the left and right of Necho. In one squatted a fierce-eyed bird. The other housed some sort of monkey, leaping excitedly about the cage. The bird, Laman explained, was the golden sparrow-hawk of Horus, while the monkey was the sacred baboon of the realm of the dead. Pharaoh never traveled anywhere without these living images at his side.

After the portable chariot of Pharaoh Necho had passed, there was a lull in the parade. The people began to feel it was safe to stand. But as the next spectacle arrived in the square, everyone shamefully dropped back to their knees. A black bull of enormous proportions made its way down the avenue on a golden halter led by two priestly attendants. Its pendulous dewlap shook and swayed. An enraptured gasp gripped the crowd. Even Laman's mouth hung open in awe.

"The Apis," Laman whispered with a reverence rivaling the most devout Egyptian.

"The Apis?" repeated Daniel.

"The most perfect incarnation of Osiris the redeemer," said Laman. "Do you realize how fortunate we are to see this? Sometimes entire generations pass without the birth of a divine bull. There are twenty-nine essential signs . . ."

Laman appeared barely conscious of his own voice as he chanted out the signs that had to be present before a bull could be considered the reborn Apis. It had to be exceptionally large. It had to have a white triangular patch on its forehead and another patch on its back in the clear shape of a sparrow-hawk. The hair of its tail had to be two separate colors. Even if all twenty-nine signs were present without exception, there had to be a certain spiritual quality about the bull—an ethereal gentleness that encouraged tears from every onlooker. In short, the Apis needed to be the best-behaved creature on the face of the earth.

As the massive bull trotted closer, Daniel braced himself for the shudder of terror that had accompanied every encounter he'd ever had with a large animal. For the first time in Daniel's life, he felt no sense of fear. Absolutely none. Was it the gentle nature of the beast or something else?

Nephi felt a similar sense of peace. The entire evening might have passed into his memory as quite harmonious, except for what happened next.

The Apis stopped.

When the crowd realized what had happened, they felt a tremor of shock. Nothing like this had ever occurred in Egyptian memory. The bull planted its feet directly in front of the place where Daniel and Nephi stood. The priests who led the bull were also dumb-founded. They considered drawing the slack on the halter, but nothing could be more disrespectful. If the Apis wished to halt the procession, then the Apis would be allowed to halt the procession. The bull sniffed the air mournfully.

It turned its head.

The eyes of the bull seemed to connect directly with the eyes of Daniel and Nephi. The crowd in front of the beast, including Laman, cautiously backed away. Daniel and Nephi did not move. A force, a shield, an unconscious awareness held them in their place. They would not relinquish ground to this heathen incorporation.

The Apis uttered a threatening snort. It kicked at the street with its legs and released a piercing, almost human scream. The beast's broad horns inclined downward, as if preparing to pummel these two Israelite urchins into dust. It screamed again and shook its massive head. Daniel and Nephi stood firm.

The bull began spinning in a dizzy, frustrated circle. Finally, it lost its balance and dropped to the earth. There on the ground, the Apis started to whimper. Its eyelids closed. Its head turned away. The beast would not, or could not, make eye contact with either boy again.

From behind, a tall priest with a yellowed, closely shaven skull approached the fallen bull. In his hands he carried a scepter and scroll. Even Laman recognized this personage, although nobody knew his real name. In Noph he was known only as "Har-Habe-Hartub" or "the Master of Ceremonies of Death." What Pharaoh Necho was to the souls of the living, the Hartub was to the souls of the dead.

The Hartub stepped up close to the Apis and laid his left hand, which carried the scepter, lightly on the bull's neck. He stroked it imperceptibly. He inclined his ear toward the head of the Apis, as if in all humility he were determined to hear what the frightened spirit which possessed the body of this innocent animal had to say. After a message from Osiris had apparently been delivered, the Hartub leaned into the ear of the bull and whispered a few soothing words of his own.

A trembling sense of relief rushed through the divine bull from its horns to its hooves. Its brownish tongue caressed the Hartub's sallow cheeks. At last, the Apis arose. With tripping hooves and swishing tail, it continued with the sacred procession, as if nothing had happened at all.

The anxiety of the crowd released with a rushing sigh. No one sustained any belief that the boys had caused the Apis' disturbance. Clearly, the soul of Osiris, which possessed the body of the bull, had experienced a moment of grave danger from unseen forces in the underworld. When Osiris had overcome these dangers, a shudder of relief had passed through his pleasing image. Could the armies of Egypt have requested a more glorious oracle? A new epoch was about to begin for the reborn empire! An era of prosperity, power and peace!

Only the Hartub himself might have interpreted the event differently. Before following the Apis, he looked at Daniel and Nephi. To the crowd, his expression was solemn and inscrutable, but to Daniel and Nephi, a subtle wrath gleamed in his eyes. The Hartub seemed to know that a confrontation had taken place this day. He also knew that the power he served had been defeated. If he could have ordered the crowd to pounce on these two miscreants and tear them to ribbons, he surely would have done it. But like the Apis, his soul would not rise to the task. Instead, the Hartub turned on his heel, and with short, sprightly steps, he followed in the path of the master he'd chosen long ago.

Laman stepped in front of his brother and the prince."You both might have been killed!" he exclaimed. "Never freeze up when you're frightened. Run! Or you'll both end up corpses before you're twenty."

"But I wasn't frightened," said Nephi.

Laman utterly failed to comprehend such a response. Obviously, his little brother was embarrassed and disturbed.

Even Daniel and Nephi hadn't fully understood the significance of their confrontation with the Apis bull, that is, if hidden within the event existed some hint of their future destinies. But from that day forward, whenever the God of Israel was made to stand beside the thousand deities of Egypt, or beside the gods of any other nation, Daniel and Nephi had no doubt which ones represented pomp and pageantry and which one represented power.

ATOP THE HIGHEST STEP OF THE OUTER HALL OF COLUMNS, ONE FIGURE no longer watched the procession. From beneath his hooded cloak, Zaavan had witnessed the confrontation with the Apis bull along with all the other thousands of spectators in Noph's central square. Like everyone else, the faces of the two boys who stood their ground were indelibly carved into his memory.

Zaavan dropped his hands quickly to his side. *Could it really be him?* With all of the luck of the gods behind him, Zaavan would have never expected to locate Daniel, son of Maaseiah, so easily among all these citizens and pilgrims. The gods truly must have wanted this boy dead.

Zaavan pointed out the youth to his cohorts. They, too, were stupefied at such good fortune. The plan had been to reside in this foreign land for weeks, maybe months. Now they were one mere thrust of the dagger away from returning home to collect their reward.

The final spectacle of the parade now passed through the square. One hundred virgins, clad in gauze-like pleated dresses and wreaths of flowers, danced behind the rest of the procession. In each of their hands they carried a little papyrus boat, each one a miniature of the sacred barque of Ptah. A light illuminated the little boats from within, making them appear as transparent lanterns. As the maidens danced into the avenues of the market district, the crowd gathered in behind them. The people would follow the procession all the way to the banks of the Nile and watch as the maidens set the little boats free in the river's current.

Zaavan kept his eyes on Daniel. He and his companions joined with the crowd in its pilgrimage to the riverfront.

"Spread out," Zaavan instructed his men. "Don't lose sight of him or I'll see to it that all your noses are severed off to match my own."

Zaavan's hood continued to shroud his scarred features. He let himself be carried forward by the human current, never allowing the unsuspecting prince to escape his sight.

Daniel and his companions stopped to purchase a snack at one of the booths. Zaavan and his minions closed in a little tighter. A few of his men positioned themselves ahead of the prince.

At last, the crowd gathered on the banks of the Nile. Daniel and his friends were fortunate enough to find a spot on the landing where they could view the launching of the little boats in all its splendor.

The maidens danced down to the water's edge. As each boat was set free in the current, a shout erupted from the crowd. The shouting intensified with every release.

Zaavan crept toward the prince, his face still hidden. He drew close enough to see the torchlight reflected in Daniel's eyes. The assassin drew his dagger and hid it inside the arm of his cloak. Only a moment now and it would all be over. When the shouting ceased, Prince Daniel would certainly walk toward him. He might see a blade flash in the torchlight, but that would be all. Before the prince's limp body hit the ground, Zaavan would have already slipped away into the anonymous masses.

The other boy, the one who always seemed glued to Daniel's side, looked in Zaavan's direction. His eyes stopped. Did this youngster recognize him? Impossible! But just to be sure, Zaavan faded back. There was no need to be impatient.

Nephi watched the man in the hooded cloak slip behind a line of cheering Egyptians. Something about the man had bothered him. What was it? There seemed to be something familiar about that cloak. Had he seen this person before? The memory made him uneasy.

*Of course!* thought Nephi. That day in the Jerusalem market! The day the governor was killed! After he and Prince Daniel had argued over the silk, Nephi noticed an identically-clad figure across the street, watching them. For some reason, the image of this person had never faded from his mind.

Nephi turned abruptly to his brother. "Where are we staying tonight?"

"I've purchased rooms at an inn not far from here," said Laman. "The animals and the other servants are already there. Why do you ask?"

"I think we should go to the inn."

"Now? The celebrations haven't ended. Aren't you enjoying yourself?"

"Yes. It's just . . . I'm a little nervous."

"Nervous? What are you afraid of?"

"Nothing. What I mean to say is, I don't *feel* very well."

Nephi knew that feigning illness was the only way Laman might reluctantly agree.

"All right," Laman sighed. "But after I get you two settled, I'm coming back."

Nephi, Laman, Daniel, and the servant pried their way through the crowd until people started to thin and the open street lay before them. Merchants had left lamps burning outside their closed-up shops throughout the night. Still, there were many shadows and lengthy stretches ruled by darkness.

As they made their way toward the inn, Laman whistled the tune of one of the bawdier Egyptian love songs. Nephi peered into every darkened corner. Daniel noted his cautious behavior.

"What's the matter?" Daniel asked softly. "You seem jumpy."

Nephi's eyes darted to his right to watch something leap out of the shadows. It whined contemptuously.

"It's only a house cat," said Laman.

The feline scurried between some planks.

They'd entered the fish market beside the river so, in fact, they saw dozens of cats, having wandered down from the shrine of Bastet. The stalls and hanging lines had been cleared of meat; nevertheless, the cats picked at the scales and licked at the drying blood, now and then locating a backbone or fin with enough flesh to warrant attention. Nephi had never seen so many cats wandering loose. The house cat was said to be sacred in Egypt. Rummaging through rotting garbage hardly seemed a worthy activity for sacred creatures.

Nephi allowed himself to be distracted a moment too long. He looked ahead and saw men in the street. One wore the familiar hooded cloak. Nephi stopped and grabbed Daniel's arm. Laman continued walking forward with the servant.

Nephi looked back. Men had also entered the street behind them. Nephi turned forward again to see Laman greeting the men casually. Their conversation seemed polite enough until the figure in the hooded cloak raised his arm and stabbed downward. Laman shrieked and collapsed. The servant fell to his knees, pleading for mercy. The villains ignored him. They also ignored the writhing Laman so that they might stalk their *real* prey.

"Run!" Nephi shouted and dashed back several steps, but the men behind them were also closing in. Nephi glanced to his left. Just beyond the fish stalls flowed the mighty Nile. There were spaces between the stalls.

"Jophy! The river!" cried Nephi desperately.

What was wrong with the prince? He wasn't moving! He just stood there, facing his murderers. Did Daniel sense an invisible force protecting him, as when they'd faced the Apis bull?

Nephi sensed no such phenomenon. He turned on his heel, brought his elbows in tight and slipped between the fish stalls. He reached the edge of the stone embankment over the river. Beyond it loomed only blackness. There was no way to know if he'd land in water or smash himself on a wooden dock. The boy sprang into nothingness and tucked his knees.

Nephi's splash stirred the prince back to reality. For an instant everything around him had fazed out—everything except the man in the hooded cloak. Daniel knew him. The man from his nightmares! His face was hidden, but Daniel knew its appearance. Under that hood brooded a hideous, naked skull with bulging, blood-red eyes and a forked tongue surrounded by a thousand dripping fangs.

Nephi's voice echoed in Daniel's mind: "Jophy! The river!"

Daniel faced the Nile. The thin escape gap that Nephi had selected was well below Daniel's position. Daniel chose a much wider gap to his left.

Daggers thrust at the prince as he lurched toward the embankment, ready to join Nephi in the Nile current. But Daniel hadn't bounded more than five steps when his foot slipped out from beneath him. He tripped. His chin struck a knot of wood, inflicting a gash. A crossing of poles supported his torso. An abyss of indeterminable depth sank beneath his dangling legs. In the dim light he hadn't noticed the pit. Something stirred underneath him. And then Daniel remembered.

Earlier that afternoon he'd seen four crocodiles wallowing down there. At present, he could only make out their spectral shadows like phantoms rising out of the Egyptian underworld and he could hear their throaty snarls.

Hands grasped at Daniel's cloak. He dragged himself beyond the assassins' reach, across the poles, out toward the middle of the pit. The wooden crossings, tied with thongs at each intersection, created squares of space an arm's length in diameter. Carefully, Daniel balanced himself. Some of the men were laughing at him. Others angrily urged him to crawl back. The man in the hooded cloak watched his victim in utter silence.

Then he threw off the hood.

Daniel took in the man's features. Hideous—yes—but not quite the monster from his dreams. Another monster! Somehow this one was just as familiar. He gazed into the man's eyes. They were lifeless eyes. And yet piercing. That face was the last thing he'd seen before . . .

A universe of information began flooding into Daniel's mind—like a cascade of oceans at the edge of the world. *Jerusalem. The king. My father. That terrible day. The assassin in the dark.*

Zaavan's men began joggling the poles. The crocodiles stirred more restlessly. Daniel held on firmly. He could not be dislodged.

"Come here, boy," coaxed Zaavan. "We won't hurt you if you'll make this easy. We only wish to take you home. There are people who miss you very much."

Daniel shook his head.

Zaavan huffed in aggravation. His patience had run short. Any moment these streets would be filled with citizens returning home from the parade. Zaavan's fingers pinched the blade of his dagger. Squinting, he held the weapon up between his eyes and took careful aim.

Just as Zaavan flung the knife, Daniel dropped down inside the poles, clinging with both arms. Zaavan's dagger hit the beam beside Daniel's hand, splintering the wood. The weapon dropped inside the pit. Zaavan cursed.

Daniel continued hanging, knowing the other men had their own daggers to throw. Daniel looked down at the moving shadows below him. Was one of the shadows preparing to lurch upward? Frantically, Daniel swung his legs high and wrapped his ankles around two of the poles. The crocodile's jaws came together in a terrible thunderclap beside Daniel's ear before the creature fell back into the blackness. A tooth had nicked the prince's sleeve! Daniel realized that he was still in range to be picked off like a monkey dangling from a limb! After pulling himself as tight as he could against the underside of the poles, he held perfectly still. Any sharp movement would certainly inspire the crocodile to make another attempt.

Zaavan could see people approaching, some distance away. The parade had ended. Time was running out. The prince had to die this instant.

Zaavan snatched a dagger from one of his men and placed the shaft in his teeth. He dropped down on all fours and began crawling across the pit. The crocodiles thrust upward at the new moving target. Zaavan snickered at their futility. The poles were sturdy. They would have supported a man twice his weight.

Zaavan brought one knee forward and then the other, bunching up the folds of his cloak so they wouldn't hamper his progress. Steadily, he made his way out toward the center, where Daniel's white knuckles gripped the pole. Zaavan would cut off the prince's fingers one by one, until the boy dropped.

A crocodile leaped. Its jaws clasped onto a hanging sag in the fold of Zaavan's cloak. Had the spaces been wider, Zaavan might have been pulled through. Instead, the assassin flattened against the poles, his eyes bulging, the wind knocked from his lungs. The thousand-pound lizard hung on to Zaavan's cloak. Its weight snapped the entire roof of the pit. Daniel gripped his fists more tightly as the poles collapsed. An instant later, the prince found himself pinned between the poles and the cold stone of the pit's inner wall.

Zaavan's final thought before the jaws of a second crocodile lunged for his head may have been one of regret—regret for having purchased a cloak of such well-woven material. A cheaper garment might have torn off in the lizard's teeth instead of collapsing the roof. Daniel listened to the assassin's blood-chilling scream, but he did not watch as the crocodiles fought for equal portions.

Daniel worried about his *own* predicament. Any instant a crocodile might turn on him, tearing through the poles between itself and the boy like so many threads of straw. Daniel's limbs ached from having hung for so long. Using all his remaining strength, he freed himself, hoisting his body through a square in the poles. The broken roof provided a ready ladder. Grasping at any support he could find, the prince dragged himself higher. Before the crocodiles had noticed his escape, Daniel's legs were well out of range.

But what predators would be waiting for him at the top?

THE CURRENT CARRIED NEPHI FURTHER OUT FROM THE RIVERBANK. At first this hadn't bothered him. Anything that carried him away from the men who'd stabbed his brother had to be God-sent. But now that he'd been swept several hundred ells down the Nile, it began to occur to him how difficult it might be to swim back to shore.

Nephi kicked his legs. His arms raked the water. It had become difficult to pant without swallowing huge gulps of river. Nephi looked toward shore. He'd only closed the distance between himself and the bank by a fraction.

The boy's heart started racing. Reaching the riverbank before drowning appeared impossible. Nephi began to panic, flailing his arms.

"Help!" he cried.

Was he too far from shore to be heard? There were lights along the riverfront—a dock of some sort. Through the blur of his own splashing, Nephi noticed men loading supplies onto a string of rivercrafts.

"Help!" Nephi cried again.

It was difficult for Nephi to tell if anyone had responded to his shouts. Did he see someone tear off his upper garment? Had someone plunged into the river from the dock? The boy continued gulping water. His arms ceased their struggle. The undercurrent prepared to swallow him.

A pair of hands rose out of the Nile before Nephi's face. Nephi grabbed at the man's hair, at his shoulders, at his neck and at his ears. The man spun Nephi around, cupping his palm under the boy's chin and muttering something in Egyptian. Nephi continued flailing his arms, desperate to grasp something solid. The man punched Nephi's arm. He punched it hard!—and repeated his Egyptian word. Nephi understood this time. The word was "Hotp!" or "Relax!" Using one arm, the man swam toward shore, keeping Nephi afloat with the other.

Nephi faded in and out of consciousness. The next thing he knew, he was coughing up water on the muddy bank. He lay on his back beside a nest of reeds. The men who stood around him were Egyptian soldiers, still wearing their heavy armor from the parade.

His rescuer spoke again in Egyptian. "Perhaps I should feel sorry to have rescued you," he said. "To drown in the Nile is to become the eternal praise of Ra."

*An honor I could do without,* thought Nephi. Suddenly, the boy remembered the plight of Daniel and his brother. After a fit of coughing, he began ranting in Egyptian, "Please help me! We were attacked! I jumped in the river to escape! They stabbed my brother!"

The men strained to understand the boy through his heavy accent and continuous coughing. Nephi tried to stand. He nearly fainted. His rescuer held him upright. Momentarily, Nephi felt steady enough to walk. The avenue along the loading docks was the same street that ran beside fish market. Nephi coaxed a few of the men to follow him.

*Was Laman dead?* wondered Nephi. *Why didn't Daniel follow me into the river?* These thoughts strengthened him further. Nephi walked faster.

Just ahead, the street bustled with onlookers. Nephi scanned the crowd for the man in the hooded cloak or any of his cohorts. He saw none of them. Where had they gone?

The men in the street had gathered around someone on the ground. Nephi pried his way into the middle and found his brother. The knife wound had pierced Laman's shoulder. Laman had lost much blood, but he was coherent enough to speak.

"Nephi? Is that you?" His voice was weak.

"It's me. What do you want me to do, Laman?"

"Ask them to fetch a physician."

Laman recited the necessary Egyptian phrases. Nephi loudly repeated Laman's words. The onlookers understood. The soldiers who'd followed Nephi from the loading docks appeared to know the readiest solution. Two of them rushed back toward the docks.

Nephi looked around for Daniel. He expected to see only the boy's twisted corpse, perhaps a little further up the street. A short distance away, Nephi spotted someone. A boy sat against an empty fish stall, his head in his hands. Daniel was alive! But his mind seemed focused a thousand leagues away.

"Jophy!" Nephi rushed to the boy's side. "What happened?"

Daniel's chin still bled from the gash he'd received on the wooden pole as he tripped.

"Are you hurt?" asked Nephi. "Why didn't you follow me?"

At first, Daniel didn't react to Nephi's voice. Nephi feared the prince had lost his mind completely.

At last, Daniel looked up. He studied Nephi's features, apparently trying to determine if he recalled even knowing this wet and mud-speckled person.

"It's me! Nephi!"

A glint of recognition entered Daniel's eyes.

"Speak to me, Jophy," Nephi persisted.

"My name is not Jophy," he replied. "My name is Daniel. I am the son of Maaseiah. I am a prince of the house of David."

# Chapter 10
## THE WILDERNESS OF SHUR

LAMAN WAS RESTING PEACEFULLY NOW. INSTEAD OF SLEEPING IN the inn courtyard with the tents and servants, he'd decided to splurge for one of the upper rooms with a straw mattress. Beds were prepared for Daniel and Nephi as well. The boys looked on as the Egyptian physician dressed Laman's wound with unfamiliar balms and left him a narcotic root for the pain and fever. Laman consumed a portion of the root and drifted away into slumber.

Daniel and Nephi no longer felt imminent danger in the streets of Noph. Zaavan's men had scattered the instant the crocodiles had killed their leader. As Daniel climbed out of the pit, he'd have been an easy target, but as it turned out, Zaavan had never revealed the names of those in Jerusalem who had masterminded the assassination. None of Zaavan's men would have known who to approach for payment after accomplishing the deed. Any motives they had for murdering this eleven-year-old boy had died with Zaavan.

For the rest of the evening, the prince appeared deep in thought. His memories had been restored, but it took a while for him to put all of them in order. Nephi tended to Laman's needs and then to his own. He cleaned himself up and found fresh clothing. Nephi avoided talking with Daniel or even looking at him. *How might the prince interpret the previous month?* Nephi wondered. His concern heightened when Daniel stopped him under the bright lamps of the inn courtyard to say, "I know who you are now. You're the boy from the Jerusalem bazaar. The boy who wanted the patch of purple silk."

Nephi couldn't deny having treated a royal prince like a common slave. The consequences for Nephi and his family might well be devastating. But it wasn't this realization that brought Nephi the most remorse.

For a month he'd found himself on equal footing with royalty. He'd thought a friendship had been forged, a friendship which transcended any and all distinctions of class or rank. Nephi had started to think there was nothing he and Daniel couldn't accomplish together, whether crossing a desert or conquering a lion. He'd never had such a friend before and he sincerely wondered if he'd ever have such a friend again. Only a couple of hours had passed and he already missed Jophy terribly. But Jophy was gone. Strangely, Nephi felt a stabbing in his heart similar to the one he'd felt when he lost Hannah.

As Daniel tried to fall asleep that night, he silently shed many tears. The prince had a great deal of mourning to catch up on—the death of his father, the betrayal of people he'd trusted. Daniel's despair intensified as the evening progressed, as if the allotted time for mourning had passed him by and all his emotions had to be expended at once.

In the early hours of the morning, Nephi opened his eyes. The prince was sitting at the edge of his bed, seeking warmth from a single flame in the lamp. As Nephi stirred, Daniel turned his head. Nephi shut his eyes again, pretending to be asleep.

Daniel studied Nephi's face. As the prince contemplated all that he and this boy had been through, a similar pang of loss welled up in his soul. But the facts couldn't be ignored. He was a prince. Nephi was a commoner. They could never be friends again, not like they had been. Such things just weren't proper. Centuries of tradition dictated this. Traditions could be very cruel.

*But Nephi saved my life,* thought Daniel. He'd taught the prince how to survive on the desert. Then again . . . he'd also forced Daniel to clean manure out of the stable.

Daniel winced at the memory. Then he laughed inside. What a brat he must have been! Daniel may not have understood all of their reasons for not telling him who he was, but he felt certain that he knew their motives. Lehi and his family had been trying to protect him—from others and from himself. Truly some of the treatment Nephi had heaped on him was well deserved. But scrubbing manure out of a stable? Getting even for that might be justified.

Daniel feared he would deeply miss his association with this boy.

If the last month had proven anything, it had proven that the wall between commoners and royalty was not impregnable. Shaphan, his teacher at the palace, had once taught him that the Law of Moses never meant for men to become distinguished by class or rank. All men were equal in God's eyes. The prevailing distinctions were the result of sin. Perhaps it was time for a prince of the house of David to return to the true attitude of God.

But at this moment, Daniel needed Nephi for much more than his friendship. He needed Nephi's help—now more desperately than ever. Within the last hour, the true state of world affairs had congealed in Daniel's mind. As he gazed upon Nephi, this realization rushed back on him again, causing him to shudder. Assasiah's betrayal. His father's murder. The Egyptian armies sailing north. When he remembered the secret visit of the Chaldean emissaries, the final piece of the puzzle fell into place. Daniel had planned to wait until sunrise to rouse Nephi, but his pounding heart convinced him that he could not.

"Nephi, are you awake?"

Nephi opened his eyes. "Yes?"

"We must leave in the morning."

Nephi sighed. Daniel had been a prince again for less than eight hours and he was already giving orders.

"Leave?" Nephi repeated.

"Return to Jerusalem."

"How?" asked Nephi. "My brother is in no condition—"

Daniel dropped to his knees at the foot of Nephi's bed. Such humility took Nephi by surprise.

"Something terrible will happen if I don't reach my uncle before the Egyptians arrive in Israel," Daniel explained. "I know that King Josiah's armies are planning to oppose Pharaoh."

"Then the rumors are true?"

Daniel nodded. "Our king has some kind of pact with Babylon. I don't know all the details, but I *do* know that if King Josiah attacks before I reach him, the campaign may be a disaster."

"How do you know that?"

"Don't you see? They killed my father. The man next in line to take his place as first commander of the king's army is a traitor to the throne. I'm certain of it. That's why they wanted me dead. For all I know, the conspiracy runs even deeper. Before the battle begins, when King Josiah shouts his battle charge, his chariot might be the only one rolling forth. If I don't warn him, the Egyptians may be free to pillage and burn every house in Judah. They'll kill the king! They might kill thousands! Your own family! Please, Nephi. Please help me."

"What is it that you intend to do?" asked Laman.

The boys turned. Laman had been awakened by the lively conversation.

"Do you intend to take my caravan?" Laman continued. "Take all my servants? Leave me here by myself?"

Daniel came to his feet. There was a time for polite appeals and a time to properly exert his authority. "I'm sorry, but it must be so. The security of our nation is at stake."

"Then send a messenger," Laman proposed.

"I can't risk it," said Daniel. "What if the message fell into the wrong hands?"

"You speak utter foolishness!" cried Laman. "Two children leading a caravan into the desert? It's like an open invitation: *'Come hither! Would you please slit our throats and take everything that we own?'*" Laman's wound launched a stab of pain. He leaned back and spoke more softly. "My servants would never go with you."

"We could hire a driver," suggested Nephi. "A Philistine or an Arab. Someone who knows the roads across the Sinai."

Daniel smiled at Nephi, gratified to know that he had at least one ally.

"You don't know what you're saying," said Laman. "There isn't one man in twenty who wouldn't steal your camels the instant you reached the frontier."

"They would think twice before wronging a prince of Judah," stated Daniel.

Laman shook his head and chuckled. "So naive. If they learned your identity, you'd only die sooner. If you were lucky, they might hand you over to Pharaoh so that he could ransom your life to King Josiah."

Nephi seemed absorbed in thought as Laman spoke. When his brother had finished, he blurted out to Daniel, "We can do it."

"No, you can't!" Laman ranted. "Listen to reason, little brother! Haven't you heard anything I've been telling you?"

"I don't believe this is a matter of reason," said Nephi. "It's a matter of faith. If the Lord wants us to reach the king, then He'll prepare a way for us to do it."

Laman's face boiled red. His anger required so much energy that it acted like a blow to the skull. Laman fainted. An exasperated sigh seeped out of his lungs as he fell fast asleep.

LAMAN WAS RIGHT ABOUT THE SERVANTS.

The boys tried desperately to convince three of them to come along, but to no avail. They revised their offer to two, and then to one, but every effort failed. Nephi finally announced to them that Jophy was actually Daniel, a prince of Judah, but whether they believed him or not, the announcement carried no weight. The servants were staying with Laman. Daniel would have threatened them with their lives if he'd have thought it would make a difference. To the servants, a trip into the desert without an experienced caravaneer was suicide anyway.

In Laman's weakened state, he couldn't stop his little brother from collecting as much silver from his purse as they would need. Nephi left well over three-quarters of the exchange that Laman had received for his bales. This amount would support Laman and his servants in Egypt for six months, if necessary. Actually, Nephi expected that his older brother would follow them in two or three weeks.

The servants watched as the boys hoisted the wooden platforms onto the humps of three of the camels and tied the cords under the animals' chests. The servants did nothing to hinder them. Nephi was still part of their master's family. But none of the servants ever expected to see the camels or the boys alive again. After Daniel and Nephi had loaded the last provisions, they climbed aboard and aimed their beasts into the sunrise.

After crossing the Nile, they turned north. The first night they stayed in a caravanserai at On, or as it was known in the language of the Greeks, Heliopolis. Already, men's eyes were watching them curiously. Two boys alone on the road with three strong camels? The prospect was tempting.

The following morning Nephi acquainted himself with the leaders of another Jewish caravan en route across the Sinai to Hebron. This one had almost thirty camels. Nephi asked them if he and Daniel could tag along. They didn't mind at all, for the price of two gerah of silver per day. To Nephi, the protection of a larger caravan was worth twice that much.

On the third day, as they neared the Egyptian borders, they began to notice foreign caravans turning back.

"What's the matter?" Nephi called over to the lead driver of one of the returning trains.

"The Egyptians have closed the Way of the Sea!" the rider called back.

The road had been closed to accommodate Pharaoh's northbound war chariots. The nearest open road to Jerusalem would lead them into the treacherous Wilderness of Shur in the heart of the Sinai. Nephi had heard stories about the Way of Shur. Few wadis ran through the desolate landscape and the wadis which did run through it dried up early in the year. Wells were few and far between and the ones which did exist were owned by nomads who charged "per camel" to drink and high tariffs for safe passage. If a caravan lost its way, nothing could save it from disaster. It was said the vultures were fat in the Wilderness of Shur.

The Way of the Sea was expected to open again in about a week, but the Jewish caravan to which Daniel and Nephi had attached themselves was just as impatient as the boys. Besides, some of the caravan's men had traveled the Way of Shur before. They claimed it was a good route, even slightly shorter since it cut straight across rather than hanging near the coast.

During their second day along the new road, unseasonal rains fell heavily, but no caravaneer viewed rain as anything less than a blessing —a sign that the gods wandered with them. So in spite of the downpour, the camels plodded on.

The rains stopped late the following afternoon, just as the caravan broke camp. The men were wet and tired. They decided that tonight was a good night to break out a stash of wine they'd been saving. Daniel and Nephi were invited to join them, but the boys declined.

After erecting their tents, the boys wandered along a graveled hillside overlooking the camp. A blade of sunlight stabbed through the clouds in the west. Daniel knelt and focused his eyes across the desert. He'd never imagined a land so desolate. Not so much as a lone weed sprouted out of the earth.

The skies in the east remained dark and ominous. Further inland the storms continued. Daniel peered into the wide canyon which swept toward the east. The canyon floor was smooth and featureless except for a lone pillar of stone. Something about that pillar seemed familiar to Daniel.

"I've seen that before," said the prince.

"Seen what before?" asked Nephi.

"That pillar of stone, like a dagger stabbing the earth."

Nephi spotted the pillar. A web of lightning flashed in the skies behind it. "You're right. It does sort of look like a dagger."

"There's something missing," said Daniel.

"Something missing?"

"There should be a wave of blood."

Nephi looked perplexed. "What are you talking about?"

"I saw it on the desert, the day before we arrived in Egypt. At the time I thought it was only a mirage. You told me people who spend long periods out here sometimes see false visions. This one was not completely false."

"So what does it mean?" asked Nephi.

Daniel opened his mouth to speak, but he could only shrug.

All evening, Daniel remained uneasy, staring off at the pillar of stone until it was too dark to make out its outline. Sometimes its shape was illuminated by a flash of lightning. Before settling down to sleep, Daniel waited outside the tent. He watched the lightning brighten the pillar one more time, and then he sighed and climbed inside.

Nephi was already bundled up in his blankets. "What is it that you're looking for out there?"

"I'm not sure. Something isn't right."

Nephi groaned. "You've been saying that all evening! What do you mean?"

"I don't think we're safe here."

"You mean we're not safe on this spot? We're not safe in this wilderness? We're not safe in the world? What!?"

"I don't know."

Nephi rolled away. "Well, wake me up as soon as you figure it out."

Nephi had great respect for visions and premonitions. His father's were always reliable, but Daniel's visions tended to exaggerate things a bit. That first night at On, Daniel told Nephi all about his premonitions concerning the man in the hooded cloak, but every day Daniel's visions had transformed the man's face into something more hideous. Perhaps Daniel's lack of experience allowed him to mingle imagination and fear with his spiritual gift.

A thought struck Nephi. He, too, had always felt he possessed a similar gift of the Spirit, though perhaps equally unrefined. He started to pray. He asked the Lord for clarification. Why was Daniel so uneasy? What had he seen?

Nephi prayed for a long time, longer than he remembered. He didn't recall falling asleep, but he remembered very well the moment he awakened abruptly and sat up.

Nephi shook the prince. "Daniel!"

"Hmmm?"

"I've seen it too."

"Seen what?"

"The vision."

"What did you see?"

Nephi grabbed Daniel's arm to silence him. "Listen."

After a moment the boys heard a crack of thunder.

"There it is!" said Nephi. "I *knew* the thunder was coming. Now lightning. Two flashes."

The walls of the tent were ignited with two pulses of light. Daniel also sat up. Nephi's perceptions had inspired him. He tried to extinguish all fear and concentrate solely on the voice of the Spirit.

"And now the rain will start again," prophesied Daniel.

Instantly the pitter-patter of raindrops struck the roof of the tent.

"Lightning!" the boys cried in unison.

And the lighting struck according to their word.

"And now . . ." Nephi struggled for a word to describe the next phenomenon.

Daniel found the word. "Now comes the *sound*."

Nephi put his hand to the ground. The sound was more of a vibration in the earth, a low rumble rising in the distance like a stampeding herd of ten thousand horses.

"Let's get out of here!" Nephi declared. "We must warn the camp!"

The boys burst out of the tent. Other than the glowing coals of two camel-dung fires, there wasn't an ounce of light in any direction. Everyone was fast asleep.

"Wake up!" Nephi cried. "Wake up! It's coming!"

The wine had lulled the caravaneers into an unnaturally deep slumber. Not a soul stirred at Nephi's voice, but the rumble in the earth grew louder.

"Daniel, where are you?" shouted Nephi.

The prince was attempting to locate their camels. Nephi heard the beasts' snorting. He dashed toward the noise and found Daniel trying to undo the hobbles on the camels' legs. He pulled the prince away.

"There's no time!" Nephi insisted.

The boys began running. They rushed toward the graveled hill overlooking camp. Only as lightning flashed again could they confirm that they were headed in the right direction. They tripped many times while groping to the top. At the summit they dropped down on all fours, panting, and then they looked off toward the pillar of stone.

The canyon floor ignited under a web of lightning which stretched on for leagues. Daniel and Nephi saw something moving in the brief illumination. It rolled toward them along the wide floor of the canyon, burying everything in its path.

"A wave of blood," muttered the prince.

"The wave of a flash flood," clarified Nephi.

The wall of water, as tall as a man, crept menacingly toward the camp. Even the drunken caravaneers couldn't sleep any longer under its terrible roar. The boys heard voices crying out in the night, but it was too late for the men to save themselves. The wave crashed against the hill. Water inundated the camp, washing away the tents, the provisions, the camels—everything. Nephi and Daniel listened helplessly to the shrieks of men and beasts. Now and then a bolt of lightning revealed the swirling destruction. The wave continued down into the valley.

After a period of time, the voices faded away and the roar of water subsided. A crystal-silent darkness returned to the desert. The boys shivered on the graveled hilltop until morning. At first light, they wandered down the hill.

The lay of the canyon floor had totally changed. Except for the moistened earth and a few shallow puddles, nothing was left as evidence that a great flood had even passed through. The camp was entirely gone. Though the boys looked and looked, they couldn't find a single scrap of tent or even a meager bit of rope. Nothing remained to prove that any caravan had camped in this spot for a thousand years.

# Chapter 11
## COMING OF THE SAGES

Wᴴᴱɴ ᴅᴏ ʏᴏᴜ ᴛʜɪɴᴋ ᴛʜᴇʏ'ʟʟ sᴛᴀʀᴛ ᴄɪʀᴄʟɪɴɢ?" ᴀsᴋᴇᴅ Dᴀɴɪᴇʟ as he gazed up in the sky, looking for vultures.

"Not for a while," Nephi replied. "I'm sure they're plenty busy. Even if *we* can't spot any camel carcasses, I'm sure the vultures can. Who knows? If we die, they might even find themselves too gorged to care."

"Would the Lord save us only to let us die of hunger and thirst?" asked Daniel. "We *were* saved, weren't we? We both saw a vision. Am I right?"

"Are you starting to doubt?" asked Nephi.

"No!" said Daniel defiantly. He repeated the word with less certainty. "No."

"It happened," said Nephi. "There's no need to doubt."

Daniel felt ashamed for having to be reassured. In truth, Daniel's witness comforted Nephi as well. As the sun bore down on them ever more fiercely, it was becoming harder to believe the vision had served any real purpose.

The boys drank at the last muddy puddle they found that hadn't yet been consumed by the desert and began walking northeast, toward what appeared to be an outcropping of rock. Perhaps they'd find shade. Perhaps they'd climb to the top and spot another caravan.

The rock face was farther away than it looked. It was mid-afternoon before they reached it. Their faces and arms were bright with sunburn and their lips had begun to crack. After locating a spot of shade where two slabs of stone leaned against one another, the boys dropped to their bellies and fell asleep.

An hour had passed when Nephi felt an odd tickling on his leg. Slowly, he lifted his neck and glanced down at his calf. A scorpion was poised there, its pincers raised, its stinger ready to strike. Nephi recognized it at once as one of the deadlier varieties. The creature seemed to be daring Nephi to issue the slightest disturbance.

"Prince Daniel."

Daniel stirred.

"Scorpion," said Nephi calmly, indicating its location with his eyes.

Daniel sat up and looked at Nephi's calf. "What should I do?"

"Brush it off."

"With my hand?"

"Only if you want to die. Use your shirt."

Daniel pulled off his garment. As he bunched it up in his hands, he happened to glance at the ground beside his knee.

The prince cried out, leaping to his feet. "There's another one! The place must be crawling with them!"

"Get it off!" Nephi whispered harshly.

With a tentative flick of his shirt, Daniel swept the creature onto the sand. Nephi sprang up and scrambled backwards, smacking into Daniel. The two boys toppled out into the sunlight. Desperately, Nephi itched at his calf. Though he hadn't been stung, he still felt the scorpion's tickling legs. He'd likely feel that tickling all day.

Somewhat strengthened from their rest, the boys climbed the rocks. At the top, they overturned a few stones to be sure the area was free of scorpions. After settling beneath a slight overhang in the cliff, the boys peered across the landscape. The day was hazy. Visibility stood at half a league. If a caravan was out there, it might pass by without anyone knowing. Nephi licked his lips, trying to moisten them. Daniel left his own lips dry. From past experience, he knew that licking them only made him more thirsty.

"It's worse the first day," said Daniel.

"What's worse?" asked Nephi.

"The thirst. The hunger. But you get used to it. It starts not to hurt as much the second day."

Nephi didn't find Daniel's statement encouraging. "Seems getting stranded in the desert is becoming a bad habit for you."

Daniel smiled a little.

Nephi's smile changed to a frown. "Prince Daniel, what do you think happens to us when we die?"

Daniel shrugged. "We return to the bosom of Abraham."

"Besides that," said Nephi. "Do you think, in the world to come, I'll still be a commoner and you'll still be a prince?"

Daniel mulled it over. He wanted to believe he'd still be a prince, but he feared his own actions had changed the equation.

"Maybe I'll be the commoner and *you'll* be the prince."

"What makes you say that?"

"I'm not much of a prince," sighed Daniel. "A true prince would have been wiser. I should have sent a messenger, like your brother suggested."

"Who's to say a messenger would have made it any farther."

"I've failed my king," said Daniel. "I've failed the whole nation of Judah."

Nephi groaned. "You're not going to go on and on about this all night, are you? I really could use the sleep."

The boys watched the sunset fade into the west, a bitter orange circle in the haze. Soon after dark, with the repeating cry of a distant jackal reminding them they were not alone in this desolate place, the boys closed their eyes for the night.

THE BURNING IN THEIR EMPTY STOMACHS MADE FOR A RESTLESS SLEEP and many cruel dreams. Only toward morning did their slumber deepen enough to be rejuvenating. After sun-up, Nephi had his final dream. In that dream, he thought he saw angels.

The airborne ministers circled the rock face like sentries guarding a regal throne. In one hand they wielded a sword with a blade like white fire. In the other, they carried a bell. The ring was so soothing and pure—a natural repellant for lurking demons or villains.

Nephi awakened. The angels were gone, but the tinkling bells remained, though perhaps the sound was not so pure as before. Nephi gazed out across the desert. The haze had become fog. He could see nothing. But the source of those bells had to be out there somewhere. Nephi's movements roused Daniel. The prince stood and listened.

"Let's see what it is!" cried Daniel.

Nephi bounded after the prince. After reaching the desert floor, both boys dashed into the fog, impervious to obstacles or danger.

The bells grew louder. Shapes began to appear—camels! A caravan!

Daniel was about to call out when Nephi threw his hand over the prince's mouth.

"Wait until we're closer!"

"Why? This may be our only—"

"I have to see who they are. If it happens to be spice and incense traders, the men will kill us both and call it an act of mercy."

"Would spice traders strap bells to their camels?"

Daniel had a point. Dealers in cinnamon and frankincense were a cautious, distrusting breed. They would never advertise their location.

The boys crept closer. They ran alongside the trotting camels, whose shapes remained blurry in the fog. The caravan was of moderate size. About eighteen animals. Daniel and Nephi noted the markings on the saddles and bales. The craftsmanship was Egyptian, but the men were not. The simple, yet elegant wardrobes of the two lead riders, along with their boastfully wavy hairstyles made it apparent. The caravan was Greek.

"Halt!" shouted the driver to his fellow travelers. He'd spotted the two shapes running beside the train.

Daniel and Nephi stopped. Timidly, they waited as the two lead camels broke ranks and strutted out to the boys' position. Both men were bearded. Their features were sharp and strong. One appeared to be in his mid-twenties. The other may have been five or six years older. Both men looked down on the bedraggled boys.

"What have we here?" asked the older one.

"A pair of sunburned and thirsty Jews, I presume," said the younger.

They spoke Egyptian, a language which Nephi and Daniel both recognized readily.

"We were caught in a flood," Nephi replied. "Our caravan was destroyed."

"Where do you hail from?"

"Egypt."

"Well, then. We have something in common. Where are you headed?"

"Jerusalem," said Daniel.

"How about that! We have even more in common!"

Nephi untied the leather purse from his waist—his only provision which had survived the flood. "I can pay you with silver if you'll take us to my father's estate, south of Hebron."

"Nonsense," said the older man. "If my life were in peril, would you expect payment before you saved it? Happy is the man who finds friends in a foreign land."

A grin climbed Nephi's cheeks. These Greeks were men of principle.

The younger man called back to the caravan. "Get these boys some water!"

After his camel had set him down, the older man stepped up to the boys. "What are your names?"

"My name is Nephi, son of Lehi."

The prince felt hesitant. "I am Daniel, son of . . . Judah."

The man directed his words to Nephi. "I know a Jewish trader named Lehi. My family has done business with him in Sidon. This man has an older son named Laman."

Nephi's eyes lit up. "Laman is my brother!"

"Glory of Zeus!" The older man called back to the younger. "I know this boy's father!" He took Nephi's hand. "I am Solon of Athens—a trader by day and a poet by night. I'm most pleased to meet you, Nephi, son of Lehi."

As the younger man approached, Solon said to him, "This boy's father may be the most enlightened Jew I've ever met."

"I'm delighted to know there is such a thing," the younger man replied. He shook Daniel's hand. "I'm Thales of Miletus—Solon's temporary business associate and reluctant traveling companion."

The other members of the caravan were not Greek, but Phoenician, with a Moabite driver. They'd ridden from the Egyptian markets at Tanis. Like Nephi and Daniel, the Egyptian war machine had detoured them into the Wilderness of Shur. They'd already been on the road this morning for five hours. Solon decided that finding two lost Israelites was ample excuse to break camp early and wait out the heat of the day. They'd brought fresh melons with them from Egypt, several of which Daniel and Nephi gratefully devoured.

One look told Nephi that these men were not regulars on the desert. Solon's family owned a ship currently at port in the Nile delta. Their cargo was, in fact, resins and spices—frankincense, myrrh, and cinnamon—purchased from Arabian merchants at Tanis after trading a shipment of olive oil.

"Why come overland with such valuable cargo when you own a ship?" asked Daniel, finishing off his last scape of melon. Solon opened the flap on his tent to let in a cooling breeze.

"Why does any man do foolish things?" he responded.

Daniel shook his head. Nephi shrugged, awaiting a profound reply.

Solon looked them in the eye. "To unnerve his parents, of course!"

Thales chuckled at his companion's wit.

Solon sat back and explained further. "With so many warships at sea, can traveling overland be so much more dangerous? Besides, I've never crossed the desert and I've always wanted to."

"You must be very rich," said Nephi, "if you cross the desert for pleasure."

"Not so rich," said Solon. "Your father likely has more wealth than Thales's family and mine put together."

"Not more than *my* family," contended Thales.

"We came for the adventure," continued Solon. "The experience."

"Simply to say that we had done it," added Thales.

That evening, the men redistributed their bales to free up the back of one of the camels for Daniel and Nephi. As the moon and stars appeared, Thales slowed his camel to ride beside the boys. For the last seven years Thales had pursued a study of mathematics and science under some prominent Egyptian teachers. He was eager to hear how his theories sounded in the ears of two malleable young minds.

"How far away do you think the stars are?" Thales asked them.

"Many leagues," Daniel answered. "Perhaps a hundred."

Thales shook his head. "Much farther. Otherwise, how would I see much the same stars in Miletus as I see in Memphis? What about the moon? Do you think it's larger or smaller than the sun? Do you think it's closer or farther away?"

"I've never thought about it," said Nephi. "They're about the same size and distance, aren't they?"

"Wrong! The moon is *much* smaller and *much* closer. Do you know how I know this?"

"How?" asked Daniel.

"Observation and calculation. If we measure the movements of either heavenly body from two known reference points, the truth becomes obvious. This is geometry, my friends. The purest science on the face of the earth."

"I'd like to learn this science," said Daniel.

"Of course you would," said Thales. "The whole world would like to learn it. But only *I* know its secrets. Well, myself and a couple of Egyptian priests, but they'd never talk. With geometry, I measured the exact height of an Egyptian pyramid without having to climb it. But that's not the most shocking discovery I made."

"What is?" asked Nephi.

Thales looked as if he were about to reveal his secret. Then he pressed his lips tight. "No, no. I couldn't tell you. You wouldn't be able to handle it. You'd renounce your religion and sell your soul to the underworld. Both of you."

"Try us," said Daniel.

"Well, all right." Thales seemed easily persuaded. He whispered so the other men wouldn't hear. "The sun does not go around the earth. It's the other way around. The earth goes around the sun."

"I know that," said Nephi.

Thales blinked his eyes. He sat up straight. "What do you mean you know that?"

"My father taught me."

"How did your father figure it out?"

"He asked the Lord."

"Impossible. Your father must be a mathematician."

"My father does know some math," Nephi admitted. "That's what brought him to ask the question."

"I don't believe it. Even the gods don't know about this."

"The God of Israel knows everything," said Daniel. "He *created* the earth and the sun."

Thales grunted and leaned away. "I should have known religion would creep into this if I discussed it with Jews. Well, I figured it out *without* the gods. I didn't need a single one of them. I did it with math and *only* math."

"Either way," said Nephi calmly. "Now we *both* know."

"I'd still love to learn how you figured it out with only math," said Daniel.

"Oh, never mind," grumbled Thales. He rode on ahead, returning to his place in the train.

## Daniel and Nephi

*  *  *

As the moon dwindled into the west, the caravan again struck camp. Daniel and Nephi were invited to rest in the spacious tent of Solon and Thales. The boys' sunburned necks and arms itched horribly. Since the skin was still tender, they scratched with great care, but, oh, how they wished they could scratch with all their fury.

Solon handed Nephi an alabaster jar. "You and Daniel may want to rub this ointment on your burns. It may cool the pain." Nephi took the ointment. He knew it was expensive. The instant he touched it to his skin, the itching stopped. "How can we ever repay your kindness?" Nephi asked.

"You can't," snapped Thales, his arms folded. The mathematician still smarted from his earlier humiliation.

Solon waxed poetic. *"Virtue's a thing that none can take away, but money changes owners all the day."*

Thales rolled his eyes. He'd heard enough of Solon's poetry this trip to last a lifetime.

Solon concluded, "It'll be payment enough to see your mother's face as I return her son."

"We're just glad the Lord sent you instead of someone . . . less kind," said Daniel.

"Yes, I'll wager there are many uncompassionate souls out here. But don't give your *god* credit for *my* good will. When men start blaming acts of good and evil on the gods, they have little reason to encourage responsibility and self-improvement."

Daniel was tempted to leave the statement alone, but he couldn't. "Can't the two work hand in hand? Faith in God and the encouragement of virtue?"

"You're a bright boy for one so young," said Solon to Daniel, patting his head. "But I'm afraid the answer is no. Men must be good because to be good is good unto itself, not because he fears punishment from some supernatural entity."

"People can be good out of love," said Daniel, "because they want to become as virtuous as God, who first loved them."

"An interesting idea," Solon admitted. "But unfortunately, there's no such thing as a virtuous god. Gods may be all-powerful and all-knowing. But they are also tyrannical, self-serving, abusive, jealous, petty—just like the men who created them. A god may perform an act of benevolence now and then, but only to satisfy some selfish whim or fancy. No, I've never heard of a god so virtuous that I'd want to pattern my life after him."

"The God of Israel is such a god," said Nephi.

"I'm glad that you think so," said Solon. "Your father and I have enjoyed long conversations about the God of Israel. But I'm afraid He's not for me either. So short-tempered. So impatient. So intolerant."

Nephi felt hurt. He was confident that Solon was a good man. So was Thales. How could good men pass such harsh judgments on the source of all goodness? "You say these things only because you don't understand Him."

"That's possible," admitted Solon, although it seemed to Nephi that he said it only to be polite. Solon changed the subject slightly. "I found it fascinating that your father was convinced that one day his god would come among your people to govern things personally."

"Yes," Nephi confirmed. "But not just us. The whole world."

"So what do we do until then?" asked Thales sarcastically. "Howl at the moon?"

"Don't sneer so soon, young Thales," said Solon. "To solve that problem this Jew and I conjured an interesting proposition. Man's pursuit of happiness can only be guaranteed if the society in which he lives is free. The government must give an equal say to every living soul, not just kings or priests or wealthy families, but all people. Rich and poor. Merchant and fisherman. Nobleman and farmer."

"*All* people?" asked Thales. "Would children have an equal say— and women?"

"No, of course not. Be serious and listen. In such a place men could live according to their own conscience, not the whims of a tyrant. Oh, what a world it would be. What a world."

Solon leaned back, his hands laced behind his head.

"Now we've made him all whimsical," Thales said to the boys.

Solon leaned forward one last time, his finger dancing like a firefly. "But the point is, your father and I did not need a god to invent such ideas. Only our intellect. If freed from injustice, the bounds of the human mind are immeasurable."

"Science has already proven this," added Thales. "One day science will explain all that there is to know. We'll no longer need gods and goddesses. What a great day that will be. I hope it will happen in my lifetime. I'm sure that it will."

A short while after Thales's final remark, Daniel and Nephi could hear the Greeks snoring vigorously. Daniel rolled over to look at Nephi.

"Are you still awake?" he asked.

"Yes," Nephi replied.

"Are you all right?" asked the prince.

"Why do you ask?"

"I don't know. You just seem a little sad."

Nephi didn't reply. He pretended to have fallen asleep. Daniel rolled over again and decided not to pursue the matter any further.

The following day the caravan continued its northward trek. Nephi spoke very little.

Daniel finally yelled at him. "Are you going to starve me for conversation the rest of the trip?"

"Sorry," said Nephi. "I was just thinking about last night. About what the Greeks said."

"Did it bother you?"

"It bothered me that I didn't know how to respond to them. I thought of standing up and bolding declaring that God lived. I thought of telling them about the visions that saved us from the flood. Something told me they would explain it away as easily as one might shoo off a gnat."

"These men are different from your brother, Laman," the prince observed. "Your brother won't commit to anything and therefore, he thinks he's free. These men have many commitments. In fact, they feel they have all the answers, but they won't give any credit to God. Shaphan, my teacher at the palace, says that no man is harder of hearing than the one who has all the answers."

"But Solon and Thales are so wise and honorable," said Nephi. "They should have been born in Judah. How come the Lord didn't make them Jews?"

"If you're going to look at it that way," said Daniel, "there are many wicked Jews who should have been born Greeks."

"You haven't answered my question," said Nephi. "You've only created another one."

Daniel thought a moment. "Maybe things are exactly as they ought to be. Look at it this way: most Jews think that being the Lord's blessed people is more of a privilege than it is an honor."

"So you think we've become too proud to have the world's wisest men born among us?"

"Maybe so. Or maybe such men *are* born among us but their ideas never see the light of day. I wonder if pride somehow suffocates new ideas. Until we get rid of it, the Lord may have to give His greater notions to the heathens."

"If we don't get rid of pride, do you think the Lord could decide to take the temple and His holy law away from us?"

"For all I know, he could even give them to the Gentiles!" said Daniel. "I know it's unthinkable. But the Lord will do what He will do. I only hope that I'll always be humble enough to follow Him wherever He takes me." Daniel sighed. "Sometimes I wonder if I can ever become that humble."

"If you're wondering about it," said Nephi, "maybe you're starting to become it."

# Chapter 12
## SHADRACH, MESHACH, AND ABEDNEGO

SARIAH RUSHED OUTSIDE THE MOMENT HER LITTLE DAUGHTER, Zeruah, mentioned that a caravan from the desert had turned off the road. Nephi's camel seemed to take forever to kneel. When it did, Nephi slid off the hump and met his mother halfway across the yard in a heartfelt embrace. Solon and Thales looked on with pride and gladness.

"What's happened?" Sariah demanded. "Where is Laman?"

"He's been injured, Mother."

Sariah's face paled.

"He'll be all right," Nephi assured. "The wound is healing. I expect him to return from Egypt in a few weeks. There's much to tell everyone. Where is Father?"

"He's gone, Nephi."

"Gone where?"

"To Jerusalem. He left four days ago with Sam. They went to look for Lemuel."

Nephi raised his eyebrows. A lot seemed to have happened around here as well. "What happened to Lemuel?"

"He ran away," said Sariah. "Lemuel wanted to join the king's army, but the law says a man must be twenty. Lemuel is only seventeen. One morning he was gone. We fear he lied about his age."

Sariah could no longer contain her emotions. It had been a trying month. A trying year. Sariah embraced Daniel as if he were one of her own and dropped a few tears on his shoulder. The boys helped

Sariah walk back toward the house. Nephi's sisters gathered around. Leah told Nephi about Dagan's murder and funeral. Nephi's chest fell. So much tragedy. What catastrophe would he learn of next?

"Who's watching the estate?" asked Nephi.

"Shamariah," Leah replied. "And now you and Jophy."

"I'm afraid we can't stay," said Nephi.

Solon and Thales remained outside to feed and water their animals while the family seated themselves in the Hall of Joseph. Nephi revealed Daniel's true identity to everyone. Sariah was surprised, but only for a moment. Her husband's behavior last month suddenly made sense.

"There's a terrible conspiracy at work in the kingdom," Daniel proclaimed. "I must speak with His Majesty as soon as possible. The Greeks will be leaving for Jerusalem within the hour. I'll go with them."

"The Greeks will take two and a half days to reach Jerusalem," Nephi objected. "On horseback we can be there in a single day."

"I haven't been on a horse for many years," confessed Daniel.

"You're a prince and you haven't been on a horse in years?"

"I rode when I was little, but . . . I was trampled by a horse when I was six. In case you haven't noticed, I'm not very fond of animals."

"It'll all come back to you," said Nephi confidently. "It's like riding a camel. You just have to hang on a little tighter." Sariah sensed the urgency. She would not try to stop her youngest son from helping the royal prince, but she insisted that Shamariah accompany them.

Nephi protested. "But Mother, you need Shamariah here."

"You and the prince are eleven years old," Sariah reminded them. "An adult will go with you."

"We practically crossed the Sinai by ourselves," Nephi defended. "We can certainly get to Jerusalem."

"You made it across the desert by the grace of God," Sariah declared. "Don't tempt Him any further. You will travel with Shamariah."

Shamariah was about as excited about going with the boys as the boys were about having him along. Daniel and Nephi feared the old man would only slow them down. Like Nephi, Shamariah was afraid of what might happen if he left Sariah and the girls alone on the estate. At sixty years old, however, Shamariah may not have been the best candidate to defend the place against intruders anyway. Shamariah asked one of the tenant families who lived near the olive grove to check on the Sariah and the girls from time to time. Nephi and Daniel prepared three horses for a swift journey.

Nephi bid farewell to his mother and sisters for what he hoped would be their last separation for a long while.

"I'll find Father and Sam and Lemuel. We'll all come home together," Nephi promised his mother.

Sariah held her son and kissed his forehead.

Nephi and Daniel also bid farewell to Solon and Thales, their saviors in the wilderness. The Greeks agreed to stay the night to help Sariah with a few chores, which might tide the family over until the father and sons returned.

"We're forever in your debt," Nephi told them.

"You're quite right," replied Thales.

"But think nothing of it," said Solon. "I hope you will do the same for another stranger when the opportunity presents itself, so the cycle may continue. Tell your father we're sorry to have missed him."

"I will," said Nephi. "And may God watch over you the rest of your journey."

"That would be fine," said Solon, "as long as He doesn't come down and interfere."

NEPHI SELECTED FOR DANIEL THE HORSE HE THOUGHT TO BE THE BEST natured, an older mare he knew would follow the other horses without much instruction.

Daniel climbed onto the mare's back with great apprehension. The horse knew Daniel was nervous. It became nervous as well.

Nephi started explaining to the prince how to turn the horse, how to go and how to stop.

"I know all this," said Daniel. "I wasn't born yesterday."

"Then you know all that's important to know." Nephi walked toward his own mount. He turned back. "Oh, and one last thing. We'll be riding rather fast. So hang on for dear life."

When his horse bolted forward, Daniel's feet kicked up higher than the animal's ears. He frantically grasped at the mane and regained his balance. The prince hunkered down low, closed his eyes, and prayed for deliverance.

Nephi drove the animals hard. They galloped the first hour, then switched between trotting and walking every half hour. Rest stops were short.

"We're going to ruin the horses!" Shamariah complained. "They have to rest!"

But in fact the horses were showing remarkable endurance. It was Shamariah's bones and muscles that ached. Daniel's stamina wasn't holding out much better. On a camel, a rider sat cross-legged to ease the weight on his rump. When he dismounted, Daniel feared he wouldn't be able to walk, or at least not correctly.

Late that night, just outside Bethlehem, the riders refreshed the horses in an old, empty stable beside the road. Before daylight, their steeds were again kicking up the dust of the highway. The sun had been up less than an hour when Jerusalem's walls appeared in the distance.

Daniel suggested they dismount and walk the horses the remaining distance toward the Gate of the Valley. Shamariah asked several travelers who were leaving Jerusalem if the king was in the city.

"No," they replied.

This came as no surprise to the prince. Certainly Josiah was with his armies. But where were the armies headquartered?

"North," one stranger told them. "In the land of Manasseh," replied another. No one seemed to know the precise location.

"Who would know for certain?" asked Nephi.

"Everyone who knows is likely already there," Daniel said. He thought a moment. The answer came. "Hamutal."

"The queen? Are you sure?"

"Josiah keeps no secrets from Hamutal. He trusts her more than he trusts himself. We must get to the palace."

Traffic into Jerusalem was moderate today, but those few visitors who entered led donkeys and camels often stacked high with provisions. These were the early birds anxious to obtain the best lodging inside Jerusalem's fortifications in case the Egyptian armies invaded southward. To the sneering guards who watched them pass beneath the gate, these people were unpatriotic pessimists. How could anyone believe that Josiah wouldn't finish off Pharaoh's forces in the very first battle?

"Hold it!" barked a guard.

Shamariah stopped. The boys stayed behind him. Daniel hung

back the farthest, turning his face toward the neck of his horse, pretending to groom the mane.

"Who are you that you think you can bring steeds into Jerusalem?" the guard demanded.

"Humble servants of Josiah the King," said Shamariah. "We've been riding a long distance. If you'd allow us to quarter our animals inside the gate for a few hours, we'll pay you well and be gone by nightfall."

"What is your business in Jerusalem?"

"We are, uh—" Shamariah was at a loss.

Nephi stepped in. "We are visiting noble relatives."

True enough. Hamutal was Daniel's aunt.

"*Noble* relatives? What are their names?" inquired the guard.

Nephi bit his tongue. He should have just said *relatives* and left out *noble*. He'd hoped the word would keep them from confiscating the horses.

"Their names? Well, their names are . . . Do you want *all* their names?"

"Yes! All of them!" growled the guard.

Nephi's steeds had blocked the way of a small caravan. The driver of the four camels had grown impatient. He began guiding his beasts around Shamariah and the boys on either side.

The commander of the garrison approached. He was a heavy-set man with a short, oily beard and a large, jeweled sword. "What's the holdup?" he asked.

Daniel gasped as he saw the commander's face.

"Commander Laban," began the guard, "this man and his two boys are trying to bring horses inside the city. They display no outward signs of rank allowing them to do so. I was preparing to take their beasts to the king's stable."

"Boys, you say?" Laban looked around. "I see no boys."

Shamariah turned. Nephi and Daniel were gone. Their horses stood abandoned. Shamariah looked just as surprised as the guard.

As the four-camel caravan was moving around them, Daniel had signaled to Nephi. The two of them slipped around the east side of the gate, keeping close to the turrets along the wall to avoid being seen.

"Who was that man?" asked Nephi.

"His name is Laban. Assasiah's right-hand man. If Assasiah took over my father's position, I'll bet Laban is now garrison commander. If Assasiah plotted my father's murder, Laban may well have known about it."

"What will happen to Shamariah?"

"They may question him," said Daniel. "Everyone is wary of spies. He'll likely be free in a few hours."

Daniel and Nephi continued along the wall until they reached the next city gate. The Gate of Potsherds pierced Jerusalem's fortifications at its southern end, forming an acute angle above the royal gardens. In front of it stretched the dreary, sloping meadow to which it owed its name. This was the refuse heap of the city. Five pyramids of broken pots and rotting garbage covered the meadow. Daniel and Nephi passed by several beggar women who picked through the litter with cracked and blackened fingernails.

The boys came to a gnarled sycamore near the meadow's edge. Nephi looked about with disdain.

"What's the matter?" asked Daniel.

Nephi shivered. "I've heard of this place. They stone criminals here, right?"

"Yes, sometimes. In fact, poor wretches who commit suicide often use this very tree."

Nephi was about to lean against the bark. He changed his mind. "Why did we stop here? This is an awful place."

"It's also the place I'm least likely to be discovered," said Daniel. "Nephi, I need you to go into the city alone. I need you to tell them I'm here."

"Tell *who* that you're here? The queen? A commoner like me would never get into the House of Solomon."

"I have three friends," said Daniel. "Mishael, Hananiah, and Mishael's little brother, Azariah. They're princes, sons of two of the king's highest chancellors. Bring them here. I'll explain to you where they live."

"But what if they don't believe me? To them you've been dead for several months!"

"You must *make* them believe you! It's the only way. The palace is watched by hundreds of guards. If any one of them is part of the plot against the king and happens to recognize me . . ."

"All right," Nephi agreed. "I'll go. Where do your friends live?"

The prince gave Nephi explicit directions and sent him on his way. From the watchtowers and bulwarks of the Gate of Potsherds, the guards observed the lone boy enter the city. They thought nothing of it. To them, the youngster was just another beggar.

Nephi walked toward the palace district and royal living quarters. Now and then, someone would stare. Nephi thought he could feel their eyes on his back. Daniel's paranoia seemed to be rubbing off on him. Nephi repeated Daniel's directions under his breath until he at last reached the specified doorway. The wood was hard and made hardly a sound as he knocked. Nephi beat on the door with the palm of his hand, creating a sound with slightly more volume.

The plate behind the peephole slid away. A pair of steely eyes leered down. "Yes?"

"I would like to speak with Mishael or Hananiah."

One look at Nephi's garb told the man this boy was not one of Mishael's regular companions.

"What do you want with them?"

"I have an urgent message to give them, from a friend."

The door opened and Nephi was allowed to enter.

"May I give them your name?" asked the servant.

"Uh, Nephi. But they won't know me."

The servant tightened his lips and scrutinized Nephi more closely. Nephi feared he was about to be cast back into the street.

"Wait here," the servant said and disappeared down the hall. There was a draft in the hallway. Nephi wrapped his arms about his chest and sat down on a chair. The three legs of the chair were all paws from a lion. Nephi leaned over and felt the tip of a claw. When he raised his head again, three boys stood before him.

"What do you want?" the oldest boy demanded.

"I have a message."

"Yes? What is it?"

Nephi noticed the servant listening a little ways down the hall.

"In private," said Nephi.

A second boy shooed the servant. The servant went about his business.

"Well?" said the first boy. "We don't have all day."

"Don't be rude, Hananiah," said the second boy. "It's obvious this Nephi person has come a long distance. I'm Prince Mishael.

Where are you from?"

"My father has an estate south of Hebron."

The smallest boy came up and stood behind Nephi's chair. He sniffed Nephi's clothes. "I smell cows on him."

"Horses, actually," said Nephi.

"Stop it, Azariah," scolded Mishael.

"Is your message from someone in Hebron?" asked Hananiah.

"No," Nephi replied. "It's from Daniel."

"Daniel?" Mishael looked perplexed. "We don't know any Daniel. Daniel *who*?"

"Daniel, son of Maaseiah. Daniel, the governor's son."

No one spoke. The room remained silent until Azariah started to laugh.

Mishael grew angry. "Daniel, the son of Maaseiah, is dead."

Hananiah laughed as well. "Did his ghost give you a message?"

"Daniel is not dead," Nephi proclaimed. "He's waiting for us. He asked me to bring you to him."

"Is this a trick?" demanded Mishael. "Some kind of practical joke?"

"Manoah!" shouted Hananiah. The servant poked his head back into the hallway. "Summon the house guards!"

"No, wait!" pleaded Nephi. "You *must* believe me. Daniel is alive!"

"We attended his funeral," said Mishael.

"Did you see his body?" asked Nephi.

"Obviously," said Hananiah.

"His face?"

"Of course not. He was wrapped in his burial clothes."

"I tell you, Prince Daniel is living and breathing. He's as healthy as you or me! They kidnapped him. They sent him into the desert. That's how he came to be with my family. How can I convince you? I know I'm a stranger, but you have to trust me. Come see for yourself. Come see with your own eyes!"

The house guards arrived. The three princes hesitated before issuing the order to remove the visitor. Was there any chance his story could be true? No, it was too crazy! Yet he'd invited them to come see with their own eyes.

"You summoned us?" asked a guard.

"A mistake," said Mishael. "You're dismissed."

The guards eyed Nephi suspiciously and left.

Hananiah was almost beside himself. "Have you lost your mind, Mishael? What if this is a trap? The Egyptians would love to take hostages."

"Rest your imagination," said Mishael. "I doubt any of us would be Pharaoh's first choice. This boy has told us we can come see for ourselves. I say we go and take a look."

"Where is this imposter?" asked Hananiah.

"Follow me," invited Nephi.

DANIEL STRUGGLED TO STAY AWAKE. HIS HEAD KEPT BOBBING, consumed by exhaustion. *Can't fall asleep*, he repeated in his mind. Daniel feared that if he slept he might never awaken. A conspirator's sword might cut off his head as he lay beneath the gnarled sycamore.

Daniel concentrated his gaze on the Mount of Olives where the playful reflections of the afternoon sun chased one another across the cedars, columns, domes, and fountains of the royal gardens. It was indeed a better view than the pot shards and garbage at his feet.

Daniel stood. He shook off the sleep.

Hananiah, Mishael, Azariah, and Nephi watched the prince from a distance. The chancellors' sons were somewhat concerned when Nephi had told them they'd meet Daniel outside the Gate of Potsherds. The city's refuse heap was a well-known resort of ghosts and evil spirits. As the three boys watched their old friend for a moment, still leaning at the base of the gnarled sycamore, the thought crossed their minds that Nephi had brought them here to communicate with an apparition.

"Come on," Nephi urged. "He's waiting for us."

Hananiah, Mishael, and Azariah followed uneasily.

Daniel finally saw them. The sight of familiar faces hit him like warm sunlight. He wanted to run to them, to embrace them all, but the sentiment stirring inside his soul weakened the muscles of his legs. If he could keep from fainting, it would be enough. Mishael's eyes were the first to well up with tears. The boys stopped a short distance from their old friend. The question had to, at least, be asked. It was little Azariah who found the courage to say it.

"Are you . . . a ghost?"

"No, Azariah. I'm not a ghost. It's me. It's Daniel."

"But how?" whispered Hananiah.

"The story is quite long," said Daniel.

Nephi, his own heart swelling with joy, stood by while Daniel's old friends edged forward, close enough to touch Daniel's hands and verify that they were flesh.

"We mourned you and your father for seven days," Hananiah said.

Mishael glanced around the meadow, wondering if the governor might also appear. Nothing, anymore, seemed impossible.

"My father is truly dead," Daniel confirmed.

Hananiah had been acquainted with the chamberlain who was executed for Maaseiah's murder. Deep in his heart, he never believed the man could have been responsible for such an act. Now he knew he'd been right.

"Who was your father's betrayer?" asked Hananiah.

"Commander Assasiah," Daniel revealed. The prince breathed deeply. How glorious to have finally told someone! Now even if he didn't survive, someone else from the house of David knew the terrible secret.

The news sent a shudder through the boys. The implications of this were clear to them. Assasiah had been promoted to become Josiah's commanding general. He was at the king's side even now, free to sabotage Judah's military objectives at will!

"What could become of us?" asked Mishael.

Daniel knew Mishael's question voiced the unspoken fears of every citizen in Judah—unspoken because their faith in King Josiah had been unwavering. Josiah was considered to be the reborn David! Everything he touched had always turned to gold. His thirty-year reign had been one of unparalleled peace. The new generation had no comprehension of the changes that might come upon them.

"If I don't reach King Josiah, there's no telling what could become of us," Daniel answered. "I need to know where Judah's armies are headquartered."

"In the land of Israel," said Hananiah.

"In the far north," added Mishael, "between Mt. Carmel and Mt. Gilboa."

Their answers weren't much more specific than the ones given by the strangers on the road.

"Would the queen know the exact location?" asked Daniel.

Mishael thought about it. "She probably would."

"Can you bring her here?"

"Bring Queen Hamutal here?" wondered Mishael. "Daniel, you should go to *her!*"

"But what if I were seen by enemies?" asked Daniel.

"You underestimate the loyalty of the kingdom," Mishael stated boldly. "Come with us! We'll march into the palace together!"

The boys surrounded Prince Daniel on all four sides. For Daniel, the journey's most suspenseful moment came as they marched under the noses of the royal garrison at the Gate of Potsherds. The guards recognized the three chancellors' sons in their princely garments, but they took little notice of the other two children. Even if something seemed familiar to the guards about the boy in the middle, they only shrugged their shoulders and concluded he must be a regular among the scavengers outside the gate.

The House of Solomon was not far from the Gate of Potsherds. As the boys drew nearer to the palace doors, heads began to turn, hearts began to skip a beat, and throats began forming lumps. Daniel heard his name whispered several times, first as a question and then as a declaration. Some of the people followed them all the way to the palace courtyard, waiting outside as the boys went in, debating among themselves if what they'd seen could be real.

To the palace guards, Mishael shouted, "His Eminence Prince Daniel, son of Maaseiah seeks audience with Her Majesty, Queen Hamutal!"

Mishael's voice echoed through every chamber and hall. The announcement was not just to the guards, it was to the entire household, every servant and chambermaid, every keeper of the various offices, every son and daughter of royal birth. A crowd began to gather, a tumult began to rise. "It's him!" people shouted. "Prince Daniel!" "The governor's son!" "But that's impossible!" "Risen from the dead?" "A specter!" "A phantom!" "A blessing from On High!" "A miracle of the great Adonai!"

As reality set in, the confusion only intensified. Without having to be told, the people realized they'd been duped! Something strange

151

had occurred in Jerusalem. Something rotten. Conspiracy! Betrayal! Who were the authors? What were the objectives? How deep did the evil run?

The first dignitary to arrive on the scene was Elnathan, son of Achbor, commander of the king's cavalry. When the clamor had begun, General Elnathan was just leaving the House of Solomon to rejoin five hundred horsemen, a late contingent of Judah's noble cavalry, awaiting departure outside the Gate of Ephraim. Elnathan crouched down and grasped Daniel's shoulders. His grip was almost painful. Daniel couldn't read Elnathan's expression. Was he a friend or foe? The powerful Elnathan could have snapped Daniel's neck like a twig, leaving the details of his story forever untold.

Elnathan's grip relaxed. His fat, calloused fingers stroked the prince's head. "God has sent an omen of hope to Judah," he said, "in the form of a boy."

With the help of several officers and secretaries, Queen Hamutal came into the center of the crowd. As her eyes fell upon Daniel, she stopped with a sense of reverence. The boy was indeed her beloved nephew, the same and yet different. Lifetimes of wisdom seemed to have blossomed upon the boy's countenance. Never before had it occurred to Hamutal how closely the features of Daniel resembled her husband, much more keenly than even her own children. But it was more than his features which reminded her of the king. It was the boy's carriage. The depth in his eyes.

Hamutal wrapped her arms around Daniel. Daniel smelled her hair, all the perfumes and balsams. It was the queen. He was really home.

In his reverie, Daniel might have forgotten the pending emergency. The urgent voices of Elnathan and the queen's secretaries as they whisked him out of the midst of the crowd reminded him of his purpose. Elnathan tried to leave everyone else behind, including Nephi, but Daniel grasped Nephi's sleeve in case he needed his friend from the desert's edge to help him explain the circumstances at hand.

In the antechamber of the queen's private quarters, with Hamutal, Elnathan and several other officers gathered around him, Daniel rehearsed the details of his father's murder in the governor's house. Elnathan recalled seeing Zaavan, the noseless vagabond in the hooded cloak, on some vague occasion. He tried to remember.

It struck him. "I saw this man in the presence of Commander Assasiah!"

The kingdom had its conspirator.

Daniel went on to tell them about his kidnapping, his rescue from the desert, and his subsequent amnesia. He called upon Nephi to confirm the story, which Nephi did with a nod. Nephi remained silent, fearing if he spoke in the presence of such lofty company his tongue might turn to stone and drop on the floor.

Daniel covered only scanty details of their trip to Egypt and the homeward flight across the Sinai. In case they'd missed the obvious revelation of his story, he pressed it on their minds.

"I must warn King Josiah before it's too late!" he cried. "Where can I find him?"

"Megiddo," Hamutal revealed. She looked to Elnathan for confirmation.

Elnathan nodded. "I was with Josiah three days ago. His headquarters are at the fortress of Megiddo on the Jezreel Plain."

"Riders should be dispatched," ordered the queen.

"I'll send my fastest horseman," promised Elnathan.

"Send *five* horsemen!" Hamutal demanded.

"Five it shall be," Elnathan agreed.

"If there are to be riders," said Daniel, "I want to be one of them. Nephi will be another."

Hamutal's heart filled with compassion at her nephew's boldness, but one look told her that Daniel and Nephi were too exhausted to go anywhere.

"I'm sure that isn't necessary," said the queen. "The horsemen will warn the king. No one could travel more swiftly."

Daniel clenched his teeth. "I will go! If Nephi and I are not issued horses, we will steal two mounts and ride to Megiddo by ourselves!"

The queen raised her eyebrows. "Daniel, you're thinking foolishly. You appear on the verge of collapse."

"I'm not tired," Daniel insisted. "Nephi and I have come this far. I should warn the king in person. I know this in my heart."

Hamutal shook her head. "Nothing could be more unwise, my nephew."

"Perhaps not so unwise," Elnathan interrupted.

The queen opened her mouth to protest, but Elnathan raised his hand.

"Hear me out, my queen. The betrayer, Assasiah, is Josiah's first general. Daniel's story is so fantastic the king might not believe it from a stranger's lips, at least not firmly enough to revise his battle plan. He may think it's a ploy the Egyptians have devised to buy enough time to pass through the country unopposed. Josiah's sword is already drawn, my queen. The sight of Daniel—the story from his own lips—might be the only force outside of God powerful enough to make him resheath his sword and rethink his strategy."

"But the boys could never travel as fast—"

"I will dispatch five horsemen as you requested," said Elnathan. "Daniel and his friend will ride with myself and the cavalry. We will reach Megiddo within a day of the riders and confirm their story."

Hamutal shut her eyes. She knew Josiah's commitment to this war was almost fanatical. Perhaps Elnathan was right. She agreed to his plan, but with great remorse. What had this nation come to that its fate should rest on the shoulders of two eleven-year-old boys?

Daniel and Nephi were fed and given fresh clothing. Nephi asked one of the guards to seek out Shamariah. The old servant wasn't hard to find. Laban, the garrison commander, had kept him detained at the Gate of the Valley. Within an hour, Shamariah rejoined the boys in the House of Solomon.

"They've promised me our horses will be returned," Nephi told Shamariah. "When will you start back to the estate?"

"I'll start back first thing in the morning," said the servant. "First I must find an inn and get some sleep. Your mother will be sick with worry, Nephi."

"Tell her everything will be fine. Tell her I have the whole army of Judah looking after me." In a quieter he tone, Nephi added, "Tell her I love her."

"I will pray that you'll soon meet up with your father," said Shamariah. "There's no doubt he and Sam are on the northern roads somewhere, trying to locate Lemuel's battalion before something terrible happens."

"We'll watch out for them. With any luck, we might find Lemuel before they do."

Nephi bid Shamariah farewell.

Soon afterwards, he and Daniel were escorted to the Ephraim Gate on Jerusalem's north wall. Elnathan's cavalry had assembled along the roadway. Hananiah, Mishael, and Azariah came to the gate to see the boys off.

"You and your friend are true heros," Mishael told Daniel.

"When you return," said Hananiah, "we'll see to it that you're given a hero's welcome."

"Maybe even a parade!" added little Azariah.

Daniel's three friends watched in pride as he and Nephi were presented with a pair of their own battle stallions. The horses were decked in sky-blue, gold-embroidered trappings with dangling tassels. On top of their heads flew a high plume of ostrich feathers.

A dispatch from Elnathan rode up requesting the boys to ride to the front where the general could keep an eye on them, for their own protection. The boys guided their horses toward Elnathan's position.

"How do you feel?" Daniel asked Nephi.

"Exhilarated," Nephi replied. "Like I may never need sleep again."

"Good," said Daniel. Then he noticed a few worry lines form on Nephi's brow. "What is it?"

"How do you feel about General Elnathan?" asked Nephi.

"He is said to be Judah's fiercest warrior. His father, Achbor, was also a general."

"But do you trust him?"

Daniel sighed. "These days it's hard to know who to trust anymore, but we have to put our trust somewhere. His family descends from King Solomon. Elnathan has served the king faithfully all of his life. In fact, Elnathan's sister, Nehushta, is the wife of Josiah's oldest son, Prince Eliakim. The two men are very close friends. Elnathan wouldn't be part of any conspiracy unless Eliakim had turned against his own father."

Daniel chuckled at the notion. Nephi did not.

"What are the chances of that?" Nephi asked.

The smile melted from Daniel's face. He looked ahead. Elnathan sat upon his horse in the roadway, ready to shout the order to move out. Daniel thought on how much he longed for the naive days before his father's murder, when questions like the one Nephi had just posed were as insane as they sounded.

# Chapter 13
# MEGIDDO

HOUGH IT WAS AFTER NOON WHEN ELNATHAN'S CAVALRY DEPARTED
from Jerusalem, they set a goal to reach the village of Shiloh in the
heart of the land of Ephraim before resting. After the five-hundred
horsemen had bypassed the city of Bethel, Daniel discovered that he
could, in fact, sleep on horseback. The sleep was not sound, nor was
it particularly refreshing, but it was, for the most part, involuntary.

Nephi did not sleep. As the sun declined in the west, he watched
for sideways glances from Elnathan and caught several. The general
wore a permanent frown. His frown seemed to dig a little deeper
whenever he made eye contact with one of the boys. No doubt
Elnathan was a hard man, a warrior who viewed the scars of battle
as trophies. But shouldn't he have expressed some hint of compassion
toward his youngest riders? The general didn't even speak to them.
His conversations while on horseback were restricted solely to his
officers. Elnathan's attitude had a subtle way of rubbing off on the
men. As the evening's ride wore on, Nephi felt more and more that
he and Daniel were regarded, not as special emissaries who might
change the fate of the war, but as special nuisances who might bog
them down.

Upon arriving at Shiloh, the weary riders bivouacked in and
around the central courtyard. Each officer slept in a neatly prepared
room with fresh blankets. Daniel and Nephi were offered such a
room. In fact, Daniel had opened his mouth to accept the offer
when Nephi politely refused, telling them that he and the prince
would rather sleep in a tent among the other riders. The officers
ignored Nephi. In fact, they thought it was terribly presumptuous of

him to answer for the prince. Daniel, however, had come to trust Nephi's instincts, though at the moment he did so reluctantly. Daniel told the officers that sleeping in the courtyard was just fine.

Moments later, Elnathan showed up, fuming.

"You are a prince of Judah!" he rumbled at Daniel. "A proper room has been prepared where your protection can be guaranteed. That is where you and your friend shall sleep."

Daniel stole a glance at Nephi for reassurance, then he puffed up his chest. "I *am* a prince of Judah, and I say we shall sleep in the courtyard."

"Do I have to pick you up by the scruff of the neck and toss you in there myself?"

"If you do, I'll see to it that you're severely punished. Besides that, I'll make so much noise, no one in this entire village will sleep tonight."

Elnathan's eyes narrowed. "You haven't changed much, have you, my young prince?"

Elnathan and Daniel glowered at one another. The exasperated general finally threw up his arms.

"Erect a tent for them at the edge of the courtyard," he commanded his officers. "Have two guards posted at all hours."

*Only two?* thought Nephi.

The tent was erected. Guards were set in place. When the boys found themselves alone inside, Daniel demanded an explanation.

"Now I've offended the general!" whispered Daniel. "I hope you have a good reason."

Nephi rolled his eyes. When did the prince become so dense? "Is your life a good enough reason? Prince Daniel, what's the matter with you? You're not thinking clearly."

"Wouldn't we have been safer in a room with four solid walls?"

"Of course not! In an enclosed room, we'd be all alone. Don't you get it? *No witnesses!*" Nephi drew a finger across his throat.

Daniel sat back, his attitude sobered. "You think they were planning to kill us?"

"Don't you feel the hostility?" asked Nephi. "The hatred?"

"Maybe that's just Elnathan's style—"

"Prince Daniel," pleaded Nephi, "you've got to stop lying to yourself! Things are not as they once were in Judah. We are *not* in friendly company."

Daniel cradled his head between his knees, gripping tufts of hair in both hands. "What's happening, Nephi? What have we done? What did my father do? Why have so many people turned against the king?"

Nephi was aware that Daniel knew the answer to that question better than himself. The weight of it all had tempted the prince toward denial, so Nephi answered it for him. "Because the king has granted his loyalty to Babylon and rejected Egypt. Half of our nation depends upon Egypt for its livelihood. My own family depends upon it."

"Then this is all about money?" Daniel stretched back on his blanket. "When did money become more powerful than the wisdom of a king or the word of God?"

"Maybe as people began collecting more silver than faith," suggested Nephi. He had no more time for Daniel's pining. "We'd best concentrate our energy toward figuring out a way to escape."

"You think we're in danger tonight?"

"I'm not sure," said Nephi. "But I know we're safer out here among the troops than anywhere else."

Nephi scooted over to the tent flap. He peeked outside. Most of the campfires had been extinguished. The courtyard was silent except for an occasional cough. The only persons wide awake may have been Daniel, Nephi, and the two guards who watched over them.

One of the guards glanced at Nephi. Nephi smiled and shut the flap.

"One of us has to stay awake at all hours," Nephi told the prince. "I'll take the first watch."

"No, I'll take it," said Daniel. "I slept a little during the ride."

"All right," Nephi agreed. "But if you feel yourself dozing off, wake me up."

"I will," Daniel promised.

Nephi curled up in his blankets. With all the tension he felt, Nephi doubted if he could even fall asleep this night. The next thing he knew, his lids had dropped and his mind had drifted. Nephi had no idea how long he slumbered. At some point, his eyes popped open.

Daniel was snoring.

"Prince Daniel!" Nephi whispered.

The prince snapped back to alertness.

"How long were you dozing?"

"I . . . I don't know. It came on so fast. I don't even remember closing my eyes."

Nephi crawled back to the tent flap and peered outside. Most of the fires were cold now. Coughing had ceased. Except for an occasional lamp over a doorway, the village was draped in total darkness. Nephi squinted to try and see better. He looked to the right and then to the left.

"Hello?" he said softly.

No one replied.

Nephi started breathing erratically.

"What's the matter?" asked Daniel.

"They're gone," said Nephi. "Both guards are gone."

Daniel heard his heart start racing. For an instant, the boys did not move. Their bodies felt as though caught in some invisible grip. Nephi needed a moment to collect his thoughts.

"We must not panic," said Nephi. "We have to get out of the tent. Let's go."

Daniel and Nephi swiftly gathered up their blankets and crept outside. Across the courtyard, they found a campfire's glowing embers. Beside the embers and between two sleeping soldiers, the boys endured the remainder of the night.

In the morning, after the wake-up horn had blared, Daniel and Nephi went back to look at their tent. The place appeared undisturbed. They both began to wonder if they'd overreacted. Then Daniel stepped around to the other side. Now they understood why Elnathan had specifically requested that their tent should be erected at the edge of the courtyard. In the goat-hair canvas wall, from top to bottom, someone's eager blade had slit an entrance hole. It wasn't hard to deduce what had been attempted. Nor was it hard to imagine how infuriated someone must have been to find his victims absent.

"WHERE DID YOU SLEEP LAST NIGHT?" DEMANDED ELNATHAN. "THE guards told me in the morning you were gone."

Moments earlier, Daniel and Nephi had decided their safest course of action was to feign ignorance toward the assassination attempt.

"We were cold," Daniel replied. "We thought it might be warmer if we slept by a fire."

Elnathan studied Daniel's face. His eyes were cold. "Next time," barked the general, "you will tell the guards!"

As Elnathan walked away, Daniel and Nephi heaved a sigh.

Tensions remained high as the cavalry continued its trek past the city of Shechem and between the arid woodland heights of Mount Gerizim and Mount Ebal. The thought of escape was never far from either boy's mind. Both of them were constantly on the lookout for the right opportunity. It had to come soon. The cavalry was due to arrive in Megiddo late that afternoon. Daniel and Nephi knew full well that Elnathan did not intend for them to reach the presence of the king.

Shortly before noon, the men guided their mounts below the ruins of Samaria. The once prestigious capital of the Northern Kingdom had not yet healed from scars inflicted by the Assyrian hordes two generations before. As the boys considered the carelessly strewn heaps of rubble and stone on the hill above the road, they felt a heavy sense of oppression in their hearts. The royal palace of Jeroboam and a few other proud structures were still partly intact, but the more undamaged a building appeared, the greater was the horror of desolation which emanated from it. A low, choking gasp seemed to echo in the shadowy entrance of every structure. Samaria appeared abandoned, not only by men, but by God. The successors of the great northern capital were jackals, wild dogs and venomous snakes which menaced several of the horses which wandered too close to the road's edge.

Samaria had once thought it could vie in magnificence with Babylon, Noph, and Nineveh. Who would have believed it could be so utterly destroyed? For a brief instant, as Daniel gazed upon one crumbled edifice, he thought he saw the smoking ruins of the holy temple at Jerusalem. The image made him cringe and turn away. Could it happen in Judah as it had in Israel? Daniel felt strongly impressed that the question was fast becoming "when," and not "if."

Late that afternoon, when the shadows of their horses stretched as tall as cedars, the cavalry came upon a fork in the road. Daniel and Nephi could read the weather-worn road sign well enough. The left fork took them to Megiddo. The right fork took them to Jezreel at the foot of Mount Gilboa. Elnathan directed the cavalry toward the right.

Daniel spurred his horse to ride up beside the general. Struggling to suppress any nervousness in his voice, the prince said, "I thought we were going to Megiddo."

Elnathan kept his eyes fixed forward. "I do not doubt that the horsemen I sent yesterday have already informed King Josiah of the plot against him. Queen Hamutal and I decided before we left that it would be equally important for you to inform His Highness, Prince Eliakim. Eliakim is stationed at Jezreel."

"And when will we see the king?"

"Tomorrow," declared the general.

"Very good," said Daniel.

The prince allowed his horse to slow its pace so he could ride beside Nephi. Nephi's face was easily readable. He knew that Queen Hamutal had made no such suggestion. The boys' suspicions had been verified. Prince Eliakim, son of Josiah, had turned against his father. No doubt an executioner's blade awaited them at Jezreel. If Daniel and Nephi did not attempt an escape this instant, it would be too late.

The boys nodded to one another. In unison, they raised their reins. Two cries. Two sharp kicks to their horses' withers. Both stallions bolted to the left and leaped off the road.

"After them!" shouted Elnathan.

Elnathan's men hesitated. What was going on? Why had the prince fled. What had he done?

"Has everyone gone deaf!" Elnathan's voice cracked from stress. "I said, after them!"

Ten horses broke free of the cavalry ranks to take up the pursuit. Elnathan himself led the way. Daniel and Nephi's mounts jumped a small stream and climbed a ravine. Their steeds knew how to run. The boys hunkered low and coaxed them faster. Soon they reconnected with the wagon grooves of the Megiddo road, dispersing a covey of sparrows. Not a moment later, the stallions of Elnathan and his men had also found the road.

Out of ten pursuing horses, one or two of them were bound to be swifter than the steeds issued to Daniel and Nephi. The swiftest horse of all belonged to Elnathan. The boys could hear his stallion's heavy gallops as it drew closer and closer, almost magnetically. When Daniel turned, the fierce-eyed general was nearly in range to snatch away the prince's reins. Daniel spurred his horse harder, but the animal had reached its maximum speed.

Elnathan's hand grasped out at Daniel like a vulture's claw. The prince held his reins away. The general nabbed the horse's mane instead. Sharply, Daniel yanked back on his horse's bit. The obedient stallion halted and reared. Elnathan's horse could not stop as fast. The general lost his grip on Daniel's steed and tumbled into the roadway. Daniel did not wait around to see if Elnathan was badly injured. He redirected his stallion back toward Megiddo and shortly caught up with Nephi.

Much to Elnathan's vexation, his men felt more inclined to investigate the condition of their leader rather than follow the boys. Elnathan rose to his feet, favoring a limp, and cried, "What's the matter with all of you! They're getting away! Don't let them reach Megiddo!"

A few of the horsemen continued the pursuit for quite some distance, but as soon the walls of Megiddo appeared, it became clear that the race was futile. The boys would reach the gate well before the horsemen could hope to catch them.

The encampments of the hosts of Judah, forty to sixty thousand strong, dotted the plain in all directions. The men of these camps appeared ready and restless with their armor and arms near at hand, but there was no evidence that any of them had yet engaged in combat. The sight of them made the boys giddy with relief. The battle had not yet begun. Their pain, their adventures, their struggles to reach this place, hadn't been for naught.

The fortress of Megiddo rose out of the green of the Jezreel Plain like an immortal pillar of power. The site was one of the world's most ancient, known to Abraham when he came from Ur to the Promised Land. Nine generations previously, King Solomon had expanded and heightened its platforms, ramparts and balconies to make it one of the most impregnable fortresses on earth.

Daniel and Nephi were not naive enough to believe that Elnathan had ever dispatched a single horseman to inform Josiah of their coming. They guided their mounts around to the northern gate. Sentries stopped them before they could enter. Daniel announced that he'd ridden all the way from Jerusalem with an urgent message for the king. The prince did not depend upon the possibility that one of the soldiers might recognize him; he said the message was from Queen Hamutal. But, in fact, nearly all of the men knew his identity. Every officer had been intimately acquainted with Daniel's father, Commander Maaseiah. A few of them had even heard Daniel speak in the temple that night during the Passover feast.

"Where is Josiah?" cried one of the officers.

"On the northwest watchtower with his commanders!" came the reply.

"Hasten the young prince and his companion to the presence of the king!"

FOR THE LAST TWO HOURS, A SACRED WAR COUNCIL HAD CONVENED under the direction of His Majesty inside the parapets of Megiddo's highest watchtower. From here the commanders could look across the plain to the northwest. On the sandy bay beaches beyond the eastern slopes of Mount Carmel, the Egyptian army had been unloading men and supplies from their deep-bellied vessels for more than two days. It had been the trusted advice of Josiah's commanding general, Assasiah, to make no move against the Egyptians while they completed their landing, allowing for the final contingents of Judah's forces to arrive at Megiddo. The Egyptian camp now resembled a massive city, many leagues in extent, a city whose temples and palaces were represented by the three-tiered monsters anchored close to shore.

Earlier that afternoon, an Egyptian messenger had knocked at Megiddo's gate and handed to the king a letter from the son of the incarnate sun god himself, Pharaoh Necho. The Egyptian monarch had added to his signature a circle with a point in the center, the symbol of his divinity. Ahikam, the king's private secretary, had earlier read the letter to all the commanders with suppressed excitement.

*"What have I to do with thee, thou king of Judah? Forbear thee from meddling with God, who is with me, that He destroy thee not!"*

Ahikam had then proceeded, in the tradition of his scholarly father, Shaphan, to offer an interpretation of Pharaoh's words. The very fact that Necho had sent a message even *recognizing* Israel's

163

God, and then to arrogantly proclaim that Israel's God supported *him* instead of *Josiah*, proved that Necho had been profoundly taken back by the impressive Jewish army that faced him. He now realized it would take much more than a casual swish of the Apis's tail to shoo off the troublesome gadfly of Israel. Though Pharaoh may not have doubted his eventual victory, he realized that his ultimate purpose—confronting the warlords of Babylon—might be indefinitely postponed or even hampered. Ahikam interpreted Pharaoh's letter as a subtle request to enter into negotiations. What it *really* meant was "What price dost thou demand, thou king of Judah?"

What a relief for Ahikam, who was not a soldier and who would have loved to have seen this conflict resolved without bloodshed. But the commanders of Judah, eager for their hour of glory and fame, shouted down the secretary's interpretation. Pharaoh's message was a confession of weakness and fear—that was all.

Commander Assasiah reserved his opinion until the end. Shrewdly, Josiah's first general insisted that a battle *must* take place. In fact, Assasiah yearned for it more desperately than any of his comrades. His motives, however, were carefully different. Assasiah was well aware of the betrayal of Eliakim and Elnathan. He knew the forces at Jezreel would not assist the king. The army at Megiddo, however, was still quite strong. Only by misdirecting the forces under his command during battle could Assasiah insure the king's total defeat. If everything went as planned, the king would be captured and taken to Egypt in chains. The nation of Judah would be spared and its profitable relationship with the Land of Bondage could continue.

When it was Assasiah's turn to speak, the commanding general stood before the king and said, "There is only one suitable answer to this letter from Pharaoh—none at all."

It was at this moment that the garrison commander of Megiddo disturbed the council.

"What is the meaning of this interruption!" snapped Josiah.

"Your Majesty, forgive me," begged the garrison commander. The officer searched for the proper introductory words, but he found none. His message could only be presented in one way—by signaling the boys to ascend the final steps.

As Daniel and Nephi stepped onto the platform, the council was gripped with silence. It took a moment for Josiah to register recognition. The instant he did, he felt a stab of trepidation. His nephew's visitation from the realms of the dead meant that God had cursed the nation of Judah! When Josiah realized he was not staring at a ghost, the sum of his various emotions could not be adequately described. There was joy—his brother's son lived! There was consternation—how could this possibly be? And there was dread—the news Daniel carried could only be abominable.

Daniel fell to his knees before his sovereign.

"I have been held worthy to look upon the countenance of the king," said Daniel, his eyes seeping tears.

The king also dropped to his knees. He hoisted his nephew back onto his feet so he could bask in the glow of Daniel's face. Josiah touched the boy's cheek. He felt Prince Daniel's hair and ruffled it between his fingers as he had a thousand times before. The king tightly embraced his nephew.

With his eyes squeezed shut, Josiah declared, "The Lord be forever praised that He would manifest unto me such a miracle this day."

The most definable emotions in the room were those felt by Commander Assasiah, who stood stiffly in the center of the platform. The sight of Prince Daniel filled his breast with pure horror. All the insurances, all the backstops he'd set in place to prevent this moment from happening, had been in vain. Before the king had released his embrace, Daniel's eyes opened and met those of Assasiah. Every general on the platform could feel an immediate energy, bitter and venomous, emanating between them. As Josiah backed away to further gaze upon Daniel's fair features, he too, felt the energy. Abruptly, the king arose so he might discover the object of Daniel's wrath. He glanced back at the prince to verify that it was, in fact, his commanding general.

Daniel slowly lifted a pointed finger.

"You murdered my father," he declared.

Assasiah tried to laugh off the accusation. "Prince Daniel. It's me, Assasiah. Don't you remember? Your friend and your father's friend on a hundred occasions."

Daniel's expression did not flinch.

Assasiah directed his pleas to the king. "Well, the boy is clearly not well. One look will tell you. I wonder, truly, if he even knows his own name."

"I remember my name," said Daniel. "I remember the face of my father as he lay in his own blood. I remember the terrible face of your hired assassin. I remember when you ordered your men to strip me of my royal robes and carry me into the desert."

"You see what I mean?" Assasiah told the king. "The boy is deluded! We have no time for this. The Egyptian armies are preparing to attack! We must return to the matter at hand. Yes! The glory of Judah! Shall we?"

Secretary Ahikam and the other generals found it difficult to recover from their shock. Assasiah's lies were so obviously unprepared. Every statement that fell from his lips reeked with slithering guilt. How could conspiracy's cancer have reached such lofty ranks? It had swollen right under their noses!

The rage burning within Josiah caused his powerful hands to tremble. Assasiah had been his most trusted advisor, a man the king would have listed as one of his closest childhood friends. Josiah might have tried to believe Assasiah. He might have listened patiently to any defense Assasiah could present, if the man's efforts to hide his desperation had not failed so miserably.

The king recalled the hasty trial of the chamberlain who'd been accused of Maaseiah's murder. The entire affair had been conducted by Assasiah. Josiah's commanders reflected on the many ill-timed comments and odd decisions their lead general had made over the last few months. They regretted that their stray thoughts and opinions had gone unexpressed. The commanders had been blinded by the uncommon faith placed in him by the king.

Two swords hung at Josiah's sides. He drew the longer one from its sheath, then he drew the shorter one.

Assasiah backed up a step. "Are you inclined to believe the word of a boy over that of your most loyal servant? His story is outrageous! Scar-faced assassins! Kidnappings in the desert!"

"How did you know that his face was scarred?" asked Daniel.

"That was *your* description," said Assasiah.

Daniel shook his head. "I was not so specific."

Josiah, each hand bristling with blades, took another step forward. Assasiah drew his own sword and raised it overhead. The king leaped into action, blocking the betrayer's downward strike. Josiah's shorter sword plunged into Assasiah's thigh. Assasiah dropped his weapon. Josiah placed his hand over the betrayer's neck, pushing him back so he could retract his sword. The wounded man staggered and fell against the battlements. His frame shook from the pain, but he did not cry out.

"Send for a physician!" shouted Josiah.

The garrison commander withdrew to pursue the king's orders. The king stood over his bleeding first general.

"Kill me!" shrieked Assasiah. "Why don't you kill me?"

Tears pricked at Josiah's eyes. "Because I have to know why."

"Why? You want to know why?" Assasiah cackled and then his voice grew calm. "All my life I've served you, my king. I've loved you. But I love Judah more than I love you. This campaign will bring ruin to our great nation. Ruin! Surrender now, before all our cities lay in smoldering heaps of ash!"

Josiah was not fooled by Assasiah's claims of love and patriotism. He knew his general had business interests with Egypt. There were others of his councilors who had similar interests, but they had all assured him that such interests had been forsaken. Now it was clear that Assasiah had forsaken nothing. He loved Egypt's money. His passions ran no deeper.

Slowly, Josiah shook his head. "How is it, my general, that you have failed so completely to understand the truth. You want riches? You want glory? You could have had both! If only you'd been a little more patient, a little more faithful." Josiah gazed up at the heavens. "Why does it seem as though the destiny of Judah is a vision reserved only for me?"

"We share the vision, Your Majesty!" declared the other commanders.

The king turned to his commanders. "How do I know that you haven't *all* betrayed me?"

The commanders looked shocked. "Never, my king!"

"It doesn't matter!" snapped Josiah. "Every one of you may betray me if you like. It will not change the destiny of Judah. The destiny of Israel is the destiny of God!"

The garrison commander returned with a Levite physician and his attendants.

"Tie off his wound," Josiah told the Levite. "But do not dress it and do not stitch it. He will live, but only long enough to see the Lord's will fulfilled in Israel."

Nephi, who had remained at the farthest edge of the parapet, watched the physician and his attendants lift Assasiah upon a stretcher and carry him off. The king's command had astounded Nephi. Certainly Assasiah was a criminal of the highest order. His actions had endangered the entire nation. It might well have been that his crimes were worthy of death. But could any man be worthy of the kind of torture Josiah had sentenced upon him? To writhe in fever and agony until his eyes glossed over? Nephi feared he would never comprehend the ways of kings.

"Leave us now," Josiah told Ahikam and the other commanders. "I would like to speak with my nephew alone."

The officers left the platform of the watchtower. Nephi lingered behind until the last. He was about to descend the stairway after the others when the king called him back.

"You! What is your name?"

Nephi hastily returned to the presence of the king. He knelt on the platform, but he couldn't bring himself to speak.

"His name is Nephi," said Daniel. "He has been my companion since near the beginning of this terrible ordeal. I owe him my life, several times over."

"Rise, Nephi."

Nephi stood. He became immobilized by the king's gaze. Josiah placed his hand on the boy's shoulder.

"You must truly be one of God's chosen to have found yourself embroiled in such a noble cause."

Nephi could only bring himself to nod.

Josiah faced the prince. "Your arrival in Megiddo is only the first of many miracles, my nephew. Before the sun sets tomorrow, we may actually see the fire of God descend upon the armies of Pharaoh."

"There is more you must know," said Daniel. "Assasiah was not alone in his betrayal."

Josiah turned away and took a few steps across the platform, as if he were only mildly interested in Daniel's information.

"Elnathan, son of Achbor, is involved." Daniel swallowed before he finished. "And so is your son, Prince Eliakim."

Josiah spun back. His surprise was apparent. He'd entrusted his oldest son with one-third of all the hosts of Judah. Eliakim's mission had been to wait in the foothills of Gilboa with the army's reserves until word reached him to launch a surprise attack. This strategy had been suggested by Assasiah. Did this mean that he could expect no help from his own son? The king opened his mouth to demand an explanation from Daniel—to demand proof! Instead, His Majesty faced Mount Carmel and the campfire-dotted plains. He cocked his fists at the darkening sky.

"How could they have all become so blind!" he raved. "Don't they understand? Isn't it clear? All my life I've sought to glorify Him who is the Father of All Creation and to glorify the people of His holy covenant. I have rebuilt and restrengthened His temple. I have re-established His holy law. I have torn down and trampled underfoot the shrines and idols of the heathens. I have reformed or destroyed every priest in the land whose words were greased with corruption. I have strived to keep His commandments all the days of my life, even until this day when I issued the command for every soldier who'd recently built a new house, planted a new vineyard, or taken a young wife to return, if he so desired, to his own home. Don't you see? My entire life has been in preparation for the events of tomorrow so that the Lord's support would be fixed and immovable. So that when it became my mission to begin the task of subjecting every earthly nation to the will of Adonai, I would be found worthy. It wouldn't matter now, my nephew, if every commander and corporal of the armies of Israel had betrayed me. Judah's warriors will not fight alone. God himself will lead them into battle. The arm of every man who wields a sword will do so with supernatural power and fury. Mark my words, young Daniel and Nephi. Tomorrow the fires of heaven will rain upon Megiddo's plain."

And even as the king made his prophecy, the minds of both boys became entranced by an unusual phenomenon taking shape in the northern skies beyond the eastern slopes of Mount Carmel. A reddish tinge was rising out of the great bay. The hour was too late and the glow was too bright for it to be a reflection of the setting sun. The glow's intensity was not fading. It was expanding.

"What is it?" asked Nephi, nearly breathless. "Is it heaven's fires?"

Josiah pondered the meaning of the glow. He almost answered Daniel's friend in the affirmative. The timing of this miracle compared with his own uttered words was too incredible! What else could it be?

And then Josiah's hopes sobered. He knew the meaning of the glow. It was not the fires of God. It was merely a symbol of Pharaoh's bitter resolve, an act designed to fix the will of Edypt and assure its warriors that there was no turning back. Just as Josiah had drawn this conclusion, one of his commanders rushed onto the platform.

"Word has been received from our lookouts on Carmel," said the commander. "Pharaoh has ceased to wait for the king's response to his letter. The Egyptians are burning their ships behind them!"

# Chapter 14
## BATTLE ON THE PLAIN

THE BATTLE BEGAN AN HOUR BEFORE DAWN, IN THE SINISTER LIGHT of the burning ships. Pharaoh's Ethiopian and Nubian auxiliaries led the attack, only to be hurled back time and again by the archers and sling-bearers of Judah.

Daniel and Nephi might have stayed awake if their exhaustion had not made them powerless against sleep. They rested in the king's plush quarters while His Majesty paced the platform of the northwest watch-tower all night. Around midnight Josiah dispatched his second son, the slow-witted Prince Jehoahaz, to return to Jerusalem with a command for the High Priest to ordain a great day of prayer and fasting. Any capable rider could have gone, but Ahikam had been quite insistent that the rider be Jehoahaz. Josiah knew what was in the mind of his secretary: The king should withdraw his oldest faithful son from the field to ensure that a descendant of David held himself ready in the capital for any emergencies that might arise. Josiah resented his secretary's advice. He felt confident that such a move was unnecessary. In the end, however, he conceded that such action was standard procedure.

Daniel arose at first light and wandered up to the platform of the watchtower to find His Majesty discussing the first reports of the battle with his generals.

"They've requested that more reinforcements be sent north," the commanders informed the king. "Without them, we may shortly be pushed back from the road, leaving the Egyptians free to move easily onto the Jezreel Plain."

Josiah fell into a spell of deep concentration. He paced the battlements again, entirely failing to notice his nephew. The nocturnal attack of Pharaoh seemed to have dreadfully interfered with his battle plan.

One of Josiah's generals put forth an appeal. "The entire army should be moved forward to confront Egypt near the beaches."

"No," said the king deliberately. "Let them through. I want to meet and defeat Pharaoh on the open plain, not on the beaches of the bay."

Daniel rushed back to the king's quarters to rouse Nephi. Nephi dressed quickly. Neither boy wanted to miss the fires of heaven when they fell upon the hosts of Egypt. They ate the breakfast that servants had prepared for the king. His Majesty had not found the time to come down and eat it himself. Afterwards, Daniel and Nephi climbed the steps of the platform and found a space at the far edge of the parapet where they could watch without getting in anyone's way.

Mornings on the Jezreel Plain were often misty and today was no exception. Only the very summit of Carmel had escaped the cloudy soup. Around mid-morning the mist began to dissipate. The vision left by the rising fog chilled the blood of the hosts of Judah.

Among the superstitious peasants of Israel there thrived a firm belief in the magical powers of Egypt. Today that belief would earn many converts. The arts of magic seemed to be the only explanation for the swiftness of Pharaoh in moving his forces onto the Jezreel Plain. As far as the northern steeps, the plain flashed with unfurled Egyptian banners.

The hordes of Pharaoh were drawn up in deep formation, wave behind wave. On the front line marched the sons of the Libyan coasts and deserts, who served Pharaoh as mercenaries. Squadrons of cavalry rode at their flanks. These were the dreaded Anu and Satiu, tribes of the Sinai who fought with whirling javelins. Behind the horsemen marched the actual Egyptians, arranged in dense divisions according to the forty-two regions. The wooden image of Ptah rose to the skies as the standard of the first division. Behind them marched the troops of Re, Seth, and Horus—each region with its god, each god with its region.

But what made the Egyptian army more terrifying than the mutated images upon their standards, was the magnificent rigidity of the armored ranks. The men of Pharaoh blanketed the plains in a silence like death.

The quiet was so impressive it stifled every other sound, even among the hosts of Israel. Apart from the neighing of horses, the scraping of hoofs, the grinding of wheels and the morning song of the wind, not a rustle was heard.

A double-trumpet blast issued from several undeterminable points among the Egyptians. The ranks of Libya, Sinai, and the forty-two regions came to a halt.

And waited.

Josiah's generals had long since returned to their posts. The king stood alone on the watchtower with his faithful secretary, Ahikam, and one watchman who held a curved trumpet. Also on the watchtower were Daniel and Nephi who kept as far down the parapet as possible.

"So," Josiah mumbled, "Egypt has decided that Judah shall make the first move on the plain." With a tight smile, he turned to Ahikam. "Pharaoh thinks that by displaying the breadth of his power and glory, my faith might waver."

Daniel and Nephi found themselves searching skyward. The timing could not have been better to fulfill Josiah's prophecy. Where were the fires of heaven?

At great personal peril, Ahikam decided to entreat the king one final time. "Pharaoh has granted us a short respite to reconsider this project. His Majesty should weigh the option carefully. Perhaps the king could go down . . . perhaps he could speak with Pharaoh . . ."

Ahikam's words struck Josiah like a blade to the springline of a catapult. Instantly, he made the sign to his watchman, who set the trumpet to his lips and blew a long, wailing note. The horns and bugles of all Israel joined in angrily, imitating the roar of a lion's whelp.

The trumpets of Egypt replied with tenfold fury and the first shower of arrows from the Libyan archers sang past the tower. Daniel and Nephi ducked as one of the arrows whistled above them. As the armies began to clash, Ahikam commanded the boys to get off the platform and wait below. Daniel and Nephi did so, but with great reluctance.

For the remainder of the morning and into the early afternoon, the boys moved about the various corners of Megiddo's courtyard, watching chariots and men arrive and depart through the northern gate. They inclined an ear toward anyone who brought news of the battle's developments. From time to time, some warrior was carried inside, the blood from his wounds pocking the dust around the gate. Sometimes the wind would carry in from the plain the whimpers of less fortunate men who lay helpless under the sun. Their cries mingled with the shrieks of dying horses.

After three assaults, the report came back that Egypt was buckling. Judah had driven a wedge through the Libyans, past Anu and Satiu, and deep into the ranks of the forty-two regions. But in time, the superior weight of Pharaoh's hosts squeezed them out of the wound they had inflicted like an obnoxious sliver. By mid-afternoon, both armies were exhausted. Judah and Egypt tacitly agreed to a temporary truce.

Josiah came down from the watchtower to be in closer proximity to his generals and messengers. Daniel watched him grip the leather cuirass of one of his officers.

"Ride to Jezreel," he commanded the officer. "Tell Prince Eliakim to launch his attack!"

The officer looked confused. Only that morning several generals had suggested taking a detachment of the army to Jezreel to have Eliakim and Elnathan arrested. Josiah had objected.

The officer requested clarification. "But the word is that Eliakim and Elnathan are—"

"I don't care what you've heard!" Josiah clamored. "My son *will* come! His forces are required. The God of Israel will turn his heart!" The king thrust the officer back and sent him on his way.

Josiah cast off his tunic. Underneath he wore only a short white garment. The steel flesh of the king shimmered in the sunlight. Servants poured pitchers of cold water over his head and shoulders. Josiah's chief chamberlain rubbed him down with rough towels. All the while, Josiah issued a continuous flow of orders to his generals. The king himself intended to lead the final and decisive assault. Every chariot, together with each contingent of cavalry and infantry still breathing, were to be concentrated for the onslaught.

After Josiah had donned his armor, his chariots were paraded before him. He selected a long, four-wheeled car with a huge brazen bow. The bowstring was stretched taut by means of a lever which the archer worked with his foot. The gold-plated quiver at the back of the car contained very long arrows whose tips were like lance-heads.

Its protective shield, however, did not reach higher than a man's hips.

The generals tried to dissuade the king from using this chariot. Such a car, they argued, with its gold and silver mountings, was fine for ceremonial processions, but no good for battle. It required no less than six chargers to haul it and the proximity of the quiver would require the presence of a driver as well as one other attendant.

Josiah gritted his teeth in displeasure at his generals' advice. How could any man understand his motives who was not himself a king? To meet the arrogance of Pharaoh in a war chariot with golden spokes and six silver-harnessed foaming stallions was precisely his intention!

The eyes of the king scanned the faces of his officers to select an appropriate attendant. They came to a rest on the face of a boy, the same boy who'd accompanied Prince Daniel to Megiddo. What was his name? Nephi. An Egyptian name. His father was certainly a merchant or trader to have selected such a name.

The previous night, Josiah had thought this boy might be chosen of God to have become embroiled in the affairs of the prince. Perhaps this youngster was as close as the camps of Israel came to having their own prophet. Daniel insisted that the boy had saved his life more than once. Could he bring the same luck to the king? Israel did not carry statues of gods into battle, but the possibilities of drawing down the just wrath of Jehovah by bringing along an innocent Jewish child with an Egyptian name seemed to Josiah to be infinitely delicious.

Nephi felt the king's eyes upon him. He knew he'd been summoned when Josiah's officer started walking in his direction. When his suspicion was verified, Nephi glanced at Prince Daniel for reassurance. The prince nodded encouragingly. Nephi shyly approached the king.

"You will bear my standard," Josiah told the boy, "and you will assist me in arming my bow when I require it. Do you understand?"

A knot snagged in Nephi's throat. As before, he tried to reply with a nod.

"Speak up, boy!" commanded the king.

"Y-yes, Your Majesty," stammered Nephi. "I would be honored."

Nephi's heart did a somersault. Had a greater honor ever been bestowed upon a common boy? At last, Nephi had found his jewel of self-worth. Never again would there be a reason to feel the slightest twinge of jealousy toward his older brothers. Laman would be honored for keeping his father's estate. Lemuel would be honored for his life of piety. But no matter what else happened in Nephi's life, he would always have this moment of heroic glory. As a teetering old man, he could still tell the tale of how he'd served at the side of Israel's greatest king as the fires of heaven finally ignited Megiddo's plain.

Nephi climbed into the car. He was shown the quiver from which he would draw the king's arrows and presented with a pole upon which hung a purple banner with the star of David embroidered in golden thread.

Josiah's driver mounted the chariot, as did the king. On either side of His Majesty would ride his generals, in less ornate but more practical chariots.

Before the crack of the driver's whip signaled the line to move out, Josiah raised his sword and called upon Ahikam and his commanders to act as witnesses.

"Hear my royal oath!" he cried. "If God will grant me victory over the House of Bondage this day, I will fulfill His law to the last detail. Not one jot or tittle shall be ignored. In the seventh year I shall force every house in the land to free their bondmen. For were not we ourselves bondmen in Egypt? Do you hear me, O ye witnesses? Let nothing come between the Lord and me!"

The charioteer's whip cracked. The rattle of wooden wheels and the clatter of hoofs commenced like a hailstorm. Nephi caught his balance as the chariots rolled across the courtyard. The warriors of Judah shouted the watch-cry: "The kingdom of David!"

There was a halt at Megiddo's gate where trumpeters blew the call for every other squadron to fall in. The outer gate opened. The soldiers screamed. Nephi watched the advance guards of Israel fling themselves against the Libyan ranks, their swords breaking in half enemy shields and their lances piercing enemy flesh.

The sky above Nephi darkened as the storm of arrows, spears, and slings resumed with venomous hissing and whirring. The king's chariot rumbled forward. Nephi tightly gripped the standard of the king. The boy's heart leaped into his throat as Josiah directed his driver to charge right into a nest of Libyan swordsmen!

Wide-eyed with horror, Nephi watched the advance warriors of Judah crush the enemy swordsmen one by one as they furiously sought to break through and grapple directly with the Jewish king. Josiah shook his fist at the Libyans, almost disappointed that no one broke through.

As the king's chariot rolled onward, Nephi tried to concentrate on keeping Israel's standard upright and straight. He had no desire to further witness the surging torrent of carnage around him, but he could not block out the rising, sweetish odor of human blood.

The stone from an enemy sling ricocheted off the chariot's rim, barely missing Nephi's hip. Nephi crouched down in the car, looking up longingly at the sky. An awful thought struck him. What if the armies of Judah were all alone? What if the Lord had withheld His support? Could the king have been left to his own resources?

The king's chariot came to a jarring halt. Josiah had again ordered his driver to charge directly into a hotbed of enemy strength. This time there were very few advance troops to protect the king. Egyptian ground soldiers surrounded Josiah's horses. The king's sword struck an enemy warrior as he tried to board the chariot. Another Egyptian leaped upon the rim directly over Nephi. Nephi looked up into a wild face with ivory-white teeth and ruby-painted lips. Josiah's sword struck a blow—nearly scalping Nephi in the process—and the man fell back. Nephi felt the moistness of splattered blood on his cheek. With quivering hands, he rubbed the moistness onto his sleeve, pressing down harder with each wipe.

One of Josiah's generals had noticed the king's predicament and sent more troops to His Majesty's aid. The Israelites cut their way through to Josiah and freed up his horses.

"Your Majesty, I beg you to keep behind the lead ranks!" urged the general.

"And why?" Josiah cried. "The enemy line is broken!"

It was true. Disordered knots of Egyptians had begun tossing away their weapons, surrendering, or fleeing toward the north. Anu and Satiu were turning their horses. Even the main armies of the forty-two regions reeled in retreat, leaving the foremost terrain empty of living men. The voice of Josiah cut through the tumult to shout a triumphant roar. Nephi's confidence returned. Josiah didn't *need* the fires of heaven! God had empowered His Majesty here on earth! The kingdom of Jehovah was near at hand! The new David had not been mistaken!

Josiah's squadrons of horsemen concentrated into a dense mass. A mighty cloud of dust arose as the ranks of Israel thundered into the swept field. Nephi set aside the standard and grasped the chariot's rim to keep from bouncing out. He glanced back at the twisted bodies of the dead, to whom none had paid heed. The bodies shrank farther and farther behind.

Shortly, a new roar of victory went up. The standard of Ptah had fallen into the hands of Judah. Josiah's chariot briefly paused as foot soldiers approached the king with the tall pole of the wooden god in their arms. Nephi backed away as Josiah raised the standard over his head and thrust it down on the ground. The image of Ptah and the poles that supported it snapped into three separate pieces. As the army of Judah rolled forth, the same fate befell the falcon-headed Re and the donkey-headed Seth. The battle-lines of Pharaoh had been shattered!

And then the charge of victory stumbled to a sudden halt. A deep ditch filled with water crossed the terrain. The king's horses reared to avoid the obstacle. Nephi saw that beyond the ditch rose the gentle slope of a hill. On the crest of that hill, perhaps a hundred and fifty ells distant, three lines of bronze giants stood sharply against the sky. Not a one had yet hurled a spear or received a wound. Rested, fresh, and alert, they awaited the frenzied, blood-spattered hosts of Josiah. Red horsetails and plumes waved calmly upon their helmets.

"Javan!" Nephi heard the Jewish soldiers whispering from mouth to mouth. "The Ionians!"

After one harsh word of command, Pharaoh's mercenary auxiliaries from the Greek islands lowered their long lances in a triple phalanx, like three gigantic scythes. But instead of attacking, the Ionian warriors remained rigid and motionless.

Josiah's driver directed Nephi to raise the banner of Judah once again. During the furious onward drive, Josiah's helmet had fallen off his head. Strands of his long hair had become plastered to his face by sweat, dust, and splashes of blood. The intoxication of battle had rendered His Majesty almost unrecognizable.

The king turned his eyes back toward Megiddo and beyond, his gaze reaching across the rolling plains, all the way to the invisible fortress of Jezreel. Nephi wondered what the king might be thinking. Did Josiah still harbor some shred of hope that his son, Eliakim, might come to the rescue? The plains toward the southeast were empty and green.

Nephi squinted toward the summit of a low hill, just above and to the northwest of the Ionian line. Looking down on the impending destruction with cool superiority sat Pharaoh Necho. The rims of his shoulder-supported chariot reflected the spiked rays of the sun. Even from this distance Nephi recognized the portable throne. It was same one Pharaoh had sat upon during the farewell parade in Noph, an event which now seemed to have occurred many lifetimes ago. Colorful counselors still kissed the chariot's rim. The sparrow-hawk of Horus and the sacred baboon of the realm of the dead still sat to the right and left of Pharaoh's armrests.

Nephi realized that, in spite of all the blood that had been shed, in spite of the shattered images of his gods, the autocrat of the Nile still wished to grant the Jewish king a chance to reconsider this futile pursuit. Continuing or ending the carnage still rested in Josiah's hands. Nephi realized, for the first time, it was not Pharaoh Necho who granted Josiah an opportunity to change his mind. It was the Lord.

Three times in the past twenty-four hours, fate had intervened to dissuade the king from engaging in this mad objective. Once with the warning report of his nephew and twice with a hesitation in the ranks of Egypt.

Nephi studied the features of the king. The eyes of the His Majesty reflected a cold metallic glint. Nephi felt the muscles of his heart constrict and his eyes welled up with tears. He knew the king would not recognize the Lord's respite.

Josiah had spent his life pursuing and restoring God's commandments to the best of his ability. He had destroyed a thousand heathen gods from off the face of the Promised Land, but his motives had never been that he might humbly submit to the will of the Lord. Instead, the quest of Josiah's life had been that the Lord might humbly submit to the will of the king.

"Arrow!" the king commanded.

Nephi looked up. Josiah's hand extended toward him, looking

for an arrow from the gold-plated quiver.

Nephi's arm felt heavy as it reached into the quiver and drew out one long projectile. Impatiently, the king snatched it away from the boy's hand. Josiah pressed down the foot lever and stretched the bowstring as taut as it would go. He aimed his weapon toward Pharaoh Necho on the height. When the arrow released, the bowstring hummed like the pluck of a psaltery. The missile flew over the heads of the Ionians in a high arch and seemed to vanish into the blue of the sky. But on the hill's crest, where Pharaoh was perched, loud groans were shortly heard. Had Necho been killed? No, not Necho. Pharaoh's counsellors gathered around one of the cages. Josiah's arrow had struck the sacred baboon of the realm of the dead!

"Lower the banner!" Josiah commanded Nephi.

The order confused Nephi and he was slow to respond. Josiah stripped the banner from his hands and tossed it out of the chariot. The star of David landed in the mud.

"If I'm to reach Pharaoh's throne and put a blade through Necho's heart, he must not know it is me until we're too close to make any difference."

More madness from the king! Did he expect to breach the Ionian ranks and grapple to the death with Necho himself? Nephi wanted to jump out! Such action would bring about certain death!

No. He could not abandon His Majesty.

The king whirled his sword overhead and gave the sign to attack. "Across the ditch!" he cried.

Nephi braced himself as the onrush recommenced. The ditch was steep and fairly wide. Horses stumbled. Riders fell into the water. Other mounts struggled laboriously up the hill to meet the Ionian lances. The six chargers of the king dragged the royal chariot to the other side of the ditch, but as the horses attempted to pull it out of the water, one front wheel bounced while its opposite back wheel sank into the soft bank. The foaming steeds dragged the chariot over on its side, spilling out Nephi, the king, and his charioteer. Nephi rolled to a stop, his clothing and arms now frosted in mud. The boy curled up to avoid the hooves of another horse as it leaped over him. Then Nephi lifted himself to his feet.

The king had already set about to commandeer another chariot. Josiah might have even considered the accident a blessing. By switching to a non-descript car, his chances of slipping through the enemy unrecognized were greatly improved. The king hoisted himself into place. His new driver continued the battle charge. Nephi, standing beside the ditch, was left far behind.

The ranks of warriors who joined the king in his assault up the hill had thinned considerably. Hundreds of stragglers, fallen horsemen, and cowards had abandoned His Majesty in his hardest fight, remaining instead on the near side of the ditch. The most faithful group seemed to be the simple foot soldiers, whose voices still carried a hoarse scream as they rushed toward their doom.

Nephi's eyes hit upon a certain ragged soldier crossing through the water. The soldier climbed out on the other side. His face glistened with hatred. Nephi almost let the soldier rush past him since very little about this person seemed familiar anymore. Instead, Nephi cried out the warrior's name.

"Lemuel!"

The soldier faltered in his steps, looking about, as if the wind itself had called to him. Then Lemuel recognized the voice. He spied his little brother beside the overturned royal chariot. Lowering his spear, Lemuel went up to Nephi.

The two brothers gaped at one another. The sight of a familiar face thrilled their souls, but the frenzy around them presented no opportunity to express it. Lemuel became scolding and impatient.

"Nephi! What are you *doing* here?"

Nephi turned the question back on his brother. "What are *you* doing here? Father and Sam have been searching for you. You shouldn't *be* here."

A shower of arrows discharged from the Ionian ranks. Two of the missiles impacted the ground to the right and left of Nephi and Lemuel. Lemuel took his little brother by the arm and guided him down beside the overturned chariot.

"Get under it," said Lemuel. "Stay here until the battle is over."

"Stay with me," Nephi urged. "It's over already."

"No! It's just begun!" Lemuel's features radiated with the same mad, misdirected faith as the king. "Now get underneath!"

Responding to the voice that had told him what to do so many times before, Nephi crawled beneath the overturned chariot. The ground was wet and Nephi's clothes soaked in the moisture. The curve of the chariot's rim left a peephole at the other side wide enough for the boy to watch the onslaught. Lemuel charged into Nephi's frame of vision. His older brother glanced back once, then lurched up the hill with the point of his spear projected forward.

The king had disappeared into a dust cloud raised by the advancing Ionians. From within that cloud emerged only shrieks of agony and the lightning flashes of lances and swords. The dust cloud danced and circled on its axis like a whirlwind. As Lemuel disappeared into the cloud, Nephi was convinced he would never again see the living face of his brother.

To the north of Pharaoh's hill, Nephi caught sight of another advancing Egyptian army, as fresh as the Ionians. Nephi turned his face into the dirt and wept bitterly. He had no doubt that behind that army marched another. And behind that one, another.

New fighting had also broken out in front of Megiddo, where the Libyans had rallied. The Ethiopians and Nubians who pressed the northeastern slopes of Carmel were swiftly rendering the Jewish defenders in that quarter entirely extinct. The fleeing ranks of the forty-two regions had turned. Disaster was closing in on Judah from every direction.

All at once, the dancing black cloud stopped swirling. The roar of battle suddenly hushed. Nephi looked up. A single chariot emerged from the cloud, racing back toward the ditch. Nephi recognized the chariot as the one Josiah had commandeered. Only one man stood inside, Josiah's driver, gripping the reins. Where was the king?

Shortly after the chariot appeared, several dozen retreating soldiers followed. Among them, Nephi spotted his brother, Lemuel, hollow-eyed with despair.

As the chariot reached the ditch and came to a halt, Nephi climbed out from under the royal car. Before Nephi was pressed back by hundreds of anxious, panicked men, he glimpsed another man inside the chariot. This man lay on the floor, his head upright, leaning awkwardly against the back wall. The shaft of an arrow protruded from his breast. The king of Judah had been gravely wounded.

As Josiah opened his eyes a slit, the pupils rolled back in his head. Reaching out to his driver, Josiah uttered one last thirsty command before fainting: "To Jerusalem!"

The king would not speak again until his command was fulfilled.

# Chapter 15
## THE GREAT MOURNING

A TELEPATHIC AWARENESS OF WHAT HAD HAPPENED SEEMED TO strike the entire Egyptian army at once. Fighting resumed, and with more fury than ever before. The hundreds of Jews who thronged mournfully around the wounded king were forced to turn their attention back on the advancing Ionians. Nephi heard one of Josiah's generals shout a vow to fight until the last man. It would be his last act of obeisance to the fallen king in an effort to distract Egypt's ranks long enough to allow Josiah's chariot to escape.

Since Nephi had been with His Majesty during the charge, no one disputed him when he climbed inside the chariot where Josiah was lain. Carefully, Nephi rested the head of the unconscious monarch in his lap. Lemuel caught one of the unscathed horses of a dead cavalryman, determined to join the king's escort back to Megiddo. Over a hundred of Judah's warriors had also determined to shield the king. Almost immediately, the cluster of horsemen and the chariot of the wounded king broke away from the battling masses.

The king's escort fled into a pocket of hills to the south which hid them temporarily from the view of Pharaoh and the largest grouping of enemy soldiers. The escort made its way back to Megiddo's northern gate by every side-track available to them.

Inside Megiddo's central courtyard, a physician examined Josiah's wound. Ahikam and Prince Daniel stood by with the other officers. They could read the Levite physician's dark opinion even before he revealed it. The generals who'd accompanied the king from the battlefield reminded everyone of Josiah's request to return to Jerusalem.

The best of Megiddo's traveling chariots was heaped with cushions and rugs to make His Majesty as comfortable as possible. Ahikam and Prince Daniel would ride inside the chariot with Josiah, one propping his head while the other held his feet. Nephi and Lemuel were granted permission to ride beside them with a dozen other guards. Within the hour, they departed Megiddo.

The sky had started to darken as the king's chariot stopped briefly at the reinforcement camp of Ibleam to change horses. Ahikam requested a draught of water, which he attempted, with limited success, to get the now semiconscious Josiah to drink. The men of Ibleam silently gathered around to gaze at the face of their dying king. Nephi studied the many expressions. The men bore the appearance of lost souls. But none looked more forlorn than Nephi's brother, Lemuel, who hadn't spoken a word since leaving Megiddo.

As Nephi scanned the crowd, he caught sight of a middle-aged pilgrim in a faded red traveling shawl. At the bearded man's side stood a boy in a dusty headcloth. Nephi squinted his eyes for a better focus. Could it be true? His delighted heart skipped a beat.

"Lemuel, look!" he called to his brother.

Father Lehi and Sam heard Nephi's voice. They looked about, trying to isolate its source. They spotted Nephi running toward them. Lemuel was close behind. In the midst of such a gloomy and dismal depression, there existed one happy reunion between a father and his sons.

Lehi and Sam had learned days before that the main army was stationed at Megiddo. He and Sam had tried to reach the fortress by way of the main road, their objective to tell the commander of Lemuel's contingent that Lemuel was underage, and thus see to it that the teenager was dismissed from duty before getting himself killed. The citadel at Ibleam was as far north as they got before frontier sentries had forced them to stop. Lehi and Sam were ordered to remain at Ibleam for their own protection.

Lehi had no words of reproach for his adventurous sons, especially Lemuel. One look at Lemuel told Lehi that something about him had changed significantly. A bitterness had taken root in Lemuel that reached much deeper than Israel's prevailing depression. The change reflected on Lemuel's whole countenance.

"Do not harden your heart, Lemuel," said Lehi insightfully.

"When everything is black among the people of God, let there still shine a light in your own soul."

"People of God?" Lemuel responded. "The Lord would never have allowed His chosen people to become so humiliated. Better to believe there is no such thing as a people of God. Better to believe there never was."

Lemuel wandered away from his father and brothers and continued his brooding silence.

Nephi approached Daniel to tell him the happy news of finding Sam and his father. Prince Daniel had left the side of King Josiah only long enough to wash his face and swallow some water. He was glad for Nephi, but it was clear that there existed no news in this world which might have lightened his heart. His uncle, the king—the only soul in the kingdom who might have taken the place of his father—lay dying. Even if His Majesty survived the trip home, which the physician had said was highly unlikely, it was still only a matter of time. No man had been known to survive such a wound.

Prince Daniel leaned over the well, staring into the darkness. "After all we went through, all our struggles and pain, we still couldn't save him. Why, Nephi? What was it all for? I thought God was with us. What did we accomplish? What did we change?"

Nephi hung his head. The same frustration burned inside him as well. And then the words of his father sprang to mind, the same words that Lehi had spoken the day before their caravan had departed toward Egypt.

"We changed ourselves," Nephi answered the prince. "When we pursue a noble cause, the noblest change may only be that which takes place in our hearts." At last Nephi felt he understood his father's words.

Daniel's grief would keep the meaning of Nephi's statement from sinking in for many days to come.

"You'll be staying with your father in Ibleam then?" asked the prince.

Nephi hadn't yet realized the implications of the reunion. "No," he replied. "We will all ride to Jerusalem with you."

Daniel shook his head. "We'll be traveling far too swiftly and we can't spare the horses."

"Then I'll come alone."

"No, my friend," said Daniel. "Our quest is finished. Our adventure is at an end. Every spare moment I have must now be spent with my uncle, the king. No one knows how long it will be."

Nephi's stomach coiled up in knots. "So this is good-bye?"

"Not good-bye," said Daniel. "We won't be apart long enough for it to be good-bye. We'll see each other in Jerusalem in a few weeks. Or else I'll travel to the edge of the desert with my chamberlains. We'll set out into the hills above the olive groves again to target practice with your bow. I'm afraid you may have forgotten how it's done."

Nephi laughed, but his eyes were moist.

The two boys embraced briefly. Daniel's mind had no time to concentrate on farewells. He was anxious to return to the side of the king.

"In a few weeks," Daniel shouted back at his friend.

"In a few weeks," Nephi repeated.

The caravan of the fallen king prepared to depart. Lehi and his sons watched as the chariot and its mounted escorts rode off under the moonlight which bathed the Jerusalem road.

THE KING'S CHARIOT REACHED JERUSALEM'S EPHRAIM GATE ON THE second morning after departing Megiddo. The king survived the terrible journey only by a miracle. Couriers had arrived ahead of Josiah's caravan to forewarn the palace of His Majesty's grave injuries and the disastrous defeat at Megiddo. The priests and dignitaries of the court listened to the news with blanched faces. They chose not to make the matter public.

But as soon as the king arrived, the secret could no longer be kept. Less than an hour after His Majesty's chariot entered the gate, the entire citizenry of Jerusalem knew what had happened. They watched as their wounded king was lifted out of the traveling chariot and transferred into a wide palanquin, with a deep bed, like a coffin. As the procession moved toward the palace, the crowd erupted into cries of lamentation. After such a long period of peace, the nation of Judah was like a child that did not comprehend the full extent of its danger.

That afternoon, every idler in the city gathered in the outer courtyard of the temple, their faces pale with curiosity and apprehension. Whenever a high priest or court official appeared, the man was surrounded and peppered with questions. The official would normally mumble something that sounded vaguely soothing and force his way through the throng with gentle impatience.

As the day lengthened, the weight of unanswered questions increased. Was Josiah dead? Was he mortally wounded? Had the army of Eliakim fallen into the Pharaoh's hands? Had Prince Eliakim turned traitor? Were the hosts of Egypt even now marching toward Jerusalem? Should the people flee or should they prepare for further resistance? Their questions went entirely unanswered until the following afternoon.

After reaching the palace, Josiah was laid in his private bed-chamber. Queen Hamutal veiled herself heavily. For the first time, Daniel had to concede that the queen looked old. She allowed only Ahikam and Prince Daniel, as well as her two sons, Jehoahaz and Mattaniah, to remain with her in the room as physicians and servants attended the unconscious king around the clock.

Hamutal informed Ahikam and Daniel of the other sad event that had occurred over the last few days. Ahikam's father, Shaphan, the noble and revered scholar of Israel, had passed away in his sleep. Some claimed the hour of his death was the very hour when the battle began at Megiddo.

"My father's life was devoted to bringing peace and law to the kingdom," said Ahikam. "I'm glad he did not live to see it shattered."

That night Josiah regained some small portion of coherence, enough to refuse the drink which Hamutal put to his lips and enough to prevent his physician from renewing the blood-soaked bandages or treating his wound with the famous healing balm of Gilead. Instead, Josiah directed that his second son, Jehoahaz, lean down to his ear.

"Tomorrow," moaned Josiah. His statement was interrupted by a fit of low coughing. "Tomorrow, you shall be anointed."

"No, Father," pleaded Jehoahaz. "I don't want to be king. You shall be king for a long time to come."

"Tomorrow," repeated Josiah and he fell back into a deep slumber.

The following morning, Josiah summoned his last ebbs of strength and requested that he be dressed in his royal robes and carried to the throne room of Solomon.

A large assembly had gathered. Appearances today were far

different from the assembly that had gathered the day Josiah had dismissed the Egyptian ambassador. The bench of princes sat almost vacant. A majority of Judah's princes still struggled to return home, or languished as slaves before the face of Pharaoh, or rotted as corpses on the sun-baked plain. The bench of priests also showed gaps. Only a few days before, these holy men had greeted the prospect of "the kingdom of the new David" with ear-rending excitement, but now they wanted nothing more to do with it, and blamed Josiah for having refused to recognize the inevitable failure of the campaign from the beginning.

At the back of the hall, the bench of the prophets also sat all but empty. The news from Megiddo had filled Jerusalem's soothsayers with due embarrassment. Only one man occupied the bench, a steadfast and heavy-hearted soul named Jeremiah.

The king had to be strapped to his gold and ivory throne to keep him from toppling down the steps. With a hoarse whisper, Josiah announced to the assembly his impending death. He asked the men of Judah to acknowledge his second son as the lawful heir to the throne of David. The people wondered if the vacant-eyed Jehoahaz even comprehended what was happening; nevertheless they raised their hands one by one to signify their assent to a dying man's wish.

Josiah went to lift the crown of David off his brow and set it upon the brow of his son, but in the attempt, the crown slipped out of his hands and bounced into the assembly. Josiah fainted. The Sagan of the temple had to be called upon to finish the ceremony.

"AHIKAM!"

After a full night, a day, and another half-night of feverish tossing upon his bed, the king returned to coherence and beckoned his secretary to his side. Ahikam leaned over Josiah's face. Hamutal and Prince Daniel had also awakened.

Josiah's eyes appeared clouded and sightless. "Answer me, Ahikam," the king continued. "The words of the seer. Why were they not fulfilled?"

Everyone present knew to which words Josiah referred. The promise of Huldah the seeress, who eleven years before had been sought by Shaphan and the High Priest to learn if the words of the rediscovered Book of the Law were authentic. Huldah had added to her authentication, a prophecy. Josiah repeated the promise.

"*'Thou shalt be gathered unto thy grave in peace.'* Were these not the words of the seeress? *'Thou shalt go in peace and thine eyes shall not see evil'* Was this not the promise bestowed upon me by the Lord?"

Ahikam didn't know how to reply. The quotation was accurate. Huldah had indeed spoken this prophecy. Daniel felt he had an answer for the king, but of what use was it to burden the heart of a dying man by telling him he might have nullified the prophecy through his own rash decisions? And yet, everyone who'd been present to hear the prophecy that day had not felt it was a conditional promise, but an open vision of what must surely come to pass.

"Answer me, Ahikam!" Josiah demanded. "What of the promise? Wh—why was I forsaken?"

Ahikam shook his head.

Josiah's voice rattled with fury. "I reject the prophets! I reject the Law! I reject Adonai! Our Lord has only brought evil to Israel! God sanctified Israel only to be the plaything of His hatred! I hate Him in return! I hate . . . I hate . . ."

The king shut his eyes and gritted his teeth, struggling desperately to pinch off his tears and suppress his sobs. He failed at both. The sheer force of Josiah's blasphemy also left the faces of everyone in the room wet with tears. After a moment, the mind of the king faded back into oblivion. Daniel sank into a corner. This was not how he wished to remember his uncle, a warped and bitter husk of a man. After half an hour, Daniel lulled himself to sleep with his tears.

When Daniel awakened, it was very late, or perhaps, very early. He almost felt as if he'd been nudged, but the others were fast asleep. Daniel glanced at the king's face. Josiah also slept, but his features were different somehow. The boy lifted himself and went to the king's bed. His Majesty's face looked unnaturally calm. He appeared to have stopped breathing and grief began to curdle in Daniel's stomach.

Then Josiah's eyes opened wide. Daniel gasped and withdrew a step to rouse Hamutel. At the queen's movement, Ahikam also awoke. The three figures hovered over Josiah. The king's eyes were clear and bright, so full of life. His pupils darted back and forth, but they did not seem to be looking at anything about the room.

"What is he seeing?" asked the queen.

"Only God may know," Ahikam replied.

Indeed, the king's vision seemed filled with things beyond the sight of anyone else in the room. Josiah spoke, but his voice was not shrill like before. It was clear and resonant, as in the days of his prime. He repeated the same words three times, but each time he gave the words a different intonation.

"The fathers . . ."

The first time he said it, the statement resembled frightened understanding. The second time, it sounded like an uncertain question. But the third time, his words sang out like a phrase from one of the melodies of the Sons of Asaph.

Daniel crowded more closely, as if his proximity might help him to share in Josiah's vision. What fathers did Josiah speak of? Daniel felt instinctively that Josiah witnessed the fathers of old. Had his first utterance meant that he saw the corrupted images of his most recent fathers, Amon and Manasseh? If so, His Majesty now seemed surrounded by the glorious appearances of Abraham, Isaac, Jacob, and Moses.

After a further silence in which none of the listeners dared stir even a fold of their robes for fear it would injure the spirit, the king uttered two more words, repeated three times.

"The children . . ."

Each time he said them, the words were again given a different intonation. The first utterance rang out with sighing compassion, the next with uncertainty, and the last with blissful amazement. More glorious than the vision of the gathering of the fathers seemed to be the procession of Israel's children until the end of time. In the hour of his death, Daniel knew the king had embraced both the beginning and the end in one commanding glance. After his vision had come to an end, Josiah looked at Ahikam and gently gripped his secretary's arm.

"Ahikam. To go in peace . . . it was no falsehood after all." Next, the king reached toward his nephew. "Daniel."

Daniel leaned down to his uncle's lips.

"Speak to the Lord for me, Daniel," whispered the king. "He is with you. . . . Tell Him I love Him . . . again . . . still . . ."

With that whisper, King Josiah, the son of Amon, turned his face to the wall and died.

Daniel did not tell the Lord of his uncle's love. For he knew it was true. And because he knew it, he knew that his uncle had already declared it in person.

ON THE EVENING OF JEHOAHAZ'S CORONATION, LEHI AND HIS SONS passed through Jerusalem, but they did not stop. King Josiah was reportedly in his last hours of life and Nephi knew that disturbing Prince Daniel would be inappropriate. Besides, the mood in Jerusalem's streets had grown frantic. Any day the populace expected a vicious assault from the hordes of Egypt. Lehi decided it would be best to return swiftly to his estate at the edge of the desert, where the affairs of nations had been felt only mildly since the beginning of time.

Laman returned from Egypt with his arm in a sling. The harvest of olives and grapes and their subsequent pressing into oil and wine proceeded as it had in years past.

In a few weeks, life on Lehi's estate took on every appearance of having returned to normal, except that Lemuel no longer uttered his sanctimonious speeches at the supper table. Lehi tried to get his second son to discuss the feelings of his heart, but Lemuel resisted his father's efforts. As far as Lemuel was concerned, the Lord had not lived up to his expectations, therefore, he no longer felt inclined to live up to the expectations of the Lord. Over the months, Lemuel seemed to grow much more comfortable with Laman's philosophies on life. The two oldest brothers still argued heatedly from time to time, but overall, they seemed to have found a common bond.

Sometimes Nephi would watch the road from the window of the Hall of Joseph, expecting any moment that Prince Daniel's palanquin would appear on the horizon. One gloomy day toward the end of the summer, a large and decorated caravan did appear, but it was heavily guarded by a contingent of Egyptian cavalry. Three Jewish palanquins swayed in the train, but none of the occupants was Prince Daniel.

Within the largest litter rode the newly ordained king of Judah, fettered in golden chains. After only three months of rule, the befuddled Jehoahaz was ordered by Pharaoh Necho to step down from his throne or Israel would face destructive consequences. In his place, Pharaoh installed Jehoahaz's older brother, Eliakim. Eliakim's first decree as king was to change his own name to Jehoiakim. His second decree was to send into exile his brother, his stepmother, and the young Mattaniah. They were consigned to live out the rest of their days on the banks of the Nile.

As autumn became winter, Nephi began to wonder if Daniel was even alive. The chance seemed high that the vengeful Jehoiakim had murdered his cousin and anyone else who knew the details of the sinister conspiracy which Jehoiakim had orchestrated.

The following spring, Nephi travelled with Sam and his father to the Passover festival in Jerusalem. In his search for Daniel, Nephi strode right up to the door of the House of Solomon. The official who barred his entrance to the palace refused to answer any of the boy's inquiries about the prince. At the house where Nephi had once made contact with Hananiah, Mishael, and Azariah, an unfamiliar pair of eyes appeared behind the peephole. None of the same servants were employed there anymore. Daniel and his three friends seemed to have vanished into thin air.

Lehi noted that the once joyous spirit of the Passover had now disappeared altogether. Outbreaks of brawling and drunkenness, infrequent in the days of Josiah, had become commonplace. Men with mean, brutal natures seemed to have gained new prominence and respect in Judah's capital. And with the appointment of a Jewish king under the hand of an Egyptian Pharaoh, the gods of Ra, Ptah, and Osiris had received a fresh mandate. Nephi, Sam, and his father left Jerusalem early the next morning.

Lehi wondered if he would ever celebrate the Lord's Passover in the capital again. Rejecting Jerusalem as the fountainhead of religious policy seemed to be a natural progression for Lehi. Already that year he'd released from service all the bondmen who'd been in his employ over seven years. He didn't need Jerusalem to set the example, he needed only the confirmation of his new friend, Jeremiah, who he met with briefly while Nephi had pursued his search of the prince. Lehi gave the bondmen their portion by offering them a parcel of his land or the equivalent in silver. The only servant who refused the offer was old Shamariah, who begged that his inheritance might simply be to live out the rest of his days in the service of the family he'd grown to love.

Laman swore his father's decision would ruin the estate, and in fact, things were extremely tight for two full years. But the third year finally came, and it was the most productive and fruitful season Lehi ever remembered.

Throughout that first year in which Daniel and Nephi were separated, Nephi had no idea how to direct his grief. For all he knew, Daniel could have been murdered, imprisoned, or exiled. What if he'd lost his memory again? What if the prince was destined to wander the byways as a beggar for the rest of his days? Any way which Nephi looked at it, he appeared to have lost the greatest friend he'd ever had.

One year after Nephi had last seen the prince, a modest Jewish caravan emerged out of the desert having returned from Egypt. The caravan's leader, an older gentleman with a sagging jaw, approached Lehi's house to request if the boy Nephi was about. Sam excitedly went inside to fetch his younger brother, who was at the time receiving instructions from the family tutor.

The gentleman handed Nephi a brilliantly ornate bow with a backing of Damascus steel. Nephi recognized the object immediately. He'd seen it last spring on the wall of an elite shop in the market district at Noph. Nephi took the weapon from the man's hands and held it delicately.

"How?" Nephi asked. "Why?"

"I am the chamberlain of His Eminence, Prince Daniel, son of Maaseiah."

Nephi caught his breath. "Daniel is alive?"

"I was sent to Egypt by His Eminence to retain this piece of merchandise for one, Nephi, son of Lehi. I hope I have purchased the correct article. I feel confident I have. The prince's description was quite detailed."

"Yes, yes!" Nephi clamored. "But where is the prince? Is he well?"

"His Eminence sends you this letter."

The chamberlain drew out of his robe a square of sealed parchment. Nephi broke the seal and read the letter, his heart glowing warmer with each passing word.

*To Nephi, son of Lehi, from Prince Daniel, son of Maaseiah.*
*I pray this letter may reach you. The man who brings it risks much if he is caught. He was an attendant in the*

*house of my father and now serves us in the palace.*

*I am well. I regret that I have been unable to make contact with you before now. Hananiah, Mishael, Azariah, and I have remained in the House of Solomon since the instatement of King Jehoiakim.*

*We venture out only occasionally and then it is only under close supervision. It is my suspicion that the king would like to get rid of us somehow. There is talk of sending us to Babylon to fulfill a request recently issued by the Chaldean King whose armies are said to be badly defeating the hosts of Egypt in the north, but nothing is certain.*

*I have asked my servant to first go to Noph and obtain the fine bow we saw together there during our adventures. If he does not succeed in getting it, it is only because it was already obtained by somebody else. In such case, I have asked him to purchase for you the most expensive bow in the shop. I hope that you will consider it a token of my gratitude and an emblem of our friendship.*

*It is still my hope that we may see one another again, but if we do not, I am confident the Lord will watch over you. I will always remember you, Nephi, my friend. Though I was a prince and you were a commoner, it is my hope that in the life to come, we shall both be kings.*

# Epilogue
## THE STILLNESS
## OF THE SAPPHIRE SEA

The exhausted ocean lapped gently against the hull of the ship. Nephi closed his eyes. The harmony of the mild surf, combined with the creaking of the vessel and the warmth of a light breeze, filled the man's heart with resplendence. Utterances of profound gratitude had cried up from his soul unceasingly for the past twenty-four hours, ever since the moment the back of the raging storm had been broken.

Nephi massaged his bruised and swollen wrists, injured by the cords that his two oldest brothers had used to pinion his arms behind the mast of the ship. Only after the cords had been cut, allowing Nephi to raise his arms in fervent prayer, did the tempest cease and a breathless calm settle over the ocean. The greater part of Nephi's gratitude sprang from the fact that every person on board the ship had credited the death of the storm to the boundless mercy and power of God.

Shortly, Nephi would go below to fetch Zoram and his brother, Sam, so they might raise the ship's sails and continue their course toward a new promised land. But for now, Nephi was content to enjoy the breeze and drink in the colors of the rising sun. Nephi concluded that there was nothing so beautiful as the dance of golden diamonds upon a calm sea during sunrise, except perhaps the same rising sun upon the cool blue formations of the Sinai.

Nephi sighed deeply. It had been almost nine years since he'd last watched a sunrise on the desert of his childhood. He knew with perfect assurance that he would never see such a sunrise again. Nephi had usually done well to focus his thoughts forward to the beautiful sights that would soon belong to himself and his wife, Nadira, in the new promised land. But for a brief instant, he allowed himself to lapse into recalling the past and the wondrous things which had forever changed.

He thought on his father's estate and his boyhood frolics in the hills above the olive groves, herding sheep and hunting gazelles and red-legged partridges. He thought on the tender smile of his sister, Hannah, the way she had looked in the years before the Lord had taken her home.

He thought on the rugged face of Judah's last great king, the man who had showed Israel what it was like to feel glorious again, if only for one short season. It seemed interesting to Nephi that not just one of Josiah's sons had inherited his throne, but all three of them. After Jehoahaz, Eliakim, who changed his name to Jehoiakim, had held the throne for nine years. Then, after incurring the wrath of Nebuchadnezzar, the conspirator of Israel was executed and given the burial of an ass while his oldest son was carried off to Babylon. Josiah's youngest son, Mattaniah, returned home from his exile in Egypt to be anointed king of Judah just before Lehi and Ishmael had departed into the wilderness. Mattaniah, like his brother, changed his name to one he thought more befitting of royalty. Mattaniah became Zedekiah.

Nephi would not have been surprised to learn that Jerusalem was under siege even now by the ambitious Nebuchadnezzar, whose patience with that city had run irreconcilably thin.

Nephi sifted through these memories rather swiftly. He found himself focusing most of his thoughts on a cherished friendship he'd once enjoyed with a prince of the house of David. Though their friendship had been forged in the course of a few short months, Nephi felt certain it would linger into the world to come.

Nephi thought back on a day three years after Jehoiakim had taken power. A rumor had reached Nephi that Daniel, son of Maaseiah, was to be taken to Babylon along with his three friends, Hananiah, Mishael, and Azariah. All of them were to be renamed in the Babylonian tongue. Daniel would become Belteshazzar, while his friends would become Shadrach, Meshach, and Abednego. In

Babylon the boys would be indoctrinated in Chaldean ways of life with the intent that one day they might return as puppet leaders for Nebuchadnezzar. Nephi, who by that time fourteen years old, rode a swift horse to the capital to see if he could bid the prince a final farewell, but by the time he arrived, the Chaldean soldiers had already carted off all four of the boys.

Even the steel-backed bow that Daniel had given Nephi as a token of gratitude and an emblem of friendship had broken during their journey to the promised land—a cause of much grief in Nephi's family at that time. All Nephi had left of his friendship with Daniel were memories. But what magnificent memories they were!

As Nephi gazed out at the sapphire seas made golden by the rising sun, he tried to imagine what Prince Daniel might be doing at this moment in his Babylonian home. Just as he thought it, a vague but striking image opened up before him, mingled with the ocean's dancing golden diamonds. He saw the image of a young man in the courts of Chaldean royalty, patiently instructing his rapt listeners on a few of the more meaningful points of Israelite law.

The vision closed almost as quickly as it came, but Nephi dropped to his knees on the deck of the ship, overwhelmed by the generosity and goodness of the Lord that He would soothe Nephi's heart by such a small thing. Nephi realized how much he had learned during his brief adventurous days with the prince. During that time, much of the pattern and commitment of his life had been set.

In the lands and deserts of an ancient world had been forged not only the bonds of a friendship that would last into the eternities, but the steel of character that would give to the world two prophets of God.

# ABOUT THE AUTHOR

Chris Heimerdinger was born in Bloomington, Indiana, on August 26, 1963. He was baptized into the Church of Jesus Christ of Latter-day Saints on December 10, 1981, a month after completing his first reading of the Book of Mormon. Since that day, Chris has written three books which specifically celebrate this volume of scripture. His first novel, *Tennis Shoes Among the Nephites,* now in its eighth printing, is an amazingly believable time-travel fantasy about three modern-day kids who explore the time of Helaman and Captain Moroni. His second novel, *Gadiantons and the Silver Sword,* is a thriller that transports Gadianton Robbers to a modern-day setting to interact with the "Tennis Shoes gang" nearly a decade later.

In *Daniel and Nephi,* Chris faced his greatest challenge yet when he determined to fictionalize the childhood experiences of two well-known and celebrated prophets of God. He has always been committed to thorough research in his writing in order to achieve a high level of accuracy in the setting of his books. For *Daniel and Nephi* he went to great pains, even submitting his